BOOK #1 THE CHALLENGERS

Greg R. Fishbone

Illustrations by Ethen Beavers

Tu Books

AN IMPRINT OF LEE & LOW BOOKS

NEW YORK

Text copyright © 2011 by Greg R. Fishbone
Illustrations copyright © 2011 by Ethen Beavers

TU BOOKS, an imprint of LEE & LOW BOOKS Inc.,
95 Madison Avenue, New York, NY 10016
leeandlow.com

Manufactured in the United States of America
by Worzalla Publishing Company, September 2011

Book design by Neil Swaab
Book production by The Kids at Our House
The text is set in Charter BT
The illustrations are rendered in ink on paper
10 9 8 7 6 5 4 3 2 1
First Edition

Library of Congress Cataloging-in-Publication Data

Fishbone, Greg R., 1970-
The challengers / Greg R. Fishbone. —1st ed.
p. cm. — (Galaxy Games ; bk. #1)
Summary: On his eleventh birthday, Ty Sato gets a star named for him by his Japanese cousins, and is recruited by aliens from the planet Mrendaria to help save them from galactic humiliation in the Galaxy Games. Includes author's notes about Japanese culture and language.
ISBN 978-1-60060-660-1 (hardcover : alk. paper) —
ISBN 978-1-60060-877-3 (e-book)
[1. Extraterrestrial beings—Fiction. 2. Interplanetary voyages—Fiction. 3. Games--Fiction. 4. Cousins—Fiction. 5. Japanese Americans—Fiction. 6. Science fiction.]
I. Title.
PZ7.F498843Ch 2011
[Fic]--dc23   2011014251

For Dori and Alexi,
the two brightest stars in my galaxy.

1

PLATTE BLUFF, NEVADA:

During the night, a tiny creature had crawled out of Tyler Sato's right ear—or so the fat, inch-long footprints across his pillow seemed to indicate. Tyler traced the path with his finger across the bedsheet to the wall. From there the prints zigged and zagged through a field of NFL football cards like a running back heading for the end zone. The creature had tagged each member of Tyler's fantasy football team with a pastel-colored sticky note written in tiny print:

"You like this guy? Really? This guy?"

"Your quarterback has a rubber arm!"

"Tsk-tsk. Rookie mistake, picking this one."

"Didn't this guy tear his ACL in week two?"

"Hey! Why no Japanese American football players?"

At the top of the wall, the footprints trailed across the ceiling as if they were telling gravity to take a number and wait for service. Little steps skipped around Tyler's light fixture, then dashed toward the bedroom door. As far as Tyler could tell, the footprint maker had escaped the room through an impossibly thin crack between the door frame and the top of the door.

Tyler's fuzzy brain shook off the last haze of sleep. Those footprints looked fake. One of them even peeled off the wall when he scraped it with his fingernail. "They're stickers!"

Tyler yanked open the door and stomped into the hall. The trail of footprint stickers continued down the outside of the door, right across his "DO NOT ENTER—THIS MEANS YOU, AMANDA!" sign. Messages scrawled on his dry-erase message board read, "Mini-Boffo was here!" and "Happy bum-biddley-birthday, champ!" Tyler would have recognized the handwriting even without the colored hearts and smiley-faced clown drawings.

"Amanda!" he shouted. "What have I told you about coming into my room when I'm sleeping, putting sticker footprints all over the place, and making it look like I've been invaded by pocket-sized birthday clowns?"

"Nothing yet!" his big sister's voice called up from downstairs.

"Well . . . consider yourself warned! And don't do any other stuff I haven't imagined you doing yet, either!"

Tyler followed the footprint trail to the stairs. More sticky notes, again in pastel colors, lined the railing all the way down.

"Ready . . ."

"Set . . ."

"Go!"

"Slide! Slide! Slide!"

"Wheeee!"

"Ouch! Splinter!"

"Slide! Slide! Slide!"

"Wedgie!!!"

"Slide! Slide!"

"Faster! Faster!"

"Oof!"

An unlucky Boffo the Clown doll lay at the bottom landing with its arm in a sparkling sling and a plastic bandage across its painted face. Tyler picked the clown up and turned slowly to find the entire front of the house transformed into a shrine to Boffo the Clown. Boffo posters, Boffo balloons, and Boffo streamers hung from the ceiling and walls. A five-foot-tall inflatable Boffo stood in the middle of the room. Banners on the wall proclaimed, "CLOWNING AROUND WITH BOFFO!" and "HAVE A HAPPY, SNAPPY, DUM-DIDDLY-YAPPY BIRTHDAY!"

As if Tyler were turning five years old instead of eleven.

While Tyler gaped at the horrible sight, his sister flashed her phone's camera in his face. "Perfect!" she chirped. "It's been a lot of work since Mom and Dad put me in charge of decorating for your birthday party, but the slap-happy grin makes it all worthwhile."

Tyler shouted, "I don't have a slap-happy grin!"

Amanda laughed and patted him on the head. "No, but I do! And just wait until all your little friends see what I have planned for this afternoon. They'll be talking about your party for years to come!"

Tyler groaned into his hands. Before he could look up again, the upstairs bathroom door slammed shut and his sister's off-key humming joined the sound of running water. Tyler sighed. "There goes my chance of getting in there any time in the next hour." It always amazed him that Amanda could move so fast to reach the bathroom and then so slowly once she got inside.

At school during recess, Tyler tried to get his friends to skip the birthday disaster his sister had planned for him. "Of course I want you all to come to my completely clown-free party this afternoon," he said with his fingers crossed behind his back. "It's just that . . . my sister is sick. Very sick. And mega-contagious, too!"

"Oh, no!" wailed Brayden McKay. "What's wrong with her?"

Tyler gave his friend a sideways glance. Since when

was Brayden so concerned about Amanda's health? He hadn't spoken to her more than five times in his life! "What's wrong is—um—pus! She has so much pus, it's oozing from her eyeballs!" Tyler imagined two fountains of white goo spurting from Amanda's face and had to stifle a laugh.

"Why are you smiling like that?" asked Lucas Alvarez. "It sounds like she's really sick!"

"Or really awesome," said Eric Parker. "How much pus are we talking about, Tyler? Does it squirt? Can she aim it across the room?" He flipped up his eyeglasses and blinked at a group of second-graders on the playground equipment. "Ka-pow! Ka-pow! Ka-pow!"

John Moon glared down at Eric. "Eyeball pus is supposed to be a bad thing. Think of poor Amanda, unable to read a book without making little pus puddles on the pages. Such tragedy!"

"I wonder if the drugstore sells a 'Feel better and have pus-free eyeballs soon' card," Brayden mused.

"You spent all your money buying sugar cubes for your cube sculpture," Lucas reminded him. "But if the card is for Amanda, I guess I could go in on it with you."

Tyler frowned. "A card for Amanda? Really? You guys didn't get me a card and I was home with the flu for a whole week!"

"Of course not," said Brayden. "A 'Feel better and have

pus-free eyeballs soon' card would have been all wrong for someone with the flu."

"I sure hope your sister's eyeballs are okay," said John. "She has such pretty eyes."

Tyler made a choking sound in the back of his throat. *"What?"*

John shrugged. "I just always thought so, that's all."

"Me too," added Lucas. "They're like islands of chocolate in two lakes of vanilla."

"Her eyeballs are her best feature," Brayden agreed.

"Ew, gross!" Tyler exclaimed. "Amanda has the same eyes as me. Do you guys think my eyes are pretty?"

"Of course not!" John exclaimed in horror.

"No way," said Lucas. "Yours are more like islands of dirt in two lakes of bird poop."

"On you they're just eyes," said Brayden. "But on her they're *eyes*—except when they're full of pus."

"I don't think Amanda's eyes are all that great," said Eric.

"Thanks, Eric." Once again, Tyler was thankful that he could always count on Eric, his very best friend, to back him up when everyone else got a little crazy.

Eric nodded. "She has totally average eyes, but what I really like about Amanda is that she always smells so nice!"

Tyler shuddered and tried to shake their entire conversation out of his head.

"If Amanda's really sick, what do we do about the party?" asked Eric.

"Just drop all the presents on the front porch and back away," Tyler told him. "And don't ring the doorbell. My sister's been breathing on that doorbell all day."

"Why?" asked Lucas.

"Because . . . that's another one of her symptoms. Compulsive doorbell breathing. She can't help herself!"

Brayden reached into his backpack for a notepad and colored highlighters. "One 'Get well and stop breathing on doorbells soon' card coming right up!"

The instant school ended, Tyler sprinted the six blocks to his house. His brain buzzed with extra excuses that might keep his friends outside if any of them dared to show up for the party. Would they believe his house was haunted by vampire ghosts? Or would it be better to say there was a crocodile hive in the attic? It was a tough choice. Was it more believable that vampires could become ghosts or that crocodiles could build hives?

Tyler turned the corner and stopped short at the sight of a clown-themed inflatable Bouncy-Bounce House sitting in his front yard. Tyler suspected his sister had arranged for a kindergarten class to be delivered along with the

Bouncy-Bounce House in a special Tyler-torturing rental package because the carnival-sized vinyl structure already had a half-dozen shrieking six-year-olds bouncing around inside of it. "Amanda's really outdone herself this time," he had to admit. "All the vampire ghosts in the world couldn't distract anyone from that thing!"

Worst of all, Boffo the Clown himself stepped forward to welcome Tyler home from school. The Clown Prince of Fun extended his hand for an oversized floppy handshake. "Hi-diddley-eye, birthday boy! It's dum-diddley nice to meet you! I'm Boffo the Clown and you must be"—Boffo consulted an index card taped to the inside of his wrist— "Little Ty-Ty!"

Tyler winced at the embarrassing nickname from back when he was only a baby, unable to form the words "Don't call me Little Ty-Ty again or my friends might split their pants laughing at me!"

Tyler pushed past Boffo on his way into the house and found his mother fiddling with her laptop, the living room TV, and a mess of computer cables. It didn't seem possible but there were even more clown-themed decorations in the house than before. "Mom, we can't have the party here," said Tyler. "The house is . . . infested with termites. Clown-eating termites. It's too late for Boffo, but we can still save ourselves!"

His mother had her attention focused on splitting two

wires with her thumbnail but still managed one of her standard responses. "Tyler, what have I told you about lying?"

"That I'm not very good at it?" Tyler asked.

"Exactly." She continued to untangle the computer cables.

"So I should practice my lying skills as much I can until I get better?"

"What? No!" She craned her neck around.

Tyler smiled. "Made you look!"

Tyler's mother groaned and brushed a stray hair out of her eyes. "Honey bear, I don't have time for this. It's seven A.M. in Tokyo right now, so I need this webcam up and running before your cousins go off to school."

"Cousin Riku and Cousin Daiki are going to see all this clown stuff too?" Tyler demanded.

Tyler's mother pushed a black cable into a red slot on the side of the TV, then pulled it out and tried it in a yellow slot instead. "I think the room looks really nice, Tyler, and you should show some appreciation. Your sister put a lot of work into planning this party for you."

"It shows," Tyler stated. "It takes real effort to make a party this painful."

Tyler's mother sighed. "What's wrong, honey bear? I thought you *loved* clowns! Aren't you the little boy who talked about running away to join Boffo's Flying Circus?"

9

"*Back in kindergarten,*" Tyler told her. "Did you plan a clown-themed party for Amanda when she turned eleven?"

"Of course not! She was much too old for— Oh." Tyler's mother glanced around at the overwhelming collection of party decorations. "I'm sorry, honey bear. I should have realized you'd outgrown clowns and colored balloons. It's just hard for a mom to let her baby grow up. What can I do to make this right for you?"

"Tear it all down and tell Boffo to take a hike!"

"But we've already paid him for the day." She rubbed her chin thoughtfully. "Couldn't we just tell everyone he's your eccentric Uncle Billy?"

MIDDLE SOLAR SYSTEM:

Eight hundred eighty-five million miles from Earth, a dimpled white ball completed its 196th trip around the sun.

The space ball looked a lot like the dimpled white balls that humans have been launching toward space since the invention of golf clubs, with only a few small but telling differences: Golf balls shot from Earth almost always returned to Earth. The space ball, however, had been whacked from an orbital platform in the Milky Way's Sagittarius Arm. It had zipped around a neutron star, through a wormhole, and into a stable orbit trailing Saturn, some 6,500 light-years from the ball's actual target in the Crab Nebula. This badly botched shot had cost Planet Greeblan a slot in the Galaxy Games Tournament for five generations and inspired the popular planetary slogan, "Planet Greeblan: Can we get a do-over, please?"

As the space ball drifted into orbit number 197, its quantum transmitter began to shudder and vibrate with an incoming transmission. A quantum network controller asked the ball whether it might be available to help a Mrendarian ship complete a stepping-stone transfer. "Why not?" the ball answered. "It's not like I have anything better to do."

The space ball's entanglement engine sprang to life. Each qutrit particle in the engine core danced in sync with dozens of identical particles scattered elsewhere in the galaxy. The space ball instantaneously swapped places with a floppy purple hat in a wardrobe closet on Planet Zelbrizi more than five hundred light-years away. The hat floated in the ball's former orbit for only a moment before it swapped places with a cellulose buoy attached to a hunting trap from an asteroid field in the Large Magellanic Cloud. A bear-sized lobstronian caught in the trap kicked, flailed, and vanished as the buoy swapped places with a wind-powered trash compactor from Planet Frizzlebat at the very edge of the galactic rim.

Moments later, the trash compactor swapped places with a Mrendarian diplomatic yacht, plucked from its orbit around the smaller moon of Homabaru-Three. "Destination *achieved!" the network controller informed the wedge-shaped silver craft. "Thanks for using the stepping-stone transportation network. Have a lovely day!"*

Earth's first contact with intelligent aliens, the most important event in all of human history, was now only ninety-six hours away.

2

PLATTE BLUFF, NEVADA:

Tyler crammed an armload of Boffo banners under the couch cushions and swatted the balloons into the guest bedroom. The remaining Boffo stuff went out the window just as Brayden let himself in. He held a box wrapped in yellow MegaTruckbot paper under one arm, while his other hand clutched a pair of rubber gloves, a set of tongs, and a bouquet of flowers. "These are for Amanda and her eyeballs," he announced.

"What—?" Tyler's mother started, but Tyler shook his head. "Don't ask," he told her. "It's just Brayden being Brayden."

Tyler's mother nodded. "That's . . . very thoughtful, Brayden."

Brayden beamed. "Thanks, Mrs. Sato. These things grow wild in neat rows in front of my neighbor's house. I figured it would be a shame to just leave them there to die when they could be looked at and smelled at instead."

Tyler's mother opened and closed her mouth while trying to think of a proper response.

"Brayden being Brayden," Tyler reminded her.

She let out a long breath and took the flowers from Brayden's hand. "I'll just put these in some water."

Brayden dropped his tongs and rubber gloves onto the couch, freeing his hands to pass the birthday gift over to Tyler as if it were an oddly square-shaped basketball—which, from Brayden, wouldn't have surprised Tyler one bit. "Welcome to the Eleven-Year-Olds Club, dude!" Brayden declared.

"Thanks!" said Tyler. "I feel like this'll be a big year for me. Maybe I'll get to meet important people, or do important things, or travel really far away."

"Eleven has been a huge year so far for me," Brayden confirmed. "But I've heard it's all downhill after you turn twelve. By the way, what's with the Bouncy-Bounce House?"

"Oh, that!" Tyler felt his face flush. "It's . . . just in case some little kids show up. Something to keep them busy, you know?"

"Very cool." Brayden took a long look out the front window at the Bouncy-Bounce House before wandering to the snack table for a double-handful of pretzels.

Lucas and John arrived next. John held a birthday gift

bag overflowing with crumpled tissue. "Happy birthday, Tyler!" John also glanced through the front window. "My little sister had a Bouncy-Bounce House on her birthday. It was a lot of fun—I mean, it *looked* like a lot of fun."

"You should invite her over," Tyler suggested. "Little kids love the Bouncy-Bounce House, even though all of us are much too old for it."

"Right." Lucas pouted as he handed over a medium-sized box. "The only reason we're not bouncing around is because Tyler Sato thinks we're all too grown up."

Suddenly, Eric burst through the front door, out of breath. "Guys! Did you see the awesome Bouncy-Bounce House in the front yard? Last one in's a rotten egg!" He tossed a present at Tyler and ran back outside.

Tyler shook his head sadly. "Eric is *such* a ten-year-old."

Tyler's mother returned from the kitchen with Brayden's bouquet of stolen flowers in a large brown vase, which she placed on the coffee table. "Tyler, are you ready for your live feed from Tokyo?" she asked.

Tyler looked around to make sure he hadn't missed any clown-themed decorations. "Ready!"

"The first-ever Sato family intercontinental birthday starts . . . now!" Tyler's mother plugged in the last wire and switched on the TV. The blue blank screen lit up the room.

"Tokyo is very blue," stated Brayden.

Tyler's mother frowned at the screen. "That's not To-kyo. Tyler, what am I doing wrong?"

"You just need to press the input button on the re-mote," Tyler told her.

When Tyler's mother pressed the button, the TV flipped to a computer screen showing a video-chat program.

"Now you just need to initiate a new chat session," said Tyler.

"Thanks, honey bear. What would I do without you?" His mother picked up the laptop and began fiddling with the keyboard.

"Guys, guys, guys!" Eric came back into the house dragging Boffo the Clown along by the arm. "Look who I found outside! It's—"

"My eccentric Uncle Billy!" said Tyler.

Boffo blinked in confusion. "Dum-diddley-*what?*"

"What are you doing out of bed, Uncle Billy?" Tyler pushed the clown into the hallway toward the guest bedroom. "Rest, fluids, and complete isolation from strangers. That's what the doctors said, remember?"

"But I haven't done my super, duper, dum-diddley-ooper magic act!" Boffo protested.

Tyler opened the guest bedroom door and a bouquet of clown-face balloons popped out. He pushed them back, shoved the real Boffo through, and slammed the door. "Feel better, Uncle Billy!"

Back in the living room, the party guests looked to Tyler for an explanation. "Uncle Billy has a more advanced case of the thing my sister's got," he told them. "Pasty white skin, swollen red nose, oversized feet—"

"Rainbow-colored hair?" asked Lucas.

"That too," said Tyler. "My sister's not as bad yet, but

she'll be throwing cream pies and pulling handkerchiefs from her nostrils by the end of the week. And she's still contagious, so keep away!"

Just then, Amanda arrived from school with a huge grin on her face. "Big sister is in the house! Let's start clowning around!" She scowled at the lukewarm response. "What? Why is everyone backing away from me?"

Brayden snapped on his rubber gloves and used his tongs to hold out a homemade card that read "For Amanda: Here's to getting well, losing the pus, and resisting the temptation of doorbells."

"Really, really, really don't ask," Tyler told his mother.

"I wasn't going to," she replied. "Aargh! The chat program is asking whether I want to install a new plug-in, but I thought I'd already plugged everything in!"

Tyler walked over and pressed a button on her laptop. The dialogue box vanished and a Japanese family peered out from the TV. Uncle Kazu wore a suit and tie. Aunt Megumi wore a flowery robe and held baby Sakura on her lap. The two boys, Cousin Riku and Cousin Daiki, were dressed in Japanese school uniforms—Cousin Daiki was about Tyler's age, while Cousin Riku was fifteen, like Amanda. Tyler recognized his Tokyo relatives only from holiday pictures, since he'd never met any of them.

"*Moshi-moshi,*" said Uncle Kazu, speaking into a TV remote as if it were a phone.

"Hello!" Tyler's mother replied, speaking into her laptop mouse as if it were a microphone.

In the living room and on the screen, Amanda and Cousin Riku rolled their eyes in exactly the same impatient teenage gesture.

Aunt Megumi scowled into the screen and spoke so quickly that Tyler was just barely able to catch the words "Hiroshi-kun" and "where is he?" in Japanese. Tyler's mother made an apologetic reply, most likely explaining that Tyler's father had work to do and could not attend the party.

Aunt Megumi shook her head and clucked her tongue.

Next to Aunt Megumi, Cousin Daiki waved at the screen and shouted, *"Ohayogozaimasu!"*

"That means 'good morning,'" said Tyler's mother.

"I know at least that much Japanese, Mom." Tyler tried to roll his eyes like Amanda and Cousin Riku, but it made him so dizzy that he almost fell over.

"I was translating for your friends," his mother explained.

"Pssst," hissed Eric. "It's not morning, Mrs. Sato. It's almost four in the afternoon."

"It is morning here in Japan," said Uncle Kazu in heavily accented English. "We are seventeen time zones into your future!"

"Gomen nasai," Cousin Daiki apologized. "Good yesterday afternoon, Cousin Tyler-kun."

"Good tomorrow morning, Cousin Daiki-kun." Tyler tried not to make it obvious how closely he was studying the other boy. Looking at Daiki was like looking at a weird, alternate-universe version of himself with strange clothes and wild hair. If Tyler's parents had moved to Tokyo instead of Nevada after graduate school, and if Tyler and his sister had been born in Japan instead of America, and if Tyler spoke Japanese instead of English. . . . If all those ifs had happened, Tyler wondered whether he'd be more like Daiki or more like himself.

Tyler's mother pushed a flat package to him. "This one's from Aunt Megumi, Uncle Kazu, and your cousins. Open it now before your cousins have to leave for school."

Cousin Riku said something in a complaining tone. He sounded eerily like Amanda on every school morning of her life, except that Cousin Riku spoke Japanese words that Tyler didn't know. Tyler smiled at the thought of having a weird, alternate-universe version of his big sister who was a boy instead of a girl. Alternate Universe Boy-Amanda would teach him wrestling moves, beat up bullies for him, and never hog the bathroom—which would be a definite improvement! On the screen, Uncle Kazu rewarded the tall high schooler with a disapproving glare.

"*Arigato.*" Tyler nodded respectfully at the screen and heard a snicker from the other side of the living room. Looking over, he caught a glimpse of Lucas nudging Eric with an elbow. Eric cupped a hand over his mouth but his body still bounced up and down with silent laughter. *That's okay*, Tyler thought. A mature eleven-year-old like himself would be able to take a bit of teasing from a ten-year-old like Eric Parker.

Tyler turned the gift over in his hands and tried not to think about the electric socks his Japanese relatives had gotten him one Christmas, or the weird sampling of J-pop music from a previous birthday, or the umbrella decorated with some bug-eyed cartoon character Tyler had never heard of. This present was about the size of a hardcover book, but thinner and heavier. Tyler tore off the paper to uncover a gold frame. A certificate printed in curvy black letters was under the glass:

From this celebrated date, the following star shall be renamed TY SATO to honor the eleventh birthday of Tyler Sato, a resident of Platte Bluff, Nevada. So has it been recorded in the Galactic Registry of Celestial Objects.

"That gift was your Aunt Megumi's idea," explained Uncle Kazu.

Tyler stared at the certificate. Holding it gave him a weird feeling that his life was now connected with the cosmic fate of the universe. His mother leaned over to read the words and nodded in approval. "How exciting! Just imagine, Tyler, that star now has the same name as you!"

Tyler's friends pressed in for a better look, except for Eric. "A star?" Eric asked. "What kind of lame gift is that?"

"You're just jealous," said Tyler. "I'll be right back—this is something my dad would want to know about." Tyler grabbed the cordless phone and ran into the kitchen for a moment of privacy.

His father's number at the Mount Williamson Observatory usually went directly to voicemail, but today his father actually picked up. "Dr. Sato speaking."

"Dad, guess what! Uncle Kazu and Aunt Megumi bought me a star!"

"Did they?" His father's voice sounded skeptical. Tyler imagined him removing his glasses and pinching the bridge of his nose. "Nobody can buy a star, kiddo."

Tyler frowned. "You think it's only rented? I have a certificate and everything!"

"Describe this certificate for me."

Tyler read from the star certificate.

His father just laughed. "My dear older sister has fallen for yet another scam. The Galactic Registry of Celestial Objects? Ha!"

"So . . . I really don't have a star named after me?" Tyler asked.

"I'm afraid not, kiddo. Stars with names are ancient exceptions to the rule. These days we mostly identify stars by their catalog numbers."

"Oh." Tyler's gift suddenly didn't look as special anymore. How had he missed that flecks of gold paint were flaking off the frame, or that the glass was hopelessly smudged?

"Aside from that, how's the party?"

"You're not missing much," said Tyler. "The highlight so far was when I locked a clown in the guest bedroom."

"Ooooookay," said Tyler's father. "I'm not familiar with that particular party game."

"No, Dad, the game is that Amanda is trying to ruin everything, and I'm trying to stop her."

"Sorry about that, kiddo. Believe me, I know how older sisters can be."

Tyler wondered about that for a moment. Had his father moved out of Japan to get away from Aunt Megumi? If so, it had seemed to work, but where would Tyler have to move to in order to get away from Amanda?

"Tell you what, kiddo," his father said. "Pick three or four of your friends, and we'll have a real party for you tomorrow night at the observatory. Stars, planets, maybe a little pizza—"

"And no clowns?" asked Tyler.

"No clowns," his father promised. "Oh, and bring that certificate. We'll take a look at your namesake star through the big scope, just for laughs."

Tyler could hardly wait. Being eleven was better than being ten after all! A pizza party at the observatory with his father. It was hard to imagine how things could get any better.

MIDDLE SOLAR SYSTEM:

Eight hundred eighty-five million miles from Earth, Captain M'Frozza slid into the bridge of the silver spacecraft. "You summoned me, R'Turvo?"

"We are going back to Homabaru-Three," the pilot stated.

M'Frozza blinked each of her eyes in turn: one, two, and three. "What do you mean?" she asked. "I have a challenge here."

The pilot, an adult Mrendarian, waved a purple arm-tentacle over the communications console. "This system has no navigational beacons, no refueling facilities, no quantum responders, and no listing in the latest edition of Qoxxil's Travel Guide to the Galaxy. *There don't even seem to be any established spawn-points for entanglement objects, aside from the space ball we used for our entry. Being here is a complete waste of time. There is no challenge for you."*

"I will decide that," M'Frozza snapped. "Is there no sign of intelligent life at all?"

R'Turvo grumbled something into his face-tentacles.

"What did you say?"

"Here." He flicked an arm-tentacle at one of his displays. "The system's third planet shows life signatures, evidence of primitive industry, and thousands of sorry-looking artificial satellites."

"Ah, yes," said M'Frozza. "Exactly as it was described to me. I will meet their captain on their home world. Just don't expect any direct contact until then because . . . they're an extremely shy species."

"They're shy? And yet they have challenged you to a match?" R'Turvo asked.

"Of course," said M'Frozza. "Why else would I have us come to such a dull, backwater system?"

"I must admit, I can't think of any other possible reason. Very well. Against my better judgment we will continue onward." Pilot R'Turvo returned to his chair and programmed a course to Earth, ninety-five hours before the most important event in human history.

3

TOKYO, JAPAN:

Daiki Shindo tapped his foot against the curb. "Come on, Big Brother. We're already late for school!"

His brother, Riku, flipped through a bundle of magazines someone had left on the curb for recycling. "We have a good excuse."

"We had to watch the birthday party of an American cousin we barely know through a fuzzy video connection." Daiki frowned. "My teachers won't accept that as a real excuse."

"Tell them it was an exchange of international culture." Riku pulled out a manga their mother would never have let him buy. The bikini-clad woman drawn on the cover made Daiki blush, although he couldn't explain exactly why. "Teachers are always impressed by exchanges of international culture," Riku continued. "And we even named a star after him! That should be worth extra credit in physical sciences."

"You always know how to manipulate the adults," said Daiki with admiration. "But still, you've already missed the bell three times this month. We need to hurry!"

"Patience! I think Takeda-sempai will like these, but I need one or two more."

"*Nani?*" Daiki blinked in surprise. "All this trash picking that's making us late isn't even for yourself?"

Riku struck a pose that reminded Daiki of a heroic statue in the park. "While Takeda-sempai is training for the playoffs, my duty as his coach and as his friend is to—"

"Sort through other people's garbage?" Daiki demanded.

Riku maintained his pose but scowled in a way that heroic statues never did. "To take on some of the menial tasks that would distract him from practicing," he stated.

"This is still just for that video-game contest, *ne*?" Daiki asked. "I mean, Takeda-sama hasn't suddenly become a real athlete or anything?"

"*Tekno-Fight Xtreme* requires as much timing and coordination as any sport. You'd know that if you didn't spend all your arcade credits on that antique *RoboMaze* game."

"It's not an antique. It's a classic."

"Daiki-kun, that game is older than you are. I've got

a free version on my phone that I never even use. Why would anyone pay for it in an arcade?"

"You can't battle against something you hold in your hands. It's not the same as the arcade version and you know it!" Daiki angrily kicked over a stack of recycling. A sports magazine landed faceup at his feet. "See this, *Onii-san*? Here is a real athlete, Tomoko-san, the judo superstar!"

Riku raised an eyebrow. "Well, this is certainly a momentous day. Daiki-kun has finally started to notice cute girls!"

Daiki's face burned. "I didn't say she was cute! The important thing is that she's my age, but she could throw Takeda-sama around like an overstuffed pillow."

"Maybe," Riku admitted, "but she wouldn't last thirty seconds against him in a game of *Tekno-Fight Xtreme*."

MIDDLE SOLAR SYSTEM:

Eight hundred seventy-five million miles from Earth, ninety-four hours before the most important event in human history, the pilot of the silver spaceship ordered the ship's technician to the bridge. The technician was an older Mrendarian with an annoyingly cheerful demeanor. "What can I do for you, sir?" the technician asked.

"The toilet is making a horrible noise," Pilot R'Turvo complained. "Fix it!"

"Them, sir."

"Them?"

"Yes, sir. It's a problem with the entire waste recycling system. The toilets in all five of the ship's bathrooms are acting up in the same way. M'Frozza has already asked me to look into the matter."

"All five at once?" R'Turvo asked. "What could be causing that?"

"Dwogleys," the technician stated.

R'Turvo rubbed an arm-tentacle against his brow. "For the last time, N'Gatu, there are no such things as ghosts, spirits, or Dwogleys."

"Don't ever say that," Technician N'Gatu warned. "Once I was a rising star in the Mrendarian Science Academy. Today I'm fixing toilets. How could you explain such a change if not for the interference of Dwogleys?"

"Incompetence might have played a part," R'Turvo suggested.

N'Gatu bristled at the suggestion. "If it's not Dwogleys, my second guess would be electromagnetic interference. I've detected signals from the third innermost planet being broadcast on the same frequencies we use in our recycling and reclamation process."

"The nerve!" R'Turvo shook a tentacle in the air. "Sabotaging our toilets is an outrage upon outrages! Wars have been started for less!"

"Wars, sir?" N'Gatu flapped his face tentacles in confusion.

"Armed conflicts," R'Turvo explained.

N'Gatu continued to stare back blankly.

"Combat between military factions, each bent on destroying the other's home world."

N'Gatu blinked his three eyes and shrugged his arm-tentacles.

"Violent episodes that once wiped out billions and billions of people. You know, wars!"

"This was before the Galaxy Games, sir?" N'Gatu asked timidly.

"Yes, of course it was before the Galaxy Games. Civilized worlds no longer go to war with each other now that we can settle planetary disputes in the sporting arena. Don't you ever read history books?"

"Not if I can help it, sir. Except for the history of plumbing, of course."

TOKYO, JAPAN:

It had turned out to be a typical school day for Daiki Shindo: He had accidentally dropped his lunch onto his shoes, he'd fallen asleep in class, and with one completely innocent remark, he had somehow offended every girl in the fifth grade. Thankfully, *RoboMaze* had been invented for exactly this kind of a day. It wasn't the newest or flashiest game in the arcade, but nothing else made Daiki forget his problems better than weaving his robotic sphere through an alien landscape filled with enemy towers and floating hoops.

But as Daiki's eyes slowly adjusted to the flashing neon lights in the Pack-Punch Video Arcade, he saw his way to the *RoboMaze* game blocked by a thick knot of kids jostling around the *Tekno-Fight Xtreme* machines. Daiki couldn't see the game screens, even bouncing on his toes, but he did spot his older brother's head above most of the others.

"Riku-san! Older Brother! Oy!" Daiki waved his arms until the tall high-school freshman noticed and cleared a path to the front of the crowd.

"What's going on?" Daiki asked.

Riku shrugged. "Just an ordinary day at the Pack-Punch. Takeda-sempai is toying with some young girl. She's a first timer here and they're playing his best game."

Daiki looked at the two gamers. At one set of controls stood an upperclassman in Riku's high school, the sumo-sized Jun Takeda. A sweat-soaked *Tekno-Fight* T-shirt stretched over Jun's rolls of fat. Streams of sweat trickled from his "victory bandana" down the back of his neck. Jun jerked the control stick around and stabbed the buttons with the speed of an attacking cobra, a physical exertion that made him wheeze.

Jun's challenger was a thin girl about Daiki's age. She stood as still as a statue while her fingers played the game console as if it were a concert piano. Twin pigtails geysered from the sides of her head, bouncing in time with a colorful plastic keychain on one of her belt loops. Although the girl was facing away from Daiki as she played, something about her seemed familiar.

Jun keyed in a secret button-and-stick combination for Kaeruyasha, the frog-headed, muscle-bound demon he was controlling. His Kaeruyasha puffed out its vocal sac like a huge balloon under its chin. The sac released with a loud croak and a stream of regurgitated fireflies.

The fireflies shot across the screen at the girl's character, another Kaeruyasha wearing pink robes instead of blue ones. The girl gasped as her character's life-bar dropped by about half its strength. Daiki could see the girl's narrowed eyes reflected in the screen as she flawlessly imitated Jun's moves and sent out her own stream of deadly fireflies.

"Takeda-sama made a mistake, letting her also play Kaeruyasha," Daiki told his brother. "She's learning all his best moves."

Riku grunted at him. "She's a quick study, but nobody can play this game like Takeda-sempai. Your new girlfriend is going to crash and burn!"

Daiki frowned. "She's not my girlfriend."

32

Riku laughed and made kissy noises.

"You are an idiot," said Daiki, which only made Riku laugh harder.

Jun, now gasping for air, misplayed a sequence of buttons. His Kaeruyasha hopped around in confusion. The girl played the sequence in the proper order, causing her attack to unfold correctly. Two tuxedo-clad waiters appeared on the screen, carrying a small table between them. The girl's pink-robed Kaeruyasha pulled a chair up to the table, accepted a glass of wine, and consulted an oversized menu. Meanwhile, a French chef hacked the legs off Jun's blue-robed Kaeruyasha with a two-handed battle spatula. The frog demon's legs were dumped onto a covered plate, which one of the waiters delivered to the table. The girl's Kaeruhyasha attacked the platter with a fork and knife.

"That doesn't seem right," said Daiki. "Why would a Kaeruyasha order frog legs?"

"Fight on, *Sempai!*" Riku shouted as Jun's legless Kaeruyasha climbed into an old-fashioned wheelchair and resumed the battle. The girl's Kaeruyasha wiped the frog legs from its frog lips and leaped into a ready stance.

"That's okay," said Jun. "I don't need my kick attacks to beat you, anyway." His Kaeruyasha flailed out with its arms, but the girl's Kaeruyasha danced backward out of range.

"Stop messing around and beat her!" Riku snapped at

his friend. "Do you really want to lose to some girl with a Pandichigo keychain on her belt?"

"That's not a Pandichigo," Daiki told him. "That's a Hunter-Elf Zeita."

Riku turned on him with an angry sneer. "I'd forgotten you were such an expert on little-girl shows."

"Hunter-Elf Zeita is not a little girl," Daiki stated, amazed that his brother could be so ignorant. "Actually she's pretty tall for an elf of her age, and she gained all the rights and privileges of elf society when she inherited the Longbow of the Eldritch."

"Whatever," said Riku.

All at once, the crowd leaned forward. The life-bar above Jun's Kaeruyasha pulsed red like a dying heartbeat. His frog-demon crouched in a defensive posture, unable to attack. The champion gamer punched the console and yelled at the screen. "*Makenai, makenai, makenai!* I can't lose at this game. The machine must be broken!"

A booming voice crackled from the overhead speakers like an angry god. "The machines are perfectly maintained! Do not disrespect the machines!"

Daiki saw the girl flinch in surprise. "Is that part of the game?" she asked.

"That's Mori-sama," said Jun.

"I see." The girl stole a glance upward at the speakers. "Is he some sort of referee?"

"No, he's just . . . Mori-sama."

"Takeda-kun!" crackled the voice of Mr. Mori. "Stop sweating all over my floors. I just vacuumed that carpet!"

Jun grinned. "Actually, Mori-sama is a really interesting guy. Let me tell you all about him." He was stalling for time, Daiki realized. Jun moved his stick left and right as he spoke, allowing his Kaeruyasha to slowly recover from its injuries. Even its legs were growing back.

"Stop talking and finish him!" shouted someone in the crowd. Others turned the call into a chant: "Finish him! Finish him! Finish him!"

The girl pressed a deft three-button combination. Her Kaeruyasha grabbed Jun's Kaeruyasha and pinned it onto a giant dissection tray. The pink-robed frog-demon then sliced open the blue-robed frog-demon with a scalpel and drew pictures of its internal organs.

"A frog dissection?" asked Daiki. "Ewww, gross!"

The overhead speakers crackled. "It's not gross. It's educational!"

Thoroughly defeated, Jun slumped to the floor and gasped for breath.

The girl spun around and pumped her fist in victory. "*Yatta!* That was amazing! I can't believe I won! He was all like, 'I'm the champion of this game,' and I was all like, 'I bet I could take you,' and he was all like, 'Have you ever played before?' and I was all like, 'No, but I've been studying your moves for an hour now and I think I see the pattern,' and he was all like, 'Bring it on, little girl.' And I remembered what Obaa-chan always says about matching your strengths against an opponent's weaknesses, and that's totally what I did!"

Daiki blinked at the intensity of the girl's outburst.

Riku winced and rubbed his ears. "Ouch! They make dog whistles that aren't as high-pitched as that girl's voice."

Daiki just nodded. Now that he could see the girl's oval face and large expressive eyes, he felt stronger than ever that he had seen her before, but where? She wasn't a student at his school, and he was pretty sure he hadn't seen her around the neighborhood.

The girl took a deep breath and became much calmer again. She faced the former champion and bowed respectfully. "Thank you for teaching me your game, Takeda-sensei. It's not much like real fighting, but it was still a lot of fun."

Jun glared at her with evil eyes over the top of his asthma inhaler.

The girl bent down to face him, suddenly noticing his condition. "Hey, are you all right?"

Jun waved her away, rose unsteadily to his feet, and took another puff from the inhaler. "You got . . . lucky," he gasped.

Riku grabbed Jun's arm and steered him to a chair in the vending area. "It's okay, buddy. I know you should have won. She took advantage of your asthma attack, and that's so uncool!"

Daiki trailed after them. "Did you hear what she said?" he asked his brother. "She said that *Tekno-Fight Xtreme* wasn't much like real fighting. Don't you think that's a weird thing to say?"

"Chill out, Daiki-kun," said Riku. "Can't you see the champ needs to rest?"

"He's not the champ anymore," Daiki reminded his brother.

Riku's face turned red. "Aw, man! You don't know when to let up, do you? Go hang out with your new girl-friend and leave us alone!"

"She's not my girlfriend," said Daiki through clenched teeth, although he did want to congratulate the girl on playing such a masterful game. He was not the only one, either. It was hard to even see her through the thick crowd of well-wishers until two older kids hoisted her onto their shoulders for a victory parade around the arcade.

"Hey! Hey! Excuse me," called Daiki.

He almost had the girl's attention when a sharp voice cut through the celebration. Its angry edge seemed to draw all light and oxygen from the room. "TO-MOH-KOOOOH!"

Daiki turned, along with everybody else, to see a short, gnarled, wrinkled, white-haired figure leaning on a polished wooden stick at the arcade entrance. Her ancient eyes were angry and intense as she addressed the girl. "What are you doing in this place?"

"Obaa-chan!" The girl looked at her watch and gasped. "I'm sorry! I didn't realize it was so late. *Sumimasen!*" She dropped to the floor and ran toward the old woman.

Jun Takeda, still pale and wheezing, wrenched himself free of Riku and stepped between the girl and the old woman. "Hold on a moment, granny. Let the girl play one more game. I've got a reputation to defend."

"A reputation? Is that so?" The old woman waved her stick dangerously close to Jun's face. "Young man, I'd suggest you give up on building a reputation for fighting little girls and instead develop one for respecting your elders."

"Hey, be careful with that!" Jun put a hand on the old woman's stick. "I'm just asking for a few minutes to prove that I can defeat anybody, best two out of three."

Daiki heard the old woman's stick strike—*crack, crack, crack!*—before he ever saw it move. Jun dropped to the ground as his knees gave out. He clutched his wrist and winced in pain.

"Would you like to try that again?" The old woman cracked an amused smile. "Best two out of three?"

"No, thank you, ma'am," Jun squeaked.

The overhead speakers crackled. "Takeda-kun! If you're going to bleed, take it outside!"

"He's not bleeding!" Riku shouted at the ceiling. "Somebody must have spilled a Cherry Sweat-Water right where he fell down."

The old woman turned her back on Jun. "Hurry along, Tomoko-chan. You are already late for practice."

"Yes, Obaa-chan," said the girl wearily.

"Tomoko-chan. . . ." Daiki dug into his backpack for the judo magazine he'd found that morning, with its cover image of a young girl in a fighting uniform. She was pulling down her right eyelid and sticking out her tongue at the camera, but Daiki could still tell it was her.

He ran from the arcade to catch a final glimpse of the girl and the old woman disappearing into the street crowd. "I knew she looked familiar. She's Tomizawa Tomoko!"

4

PLATTE BLUFF, NEVADA:

On the evening after his birthday, Tyler's dad drove him up
Mount Williamson to his star-searching birthday-plus-one-
day party along with three other boys: Brayden McKay,
John Moon, and Lucas Alvarez. Tyler had decided not to
invite Eric Parker. Now that Tyler had turned eleven, he no
longer had anything in common with mere ten-year-olds
like Eric.

"This wasn't always called Mount Williamson," John
told them all as their car wound upward around the moun-
tain. "For thousands of years my grandfather's people, the
Shoshone, called it Place Where Desert Meets Sky."

"And what did your other grandfather's people call
it?" asked Tyler.

John frowned. "My other grandfather's last name is
Williamson. What do you think?"

"We should give it a new name," said Brayden. "How

about Place Where Tyler's Father Sees Stars?"

"How about Place Where Pizza Meets My Stomach?" asked Lucas.

"I'm sticking with ancient Shoshone tradition," said John. "You're the tiebreaker, Ty. What do you think we should call this *place* where the *desert* meets the *sky*?"

Tyler thought for a moment. "Mount Tyler Sato Is Awesome," he decided.

"Dude!" Brayden's nostrils flared with disapproval. "You already have a star named after you. How many things named after you does a single person need?"

At the top of Mount Williamson, the minivan crunched to a stop on a pack of fresh-fallen snow that sparkled in the vehicle's headlights. The boys got out and traced the sweeping white band of the Milky Way that stretched from east to west, surrounded by the brightest field of stars that any of them had ever seen.

John waved a hand as if to make a formal introduction. "Desert, meet the sky. Sky, meet the desert. I'm sure you two have a lot to talk about."

"I still think Mount Tyler Sato Is Awesome could catch on," said Tyler.

The only building on the summit was an observatory run by the Platte Bluff Institute of Science, where Dr. Sato had tenure as a professor of astronomy and astrophysics. The observatory roof held one large dome and two smaller ones, each containing a huge telescope with a clear view of the stars.

Tyler's dad gave the boys a tour. Tyler had seen the observatory before, but John, Lucas, and Brayden asked a lot of questions. Tyler had to admit that his dad's work really was pretty cool, which was probably why he spent so much time doing it.

Tyler's dad called to his assistants. "Victor? Joanne? Could you set up the big scope for us? Pranav, see what you can make of the coordinates on this certificate."

A short man with dark hair and a scruffy beard stepped forward to accept the certificate. He looked at it and sighed. "Professor Sato? I'm still a bit jetlagged from that quasar symposium in Tenerife. Couldn't I have the night off?"

"We brought pizza," Tyler's father offered, holding up a stack of pizza boxes.

"Oh, it's from Antonio's!" Pranav grinned. "Why didn't you say so?"

"Grad students are 90 percent stomach," Tyler's father explained to the boys.

"I could be a grad student," said Lucas as he helped himself to a slice with mushrooms and peppers.

The boys ate pizza while Tyler's dad made star certificates on one of the observatory computers. Soon Brayden, Lucas, and John all had certificates that looked at least as good as Tyler's. "Mine was supposed to be special," Tyler complained quietly to his father.

"We're not here to celebrate a worthless sheet of paper, kiddo. We're here to celebrate you and your birthday by printing out all the worthless sheets of paper we can think up."

After that, Tyler enjoyed himself more and more as he and his friends churned out star certificates by the dozen:

From this celebrated date, the following star shall be renamed Alpha Sweatsocks to honor the smell of our soccer coach, Mr. Boughis.

From this celebrated date, the following star shall be renamed Obvious Toupee to honor the hairstyle of our principal, Mr. Johansson.

From this celebrated date, the following star shall be renamed Pukeburger Minor to honor the menu in our school cafeteria.

The boys were rolling with laughter when Pranav, the grad student, ran back downstairs. He waved a set of oversized pages like a flag. "Professor Sato! Take a look at this!"

"What have you got there?" asked Tyler's dad.

Pranav spread the printouts across the floor because the table was still covered with pizza plates. "Here are the prints from tonight, and these are from the same part of the sky taken last week. The object you asked us to find wasn't there a few days ago."

Tyler and his friends crowded around. All the stars were in the same places in both printouts, except for one. The newer printout had a small spot marked "TY SATO" under a triangle of three bright stars, but in the older printout there was no "TY SATO."

"Of course Tyler's star wouldn't have been around last week," Brayden scoffed. "Tyler only got his star certificate yesterday, so that star's only one day old!"

John whispered, "All right, whose turn is it to play Let's Explain Stuff to Brayden?"

"Not me," said Lucas. "I spent twenty minutes today listening to him complain that a grapefruit doesn't taste anything like a grape."

"Well, it doesn't," said Brayden.

Tyler was still studying the printouts. "Stars don't usually pop out of nowhere like that, do they?"

"New stars are constantly forming," Tyler's father told him. "Just not overnight like we seem to see here. That's why it's safe to say this isn't a star at all. Victor, let's check this object against known comets, asteroids, and the other usual suspects." He scooped up the printouts and ran upstairs. "Stay put, boys," he called over his shoulder.

"Your dad has the coolest job in the world," Lucas told Tyler.

"Yeah, I guess." Tyler took another slice of pizza and nibbled the edge. "But he's missing my star-searching birthday-plus-one-day party, just like he missed my other birthday party."

Lucas typed up a certificate to rename the Andromeda Galaxy after his pet ferret. John typed up a certificate that said the moons of Jupiter belonged to the Western Shoshone Nation. By the time the three astronomers came back downstairs, it was almost time for the boys to leave.

"Well, Dr. Sato?" Lucas asked. "Is Tyler's star an asteroid or a comet?"

"Or maybe it's a blinky-light star that turns off and on and off and on again!" Brayden exclaimed.

"In space those are called pulsars," said Tyler's father.

"That's right," said Brayden. "Blinky-blinky pulsars."

"However, I'm almost certain we're looking at a standard-issue asteroid. We'll just need some help to calculate its trajectory."

"Help from who?" asked John.

"Come on, I'll show you." Tyler's dad led the boys to a terminal where Joanne was typing on a computer keyboard. "After Joanne enters our observations, we'll email them to a central archive called the Minor Planet Center so other astronomers can confirm the object and track it. As the Earth turns, TY SATO will come into view in Hawaii. There's a telescope on Mount Haleakala that's made for just this kind of thing. A few hours later, astronomers in Asia will get a good view. There are major observatories in South Africa, then the Canary Islands off the coast of Africa will come online, followed by the major observatories of Chile. The west coast of South America has the same longitude as the east coast of North America, and soon after that we'll be back at work here in Nevada."

"So people can watch my star twenty-four hours a day!" Tyler exclaimed.

"More or less. There are telescopes up in orbit too, if we need them. By this time tomorrow, we should have a rough idea of how TY SATO is moving, especially if we can find some additional sightings in any of the archived databases. Victor, go ahead and pull the *Palomar Sky Survey*—let's see if this thing was around in the 1950s."

"Right away, Professor Sato," said Victor.

"I'm almost ready to send," said Joanne. "All I need is a temporary designation."

"A what?" the boys all asked.

"That's a name we give to any objects we find," Joanne explained. "It's just something to call the thing until it gets a permanent name."

"Oh oh oh! Pizza Party Victory Star!" John suggested.

"What about Planetzilla?" asked Lucas.

"Blinky-Blinky-Blinkety-Blink!" Brayden insisted.

"Guys," said Tyler. "It already has a name: TY SATO. I even have a certificate to prove it." He held up his gold-framed star certificate, and none of his friends could argue with that.

Joanne typed "TY SATO" into the computer. Then she pressed a key to make the data available to observatories around the world.

MIDDLE SOLAR SYSTEM:

Six hundred and five million miles from Earth, the pilot of the silver spaceship wished that his species had hair so that he could tear his out in frustration. The noise from the toilets had only grown louder as the ship drew closer to the third innermost planet. The racket now sounded like a thousand babbling voices blended with a thousand off-key songs and a thousand tentacles drawn across sheets of glass—all mashed together and flushed through a thousand metal pipes.

The door irised open and Technician N'Gatu glided through on a jet of yellow green slime. One of his tentacles held a box of tools.

"Technician! Report!"

"Still working on the problem, sir."

"How long before you figure a way to shield us from this horrible noise?"

N'Gatu cleared his throat. "Actually, sir, I'm not trying to shield us. I believe the signals are a means of communication, so I've been trying to patch our waste systems into the ship's signal filter and translation device."

Pilot R'Turvo stared in horror. "You mean the inhabitants of this system are trying to communicate with our toilets*?"*

"The system inhabitants, or perhaps the Dwogleys."

R'Turvo's nostril-holes hissed and steamed. "For the love of freen! Get it through that thick cartilage encasement of yours that Dwogleys are a myth!"

"With all due respect, sir, I've seen things. Things you couldn't possibly imagine. Things that can only be explained by invisible creatures capable of speaking through our toilets."

"Well, then, would you mind watching the controls for a moment? I need to deliver a strongly worded message." The Mrendarian pilot slid into the bathroom and shut the door behind him, sixty-five hours before the most important event in human history.

5

Daiki ducked behind a vending card machine and braced himself for an explosion. Not the safe and fun kind of explosion that lit up the sky during a summer fireworks festival, but the unpredictable violence that happens when you taunt a bull. Or when you tease a sumo wrestler about his weight. Or when you make fun of a high-school video-game champion who's just lost to an eleven-year-old girl. Exactly that kind of explosion was only seconds away.

From his hiding spot, Daiki watched Jun Takeda swagger through the neon archway into the Pack-Punch Video Arcade, with Riku at his side pretending to be a coach. Today Riku even wore a gym sweatshirt and a whistle around his neck. On the far side of the room, a bank of five *Tekno-Fight Xtreme* machines played through their demo scenes while making *punch-kick-slap* noises over an electronic soundtrack. The middle machine was the one Tomoko Tomizawa had used to whip Jun's butt, and a taunting picture of Miss Tomizawa now hung on the wall above that machine.

My fault, thought Daiki. He turned his head slightly and spotted Mr. Mori standing at a nearby counter, next to a bank of surveillance video screens. Flashing colored lights glinted off the arcade owner's spectacles as he polished hundred-yen coins with a yellow-stained cloth. Mr. Mori didn't seem to be paying attention to anything but those coins, but Daiki knew better. All those video screens and microphone controls weren't just for show!

Ten minutes earlier, Daiki had been showing the judo magazine he'd found to his friend Katsuro Tabei. They were fifty feet away from Mr. Mori's station and masked by the sounds of *Tako-Tako Dance* and *Missile Zap* machines, but that hadn't mattered. Suddenly and without warning, Mr. Mori had appeared out of nowhere. Before Daiki could twitch his fingers, the magazine slipped out of his grasp.

"What is this?" Mr. Mori asked.

"That's Tomizawa-sama," said Katsuro in reverent tones. "She's the one who beat Takeda-sama at his own game."

A flash of red neon reflected off Mr. Mori's spectacles. "Ah yes, I remember like it was yesterday."

"It was yesterday," said Daiki.

Mr. Mori chuckled. "So much noise, such celebration, and what a look on Takeda-kun's face! It's been years since this place has been shaken up like that. Such an accomplishment deserves recognition, *ne*?"

Daiki had protested as hard as he could. He had warned Mr. Mori that Jun would get upset if he saw the picture, but the arcade owner refused to listen. Two minutes later, Mr. Mori had the magazine cover mounted in the elaborate wooden frame that used to hold a picture of Jun Takeda. The kanji characters for "grand champion" were etched into the wood and painted in red, white, black, and gold.

Dozens of gamers had cheered and laughed as Mr. Mori hung the picture above the Techno-Fight Xtreme game. Now, as Jun walked through the arcade, they all fell silent. When Jun said hello, nobody would look him in the eye. The big gamer's muscles twitched, like a deer in a hunter's crosshairs. Jun hadn't noticed the picture yet, but somehow, he sensed that something was wrong.

Riku moved and spoke his coaching patter as always. "You're still a champ, *Sempai*. You just need a little practice to get back on top. Set yourself up for a solo game and I'll put some more cash on my game card."

As Riku passed by, Daiki grabbed his brother by the arm and whispered, *"Nii-san,* you have to get Takeda-sama out of here. It's for his own good."

Riku pushed Daiki away. "For his own good, he needs to get back into the game."

"But when he sees Tomoko-san—"

"Your girlfriend? She's here?"

"No! I mean, yes! I mean, she's not my girlfriend!"

Riku glared. "Is she here?"

"Not . . . exactly." Daiki's eyes darted upward to the picture.

Riku snorted. "Don't bother us with your nonsense, Daiki-kun. That little girl got lucky. Anyone can have a lucky game, but it was just a fluke. Nobody has ever beaten Takeda-sempai two times out of three, and nobody ever will." He continued onward without paying Daiki any more attention.

Daiki glanced over at Mr. Mori. He thought about giving him one more warning about Jun's temper, until he noticed the amused smirk on Mr. Mori's face. The arcade owner knew exactly what would happen when Jun saw that picture, and he didn't even care!

Jun Takeda settled in at the machine directly under the shrine to Tomoko Tomizawa. The judo girl with the Hunter-Elf Zeita keychain seemed to be staring directly down at him. A crowd of amused gamers moved in slowly, with none of them daring to get too close.

Katsuro snapped a picture with a mobile phone.

Jun played his game, still without looking up.

A middle-school boy giggled, then slapped a hand over his mouth.

Jun whirled around. "All right, what's going on?"

Eyes flickered upward to the picture on the wall.

In a single slow-motion movement, Jun turned and looked up. His jaw dropped. His fists clenched. His ears reddened from the sudden burst of laughter at his expense, and nobody was laughing harder or louder than Mr. Mori himself.

"I am the champion!" Jun roared. "If I lose, it must be because these crummy machines were rigged against me!" He pounded his fists on the Techno-Fight Xtreme console and kicked the front of the machine hard enough to blur the screen.

Mr. Mori quickly closed the distance between himself and the teen gamer and clamped his fingers on Jun's shoulder. "Nobody abuses my game machines. Leave now and do not ever return."

"Don't worry, I won't!" Jun's words were delivered with the strength and defiance of a warrior from a samurai drama on television. He then spoiled it by crying like a baby from the pressure of Mr. Mori's hand on his shoulder. "Not so tight, not so tight, not so tiiiiiight!" he shouted as the arcade owner steered him toward the exit.

"You won't see me in here again, either," Riku announced. "Even if the world came to an end this week, I wouldn't stop by here to say good-bye. This dump doesn't deserve a grand champion like Jun Takeda!"

A few gamers applauded as Riku walked away.

Daiki cleared his throat to try his own dramatic speech. "I think . . . I will stop playing video games here . . . after my money runs out," he stated. "And I won't put any more credit on my Pack-Punch game card until tomorrow!" Somehow this speech didn't come out as strongly as Daiki had hoped. It would have been embarrassing if anyone had been paying attention to him.

MIDDLE SOLAR SYSTEM:

Five hundred seventy-five million miles from Earth and sixty-two hours before the most important event in human history, the pilot of the silver spaceship watched his screens through two bleary eyes. He kept the third closed while he took turns resting different portions of his brain. The intercom beeped and flashed. The pilot blinked his third eye open and whipped out a tentacle to slap the activation button. "Yes, Captain?"

The captain's young voice bubbled over with enthusiasm. "Pilot! Have you noticed the view outside? It's so pretty!"

The pilot glanced at his magnified screens. On the starboard bow was the approaching crescent of Jupiter with its banded atmosphere of raging storms. "Yes, Captain, it is pretty, but once you've seen one gas giant, you've seen them all."

"But you can really see these," the captain insisted. "There are no flares, transport tracks, or range icons in the way."

"Yes, thank you for pointing out the lack of navigational data provided by the inhabitants of this system," said the pilot bitterly. "It's the reason I must stare constantly at my control screen, in case a sudden course correction is required."

"Ah, yes," said the captain. "Well, then, why don't you go back to doing that, and I'll go back to enjoying the view."

"Wonderful." The pilot bit his face-tentacles and thought of all the choice words he'd have for the girl if she weren't the captain—and if she also weren't the ambassador's daughter-child.

TOKYO, JAPAN:

Daiki slid his game card into the front slot of the *Robo-Maze* game. The screen welcomed him back, recalling his robot's configuration and the last level he'd cleared. It also told him that his card had less than five hundred yen on it and would soon run out of money.

Between dodging waves of enemy drones, Daiki's eyes flicked toward the bank of *Tekno-Fight Xtreme* machines. It had been an hour since Jun Takeda had left the arcade forever, and Riku along with him. Katsuro had gone home soon after that. Mr. Mori had taken down the picture of Tomoko Tomizawa, and the arcade owner was now tinkering with a screwdriver and flashlight in the exposed guts of the broken machine.

As his robotic sphere churned through another level

of *RoboMaze*, something caught Daiki's attention at the neon archway over the entrance. A breath caught in his throat. It was her, Tomoko Tomizawa, the judo star who had beaten Jun Takeda at his own game!

Daiki watched Tomoko glance anxiously over her shoulder, causing her pigtails to whip around her shoulders. Then she nodded and ran straight at Daiki. His fingers slipped on the controls, and his robot nicked the side of a glowing hoop and disintegrated. Game over.

"*Sumimasen,*" Tomoko excused herself as she pushed past Daiki and wedged herself into the gap between his *RoboMaze* console and a *City Crisis* machine that wasn't being played just then. It was such a tight space that Daiki hardly believed anyone could fit into it, but Tomoko folded her thin arms and legs to make herself smaller. "Please, don't let me disturb your game," she whispered. "Pretend I'm not here."

"Um, okay," said Daiki. "Are you in some kind of trouble?"

"No." She winked. "Not yet."

Daiki wondered whether Jun Takeda had come after the girl to avenge his video-gaming honor, but that was a silly thought. Tomoko Tomizawa was a judo champion! In a real-life fight against her, Jun wouldn't fare any better than his sliced-up *Tekno-Fight* character had.

Daiki kept one eye on the main entrance until a

short old woman strode into the arcade. It was the same old woman who had cut short Tomoko's last visit, except that now she looked even angrier. The old woman smacked the butt of her stick against the floor, creating a sharp *clack* that sounded over the background of electronic noise. All around the arcade, gamers looked up in surprise.

"Tomoko-chan!" the woman snapped.

Daiki saw Tomoko flinch at the sound of her name. He hummed the *RoboMaze* theme song and tapped the controls to cover any noise Tomoko might make.

"I know you're in here, Tomoko-chan!" The old woman walked a circuit around the beeping and flashing machines, peering into every nook and open space. Daiki sidestepped to block Tomoko from the old woman's view just as she walked by. He tried to smile as he did so, but the intensity of the old woman's scowl made it impossible for him to look at her.

The old woman circled the arcade, ending up back at the main entrance. "You'll be sorry if you don't come with me. Do you hear me? You'll be sorry!" She glared one last time around the arcade and then she was gone.

Tomoko stretched her limbs and allowed Daiki to help her out of the cramped space between the game machines. "Okay, *now* I'm in trouble. The old witch will probably send me to bed without supper for a month!"

"Is she your grandmother?" asked Daiki.

Tomoko shook her head. "I call her 'Obaa-chan' but she's not really my grandmother. She's my grandmother's mother, and the worst taskmaster of her generation!" She made whipping gestures with her wrists. "Cha-kow! Cha-kow! Cha-kow!"

"I'm sorry to hear—"

"She never lets me have any fun," Tomoko continued. "It's always practice, practice, practice! Exhibition, exhibition, exhibition! Fight, fight, fight! I'm so sick of it all. Why can't I just play games with my friends like any other normal kid?"

"Well, why can't you?" Daiki asked.

Tomoko's eyes seemed to be focused on something very far away. Daiki listened for her reply, but all he heard for a long moment were the beeps and explosions of video-game consoles. "Because I don't have any friends," she said at last. "I mean sure, I had plenty of them in my old school, but not here in the city. Here I'm just a creepy girl with a bunch of judo moves and a scary great-grandmother."

"I'll be your friend." Daiki wanted to kick himself for sounding so dumb, but Tomoko's face brightened instantly.

"You will? That's great! My name is Tomizawa Tomoko."

"I know!"

She waited for a moment before asking, "And you are?"

Daiki slapped his forehead, hardly believing how stupid he was being. Tomoko was a famous judo star and magazine cover girl, so she hardly needed to introduce herself to him, but of course it didn't work that way for ordinary kids like him. "Shindo Daiki," he told her.

She took his arm. "Come on, Shindo-san. Let's go for an ice cream, or rent rollerblades, or maybe do some shopping. Yes, I know boys hate shopping, but what if we bought something cool? Hey! What's your favorite TV show?"

"Well . . ." He thought about the Hunter-Elf Zeita figurine on Tomoko's belt loop. Was she really a fan of the show or did she wear the character as a joke? If he said he was a Zeita fan, would she make fun of him like Riku had? "I don't watch much television," he said.

"My favorite show is *Hunter-Elf Zeita*," she told him. "You'd probably like it if you gave it a try. It's about this elf girl named Zeita who fights dragons with a magical quiver of arrows. There's a store nearby that sells nothing but Zeita shirts and toys. Come on. We can buy matching T-shirts!"

Daiki let himself be dragged along and wondered just what he was getting into.

6

Tyler's dad spent all night in the observatory. He didn't even come home the next day because that was when data came in from the other side of the world, or from telescopes up in orbit. Tyler worried even though his mom said not to.

Forty-eight hours before the most important event in human history, Tyler dialed his father's mobile phone number. Back when he was only ten, Tyler had been told to never bother his dad at work, but Tyler was eleven now and he had important things to talk about.

"Hello, Dad?" Tyler whispered.

"I can barely hear you, kiddo," his father answered. "Are you calling from inside a closet because your mother wouldn't approve of you bothering me at work?"

"Um . . . no." Tyler leaned back and brushed a

bunch of hanging jackets out of his way. "I'm calling from inside a closet because I get better reception in here. Anyway, what's going on with my star-asteroid-comet thing?"

"It's too early to tell, kiddo." Tyler's dad yawned. He'd probably gotten no sleep at all, Tyler realized. "We're compiling data from Europe right now. The object is moving too fast to be in a stable orbit around the sun, and the trajectory is all wrong. Comets and asteroids just don't move like that."

"Oh."

"TY SATO is one mystery after another, but we'll figure it out. Astronomers in sixteen countries are looking into it now. Even if nothing else comes of all our efforts, we're bringing the world community together on this, and that's never a bad thing."

"That's great," said Tyler. "With so many other astronomers on the job, you'll be able to come home sooner, right?"

"I hope so, but it's hard to say. We've never seen an object quite like this before, and there's so much work to do! I've got to go now. Say hi to your mother and Amanda for me."

"I will, Dad. Come home soon, okay?" Tyler said, but his father had already hung up.

MIDDLE SOLAR SYSTEM:

Four hundred thirty million miles from Earth, the Mrendarian captain held a book up between two of her tentacles. She flipped pages with a third tentacle and took notes with a fourth. Galactic history was such a snooze. The only thing that kept her awake through her lesson was the horrible sound from the bathroom of her quarters.

The intercom beeped and flashed. A call from the bridge, she noted with distaste. Normally the captain would be glad for an excuse to put her homework aside, but the pilot was such a grump—and more cranky than ever since they'd arrived in this system. "Yes, Pilot?" she asked.

"Quantum call for you, Captain," he stated. "It's the ambassador."

"Put him through, please."

"Of course I will," said the pilot. "It's what the ambassador has requested."

The holographic display crackled to life with an image of the Mrendarian ambassador. "Hello, Father-Parent," said the captain.

"M'Frozza, what in the Galaxy is that horrible sound?"

The captain looked back at the bathroom portal. "Oh, that. It's . . . just some local music. The natives of this system are welcoming our ship with a big parade."

64

"A parade?" her father asked skeptically. "R'Turvo did not mention a parade."

"Oh, but it is the grandest parade I have ever seen! Our embassy ship is surrounded by a flotilla of transports, and pyro displays are flaring around every planet in the system! All manner of native songs and dances are being broadcast over the local quantums!"

"Well, that does sound appropriate."

"Very appropriate," M'Frozza agreed, looking out at the empty blackness outside her cabin window. "I'm so glad you approve!"

"I applaud the sentiment, even if their musical taste is suspect. I thought at first that you were being tortured, and we'd have to dig into the government coffers for your ransom."

"Father-Parent!" M'Frozza tried her best to sound outraged. "You're the one who always taught me to tolerate the cultures of other species."

"That music makes me want to reconsider. Has the challenge been made yet?"

"Not officially. They're . . . very strict about protocol here. I won't meet the local captain until all the welcoming ceremonies are over, and that might take a couple hundred pulses yet."

"So it is not too late for you to withdraw from the system?"

"It would be a great dishonor for me to leave now."

M'Frozza's father sighed through all of his nose-holes, and she knew what would be coming next. "You established yourself already by defeating the Ossmendians. Your obligations under the Challenge Season have been met, and there is nothing else to be won by accepting an invitation to such a backward system."

"They are not backward," she stated. "They are as advanced and cultured as . . . well, not Mrendaria, but perhaps they are as advanced and cultured as the Kreegon Empire."

"My daily freen is as advanced and cultured as the Kreegon Empire, though I've never thought to meet with it in the gaming arena. Do as you wish, Daughter-Child, but be careful and mind the pilot."

"I will, Father-Parent." Quietly she added, "I love you," but the ambassador had already broken the connection.

PLATTE BLUFF, NEVADA:

Tyler went over to Eric's house after school. None of Tyler's eleven-year-old friends were around and he'd decided that hanging out with a ten-year-old wasn't so bad—especially since Eric had a basketball hoop in his driveway and Tyler always shot better there than at school or in the park.

Tyler and Eric took turns shooting from a painted free-throw line, pretending they were NBA stars playing in Eric's Driveway Stadium. "Eric Parker goes to the line to shoot two," said Eric, doubling as his own announcer.

"With the game tied, Parker only needs one to win the game."

"No way," said Tyler.

"Parker looks around at the sold-out crowd of twenty thousand fans. They've screamed themselves hoarse through five overtime periods. Now they're all silent as Parker takes his first free-throw shot."

"Except for all the Tyler Sato fans," Tyler added. "They're booing Parker and waving banners to distract him. Booo! Booooo! Booooooooo!"

"How rude." Eric threw a shot at the basket mounted on his parents' garage. The ball bounced off the rim and nearly knocked off his glasses on the rebound.

"And the crowd goes wild!" Tyler ran along the stockade fence that separated Eric's driveway from the next-door neighbor's side yard. He held out his right hand to collect high-fives from imaginary spectators on the other side. "Fifty thousand Tyler Sato fans hold up 'Eric Parker is a loser' signs."

"Eric's Driveway Stadium only holds twenty thousand," Eric reminded him.

"While Parker was taking forever to shoot, the Tyler Sato Construction Company built extra seats and sold thirty thousand more tickets."

Eric adjusted his glasses so he could glare at Tyler over top of the frames. "Eric Parker pauses between his first and second free-throw shots so Tyler Sato can wake up from the crazy dream he's having. Are you awake now, Tyler?"

Tyler pointed up at the sky. "The Tyler Sato Construction Company removes the stadium roof. Now the Goodyear blimp can zoom in on Eric Parker missing his second shot."

"In your dreams." Eric threw the ball, swish, right through the hoop. "The crowd goes wild as Eric Parker wins!"

"But Tyler Sato takes his last possession." Tyler grabbed the ball on the second bounce and dribbled past Eric and down the driveway to the sickly green shrub that marked the clearance line.

"It doesn't matter," Eric called after him. "The clock runs out."

"Except that Tyler Sato has activated his time-travel sneakers." Tyler turned to face the basket. "Now he can make one last drive down the lane!"

Eric put out his arms and positioned himself to block Tyler from approaching the hoop. "The referee blows his whistle. Sato has committed a time-traveling violation."

"The Goodyear Blimp lands on the referee's head. There's nobody left to stop Sato from taking his shot."

"Come on, Tyler. Give me the ball." Eric pushed Tyler back a few feet at a time until the driveway met the sidewalk. Tyler's sneakers landed on a yellow *X* of chalk he'd drawn on the ground before the game.

Tyler grinned, gripped the ball, and straightened up to take his shot.

"Wait," said Eric. "Come closer to the basket. You can shoot from the foul line for the win, and I won't even block you."

Tyler shook his head. In Eric's driveway he played better than anywhere else, but from his lucky spot on the sidewalk, he was invincible. "Tyler Sato takes his patented corkscrew jumpshot that only he can make." Tyler jumped, turned around in the air, and launched the ball at the basket. It bounced off the backboard and in.

"Nooooo!" Eric dropped to his knees. "Why do you always do that?"

Tyler shrugged. "I'd never make that shot in a million years on any other court, but in your driveway it just clicks." Tyler waved at his imaginary fans in the imaginary bleachers. "The game ends and a hundred thousand Tyler Sato fans pour onto the court!"

"A hundred thousand people can't fit on a basketball court," said Eric.

"They can if they're all really skinny. They follow the Tyler Sato Diet Program—delicious chocolate shakes for breakfast, delicious chocolate shakes for lunch, followed by a sensible dinner, and more chocolate shakes for dessert!"

The front door of the house opened and Eric's mom stepped onto the concrete stoop. "Who's winning?"

"I am!" they both shouted.

"Wonderful," she said, but she wasn't smiling. "It's time to come in now, Eric. Tyler, you should get back to your family before they worry."

"But it's still early," Tyler said. "My parents won't be worried yet."

"Have them put on the TV," said Eric's mom. "Then tell me they're not worried."

Tyler ran all the way home. His mom and sister were already in the living room watching the All-News network. His mom hugged him close. "Tyler, thank goodness you're here."

"Why?" he asked. "What's going on?" He looked over at the TV.

"—and so far NASA has no comments," said the All-News program host. "Right now we have Senator Archer in our studio with us. Senator, welcome."

"Thanks for having me, Casey," said an older man with hair like white cotton candy.

"Senator, what do you have there?"

Senator Archer held up a manila folder like the kind Tyler used in school. "This is a file that's come to me from a friend at NASA. For the past two days, our government has been tracking an object that's on a collision course with Earth. We have only forty-six hours until the most important event in human history, and possibly the end of human history itself."

Tyler felt something catch in his throat, and he couldn't breathe right. Was the world really about to end? He couldn't even imagine it. His mom was crying while Amanda stared at the TV.

"What can you tell us about this object?" asked the reporter.

The senator opened the folder. "There's not much information here. That's why I'm calling on the president to release anything else he has. All I can really tell you is that the government has given the object a code name. They call it TY SATO."

Tyler's mouth dropped open, and he thought it might stick that way all night.

1

MIDDLE SOLAR SYSTEM:

Aboard the silver spaceship, four hundred million miles from Earth, thousands of radio and TV stations blared through the toilet in the bathroom of the captain's quarters. The ship's technician had disassembled the wall panel, revealing a maze of pipes, cranks, wheels, and junction boxes.

With his head wedged in the wall, he reached back a tentacle. "Sonic wrench!"

"Sonic what?" asked the captain.

"Sonic wrench!" The technician had to shout to be heard above the din.

Captain M'Frozza reached into the technician's toolbox and selected a metal cylinder with a spiked ball on the end. She held it out with a hopeful expression. The technician accepted the tool, then pulled himself out of the wall and traded it for a wedge of yellow plastic that sprouted short tubes along its edge.

"Just a few final adjustments, Captain." He ducked back into the wall and the voices all buzzed together. "Almost . . . almost . . . there!" The waterfall of sound ended abruptly, except for a single voice. The technician gurgled at his accomplishment. "I've isolated one of the signals and blocked all the others out. With a little work, we should be able to select whichever signal we want."

"That's great!"

The technician listened to the voice for a moment, then sighed through his nose-holes. "It makes no sense yet. The ship's translator unit is still adjusting to the unfamiliar language. It could take a few pulses."

The captain nodded. She did not tell the technician that the more advanced language implant in her head had already made the adjustment. The transmission was a woman's voice delivering the nearby planet's first message ever to be heard and understood by alien ears:

"Cheeseburgers? For breakfast? Your parents might say no, but we say yes with new Cheeseburger Crunch cereal! Delicious bun-shaped flakes of wheat with brown patties, green pickles, red tomatoes, and yellow cheese squares that stay crunchy in milk! Fortified with ten essential vitamins, Cheeseburger Crunch is the cheesy-beefy part of this nutritious breakfast!"

M'Frozza frowned. "Father-Parent would certainly not approve."

TOKYO, JAPAN:

Daiki and his classmates puzzled over the latest announcement from Principal Usami. It was his third reminder that all after-school club meetings were canceled for the day. This time, the principal also added that classes and club meetings for the next two days would be canceled as well.

Daiki's friend, Katsuro Tabei, leaned across the aisle. "No school for two days? This is becoming serious, Daiki-kun."

Daiki was surprised that Katsuro would try to chat in the middle of a lesson, but others in the class were talking as well and Mrs. Asahina wasn't stopping them.

The teacher had been acting strange for most of the day, and now she was just reading aloud to the class from their science textbook without asking any questions. "In 1994, fragments of a comet slammed into the atmosphere of Jupiter. Scientists counted twenty-one impacts over the course of six days. The largest fragments hit with more energy than all of mankind's nuclear weapons going off at once. Together they left dark, Earth-sized scars across the face of Jupiter for many months afterward."

Mrs. Asahina continued reading, hardly seeming to care that the class was no longer paying attention to the material.

"They don't even cancel school for an earthquake drill," Katsuro persisted.

"They might, if it was a really big earthquake drill," said Daiki. "Or a giant monster drill."

"For two days?"

"It would take at least that long to run through every possible variation." Daiki counted on his fingers. "Godzilla the giant lizard, Mothra the giant moth, Rodan the giant pteradon, Gamera the giant turtle—"

"Giant monsters only attack in the movies," said Katsuro.

"So far," Daiki told him. "But shouldn't we be prepared for everything?"

Yumi Nonomura, the class know-it-all, skipped across the room and flopped into a chair at the other side of Daiki's desk, with her back to the teacher. "Mai says her brother told her that a friend of his saw Asahina-sensei crying in the stairwell during lunch."

"So what?" asked Katsuro.

"So watch this." Yumi turned to the front of the room, raised her hand, and waved it back and forth like a flag. "Oh oh oh! Asahina-sensei!"

Mrs. Asahina just continued to read. "In June of 1908, a meteor or comet fragment exploded five to ten kilometers above a remote part of Russia. The shock wave toppled eighty million trees and shattered windows hundreds of kilometers away."

Yumi lowered her hand and turned back to Daiki's

desk as if it were a conference table. "See? She's not calling on anyone. Something odd is happening at our school and now our teacher is acting odd as well. Obviously, she knows what's going on. Somebody from our class should try to make her talk, and we all think it should be you." She nodded at Daiki.

"Me?" Daiki felt his stomach clench. "Why me?"

"You're currently the most likable kid in our class, Shindo-san. You're up three notches in the rankings."

"Most likeable?" asked Daiki. "But I thought all the girls hated me."

"That was Tuesday, Shindo-san," said Yumi. "Try to keep up."

"Hey, I'm likable too," said Katsuro.

"You come in sixth. Here, I'll show you." Yumi marched to the front of the room, directly behind the teacher, and wrote the current popularity rankings on the board. "Shindo Daiki is first, then Nori, Rei, myself, and Takako."

"I'm less likable than *Takako*?" Katsuro looked back at a pale, bone-thin girl in the last row. "Takako, the girl who smells like feet, is more likable than I am? Says who?"

"All the girls," said Yumi.

"And what about the boys?"

Yumi shrugged. "Why would we ask any of them?"

Daiki studied their teacher for a while. As the room

got noisier with student chatter, Mrs. Asahina just kept reading. "Impacts from space are now suspected to have caused or contributed to several mass extinctions in Earth's past. This includes the asteroid strike that helped to kill off the mosasaurs, pterosaurs, plesiosaurs, and non-avian dinosaurs that had previously dominated our world for millions of years."

Daiki had to admit, it was unlike their teacher to ever lose control of the class this way. "If Asahina-sensei is upset about something, I don't want to bother her."

Yumi shook her head. "Shindo-san, would you really risk your new ranking by turning us down? I know you have a girlfriend already, but someday, when you're available again, you'll want all the girls to think well of you."

"Wait, hold on." Katsuro blinked from Yumi to Daiki. "You have a girlfriend, Daiki-kun? You? And you never said anything about it?"

"I don't have a girlfriend," Daiki stated.

"Don't deny it." Yumi pointed a finger in Daiki's face. "Rei's cousin's friend saw you and your girlfriend at a store. You were buying matching Hunter-Elf Zeita shirts. Must be getting pretty serious, *ne?*"

"She's not my girlfriend!" Daiki shouted, far too loud for his voice to be masked by the other voices in the classroom. He clapped a hand over his mouth, but it was too late. All conversation stopped and all eyes were on him.

At the front of the classroom, Mrs. Asahina sighed, put her book down, and looked out at the class for the first time all period. "It seems Shindo-san has something to say. Would you care to share with us, Shindo-san?"

Daiki felt his heart beating louder. He cleared his throat. "Sensei? We know something strange is happening. Can you tell us what it is?"

The teacher pursed her lips. "All the teachers have agreed that it will be up to your parents to discuss today's . . . news."

"But can you at least tell us if it's something bad?" Daiki persisted. "Is anybody going to die?"

Mrs. Asahina's gaze swept slowly across the entire class. Her eyes welled up with tears and she spoke with a tremor in her voice. "Everybody . . . everybody in this classroom . . . everybody at this school"—she took a deep breath and wiped her eyes before continuing —"thinks we should conduct our lessons today without any further discussion."

The students groaned in disappointment as Mrs. Asahina lifted her book and resumed her dry recitation of geology facts. Soon, the room was again filled with the sound of chatter. "That wasn't helpful at all," said Yumi. "She told us nothing!"

Daiki sat at his desk, hands clenched, his heart

pounding in his ears. *Everybody*. Did Mrs. Asahina really mean *everybody*?

MIDDLE SOLAR SYSTEM:

Aboard the silver spaceship three hundred eighty million miles from Earth, the captain lay in her bed-pod and listened to a song play through her toilet. It seemed to be called "It's the End of the World As We Know It (and I Feel Fine)." The words were confusing, but the tune reminded her of a Mrendarian song called "Meet Me on the Slimy Rock (and Let Me Be Your Squooshums)."

When the song ended, a tired voice said, "Just gonna keep playing it—over and over. Don't try to stop me!" "It's the End of the World As We Know It (and I Feel Fine)" started again from the beginning for at least the fifteenth time in a row.

M'Frozza stifled a yawn. It was nice, but such a shame that nobody on this planet had ever written a second or third song just to keep people from getting bored.

TOKYO, JAPAN:

Forty-one hours before the most important event in human history, Daiki's school principal waved at the rows of students filing out of the building. "Directly home, everybody! Don't dawdle, and don't talk to anyone else until you reach your parents!"

"Don't talk to anyone?" asked Katsuro. "What does he mean by that? And why are you suddenly so quiet, Daiki-kun? Have you started not talking already?"

"I'm just thinking about what Asahina-sensei told us," Daiki told his friend.

"She didn't tell us anything." Katsuro hiked his book bag higher on his shoulders. "She just read to us for the entire period. Most of it was material we're not even covering this year. What a waste!"

"What a waste," Daiki agreed. He and Katsuro lived on the same street, so they often walked together from the school. Today, Daiki kept quiet while Katsuro ranted about how teachers shouldn't be allowed to act so weird.

Suddenly, a white-haired man ran past them in an awful hurry shouting, "TY SATO is coming! TY SATO is coming! TY SATO is coming!" The man crossed the street and disappeared through the sliding glass doors of a convenience store.

Daiki frowned.

"Who is Ty Sato?" Katsuro wondered.

"My cousin from America," Daiki told him.

"Really? And he's coming to Japan?"

"Not as far as I know."

"Strange that some old man would hear the news before you did."

They walked on past an apartment building where two women were talking on a third-floor balcony. "I heard that TY SATO is four hundred meters wide and weighs a hundred thousand tons," said one of the women.

The other woman shook her head. "I heard TY SATO is a kilometer wide and weighs more than a million tons."

"Hey!" Daiki shouted up at them. "I'm pretty sure Ty Sato is less than 150 centimeters tall and weighs 50 kilograms at the most!"

The women laughed and retreated into their apartment.

"Maybe your cousin's been turned into a giant radioactive monster," Katsuro suggested. "That would explain why everyone's been acting so crazy."

"People only turn into giant radioactive monsters in comic books and movies," said Daiki.

"So far," said Katsuro.

As they approached Katsuro's house, Daiki could hear a television newscaster's report from inside. He could just make out the words, "—are reporting that TY SATO is moving toward us at more than 4,000 kilometers per second. Senator Archer of the United States is urging the use of nuclear weapons against TY SATO, but scientists are divided—"

The sound of the television cut off suddenly. A few seconds later, a window opened and a flatscreen dropped out. It shattered on the sidewalk, where it became a plastic pile of electronic junk.

Katsuro clasped his hands against the sides his head. "That was our TV!"

Katsuro's father stuck his head out the window and shook a fist at the broken television set. "Take that, television! No more bad news from you!" He turned his head. "Oh, *konnichiwa,* Katsuro-kun. *Konnichiwa,* Daiki-kun. I didn't see you there."

Daiki ran the rest of the way home.

His mother was on the phone, as angry as Daiki had ever heard her. "No, Hiroshi-kun, I don't care how important your work is. I'm sure the rest of the world's astronomers could handle things if you took a vacation for once. You haven't even been back to Tokyo even once since your university days, and now the world is about to end! I miss you, Little Brother. Kazu-san misses you, Riku-kun barely knows who you are, and poor Daiki-kun has never even met you in person."

Daiki grabbed the phone away from his mother. "Hello? *Oji-san?*" he asked. "It would be nice for you to visit Japan, but please, tell Cousin Tyler-kun not to step on Tokyo!"

PLATTE BLUFF, NEVADA:

Thirty-one hours before the most important event in human history, Tyler woke up on the couch. He'd fallen asleep watching the All-News network, and now he could hear his mom out in the kitchen. She was talking in Japanese, probably on the phone to relatives. He caught a few words he knew and some familiar names, including Daiki and Riku, so it had to be Aunt Megumi or Uncle Kazu on the other end of the phone.

The TV was still on, with the same news anchor from the night before. Tyler wondered if he'd been reporting all night, and if he'd just keep going until the end of the world.

"Striking with more energy than the asteroid or comet that wiped out the dinosaurs, TY SATO will form a crater thirty-six miles deep and more than a hundred miles wide. Even on the other side of the world, the

impact will likely cause extreme weather conditions, earthquakes, increased volcanic activity, tsunamis, and widespread disease." The anchor blinked his bleary eyes and yawned. "At the top of the hour, we'll be talking about this possibility with rock star Amy Thrush, who has just released a new song called 'Good-bye, Earth, I Never Liked You Much Anyway!'"

Amanda's head was resting in Tyler's lap. He tried to wake her, but she just flopped over and dug her face into the cushions. Tyler walked into the kitchen. His mother's phone sat on the table with its "low battery" symbol flashing. A newspaper was sprawled next to it, wrinkled as if his mother had already read it three times. Tyler had always wanted to see his name on the front page, but not like this:

TY SATO PACKS THE FORCE OF FIVE MILLION HIROSHIMA BOMBS

TY SATO'S SPEED SUGGESTS INTERSTELLAR ORIGIN

TY SATO WILL BURN SOME ALIVE, SLOWLY FREEZE OTHERS TO DEATH

"Your waffles are under the newspaper," said his mom. Her hair was a tangled mess and her rumpled bathrobe looked as if she'd slept in it.

Tyler found the long-cold waffle and tapped it experimentally with his fork. "Mom? Since the world's about to end, can I stay home from school?"

His mom wrung her bathrobe belt in her hands. "Sorry, honey bear. Your father says there's only a small chance Earth will be hit, so we're not going to panic."

Tyler instantly perked up. "You talked to Dad? What else did he say?"

"He said not to worry. He wants you and Amanda to go to school like this was any normal day," she said. Tyler thought this sounded strange coming from his mom, who was definitely not getting ready for work like this was any normal day.

Tyler slid his uneaten waffle into the trash and put his plate into the dishwasher. Back in the living room, his big sister was no longer sleeping on the couch, which meant there was only one other place in the house where she could be. "Hey, Amanda!" he shouted. "Can I get into the bathroom one more time before the world ends?"

"Leave me alone," her muffled voice came through the door. "Why did you have to have that stupid birthday? Why did you have to get that stupid star named after you? This is all your fault!"

"My fault how? Do you think I went into space and aimed that asteroid at Earth?"

Amanda didn't answer. Even worse, she didn't give up the bathroom. Tyler would have to hold it until he got to school. "Bye, Mom!" he called. "See you after soccer practice!"

"Be good today," she called from the kitchen.

On his way to the front door, Tyler took one last look at the TV in the living room. "—for years have been tracking several hundred potentially hazardous asteroids, but obviously none as threatening as this one," said a woman reporter. "If TY SATO really is made of a dense metal, as we now suspect, it would be far heavier than an ordinary asteroid. That would make it an even greater danger to Earth."

That's strange, Tyler thought. The house the reporter was standing in front of looked an awful lot like his. Tyler opened the front door.

The first thing he noticed was how bright it was outside. It was brighter than morning sunlight had ever been before. Tyler took a step back and shielded his eyes with his hand.

The next thing he noticed was that all the bright lights were mounted on video cameras that had enormous lenses—and all those lenses were pointed right at him.

Then he noticed the crowd of people. There were camera operators, reporters in nice suits, and curious neighbors gathered behind them. Tyler took another step back.

The reporters pushed their microphones through the open doorway. "Are you the son of Dr. Hiroshi Sato?" one of them asked. "Is your father the one who discovered the object? Is he home? Can we talk to him? Can we talk to you? What's your name?"

Almost too confused to think, he blurted out, "My name is Ty. Ty Sato."

The reporters stared at Tyler. He was glad to have a

moment to think, until they all leaned closer and spoke even louder. "Is the object named after you? How old are you? How does it feel to share your name with a killer asteroid?"

"Get away from him!" shouted Tyler's mom. With her angry eyes and wild hair, she looked pretty scary, even to Tyler. The reporters backed away.

"I'll drive you to school today," she told him. Louder, to the reporters, she said, "I want you all off my property right now. We're private people. We don't need our names in the news."

"Mrs. Sato," said one of the reporters, "your son's name *is* the news."

Tyler's mom pushed him past the cameras as the reporters yelled questions at her.

"Mrs. Sato, have you spoken to your husband today?"

"Do you know anything the government hasn't told us?"

"How will you spend your last day on Earth?"

Tyler's mom gnashed her teeth. "If you don't get those microphones away from me, this will be *your* last day on Earth. Come on, Tyler."

"Coming, Mom." Now that he was eleven, Tyler didn't need his mom to protect him. But he was sure glad to have her there.

MIDDLE SOLAR SYSTEM:

Two hundred eighty million miles from Earth, the technician aboard the silver spaceship finished a review of the signals from the third innermost planet. "Sir, I was wrong," he told the pilot.

"Of course you were," the pilot agreed.

The technician waited for a long moment before the pilot finally gave in and sighed through his nose-holes. "What were you wrong about this time, Technician?"

"The electromagnetic signal in our toilets is not coming from hyper-intelligent Dwogleys reaching out to us from a dimension beyond time and space. It seems the people of this system really do use electromagnetic waves as their primary means of communication. This includes military command and control, news, entertainment, emergency response, data transmission, and a comedy program called Pirate Pete and the Penguins of Doom.*"*

"They don't use quantum bands for any of that?" the pilot asked. "How inefficient! How insecure! How totally, utterly, mind-bogglingly primitive!"

"Yes, sir," the technician agreed, "although you really should give Pirate Pete's penguins a proper chance. Their icebound antics are quite amusing."

The pilot drummed his tentacles. "Aside from these . . . penguins . . . what else have you heard?"

"I'm still making adjustments to the translator system,

but there appears to be many panicked broadcasts about someone or something called TY SATO. Have you heard of it, sir?"

The pilot popped a nose-hole in thought. "No, but if the locals are worried about this TY SATO, we should be worried as well. I'll look it up on Quoogle."

The technician blinked. "Quoogle?"

"It's a quebsite used for finding information on the Galactic Quinternet. And maybe I'll check Quikipedia while I'm at it."

The technician narrowed two of his eyes. "I'm sorry, sir. I have no idea what that is. As you know, my job level doesn't allow me to access the Galactic Quinternet—even though I'm the one who has to fix the connection whenever it breaks."

9

Twenty-nine hours before the most important event in human history, Daiki turned over in bed and looked at the digital clock. His whole family had stayed up late, worrying about the killer asteroid with the same name as Daiki's cousin in Nevada. It turned out to all be because of the star certificate Daiki's mother had ordered for Tyler's birthday. The solution had seemed obvious to Daiki—just send the certificate back to the company and have them fix their defective star. But when Daiki had suggested it, Riku had laughed and called him an idiot.

The door chime rang loudly. Daiki realized that was what had woken him up in the first place. It was still the middle of the night, so who could it possibly be? Daiki put a pillow over his head, but the chiming song repeated over and over, along with the sound of his parents rushing to clean up and put stacks of dishes back into the cabinet. "Forget how the house looks," Daiki groaned. "Just answer the door!"

He heard the front door open, and the door chime thankfully stopped. After a minute or two of hushed voices, Daiki's bedroom door slid open and light spilled across his bedroll. He pretended to be asleep, but his father shook his shoulder roughly.

"Oy! Daiki-kun! Your friend is here."

Daiki rubbed his eyes. "Which friend?"

"She says her name is Tomoko." Daiki's father winked at him. "I didn't realize you were old enough for a girlfriend."

"She's not my girlfriend," said Daiki.

"Uh-huh."

Daiki wondered whether his father had been talking to Riku, because both of them used the same tone. "Really, she's not!"

"I believe you," said his father.

"So can you tell her to come back in the morning?" Daiki asked.

"Don't be rude, son," his father scolded. "If your mother and I have to be awake at this hour, so do you."

Grumbling to himself, Daiki crawled off the bedroom's rice-straw tatami mats and put on slippers to walk through the house. He found Tomoko in the main room, talking to Daiki's mother. The girl seemed calm, but her eyes were red and puffy, with dried tear tracks running down her cheeks.

"I'll make tea," said Daiki's mother, excusing herself.

"*Arigato*, Mrs. Shindo," said Tomoko with a bow.

"It's late," Daiki told Tomoko once they were alone. "What happened? Did your great-grandmother kick you out of the house for having too much fun?"

Tomoko's lower lip trembled as she struggled to hold back a wave of emotion. Then her eyes flooded over and she spoke so fast that Daiki could barely follow her words. "Obaa-chan is in the hospital, Daiki, because of her heart and also because she's worried about TY SATO—and it probably didn't help that you and I were off having fun and she didn't know where I was! I don't have any other family, so I didn't have anywhere else to go, but I couldn't stay at home by myself, so I hope your family doesn't mind if I sleep here tonight. Your parents seem so nice and are those *Hunter-Elf Zeita* pajamas?"

Daiki blinked. "Huh?"

"Your pajamas." She pointed. "They've got *Hunter-Elf Zeita* characters all over them—Zeita, Eita, Deruta, Mu, Nu, Peeto, and Queen Sukaro—so cute!"

"Thanks." Daiki frowned. "Is your great-grandmother going to be all right?"

"Are any of us going to be all right?" Tomoko buried her crying face in Daiki's shoulder. "The doctors can't tell us anything yet."

"I'm so sorry." Daiki put an arm around Tomoko to give her a reassuring hug. He heard a noise from the kitchen and looked up to see his father's face peek through the door frame. Daiki quickly pushed away from Tomoko before it looked like he was hugging her in a boyfriend-girlfriend kind of way. Judging by his father's thumbs-up gesture, he hadn't moved fast enough.

"I'm glad to have a friend to count on," Tomoko told him.

"Thanks," said Daiki. "I have only one favor I need to ask."

"Yes?"

"Please, please, please don't tell anyone at my school about my *Hunter-Elf Zeita* pajamas!"

MIDDLE SOLAR SYSTEM:

Two hundred seventy million miles from Earth, the technician of the silver spaceship stepped into the recreation lounge. The captain was there, eating a portion of gruud and humming a familiar tune.

"Is that 'Meet Me on the Slimy Rock (and Let Me Be Your Squooshums)'?" the technician asked.

The captain shook her face-tentacles in negation. "It's a

song from the third innermost planet, and I can't get it out of my head."

The technician dialed a portion of blarji from the food-synth and joined the captain at her table. "There's something that's been bothering me about this system."

"Yes?" the captain asked.

"They haven't responded to any of our quantum hails, and they don't use quantum bands for local communication. It's like they haven't even discovered quantum technology, except that you received an invitation from this system." He fixed all three eyes on her face. "You did receive an invitation from this system, M'Frozza? An invitation sent by a quantum signal?"

The captain gulped down a mouthful of gruud. "Yes. Of course I did. I wouldn't make up something like that."

"All right." The technician bobbed his head. "That's good enough for me." He ate his meal quietly while M'Frozza hummed another chorus of "It's the End of the World As We Know It (and I Feel Fine)."

PLATTE BLUFF, NEVADA:

Tyler squirmed at an unfamiliar desk in an unfamiliar classroom. His teacher, Mrs. Hogan, hadn't come to school that day and there were no substitutes available. Principal Johansson combined the class with Mr. Hartman's, and enough kids were absent that everyone fit into one classroom with empty desks to spare.

"We're going to have an open study day," said Mr. Hartman. He didn't look up from the computer on his desk. "Read your books and try to learn as much as you can before the end of the world . . . I mean, before the end of the day."

"Mr. Hartman?" Wendy Ghirardelli held her arm up like a flagpole as tears streamed down her face. "Can I use the bathroom?"

"Sure," said the teacher. "Do whatever you want."

Wendy left, and Tyler never saw her come back.

Tyler tried to study for a while. He wanted to act like everything was normal, like his mom had said, but that was hard to do when everyone else was goofing off. One of the boys was giving away his comic book collection, one book at a time. Some girls were drawing pictures on their desks. When a spitball fight broke out, Mr. Hartman did nothing to stop it.

Eric passed Tyler a note: "Brayden says you had a PARTY without ME. He says you named STARS after yourselves. He says you had PIZZA."

Tyler wrote back: "So?"

"SOOOOOO," Eric wrote, "you KNOW how MUCH I like PIZZA!! You invited BRAYDEN and JOHN and LUCAS and NOT ME . . . WHAT GIVES?!!"

Tyler wrote, "You wouldn't want a star. It wouldn't fit in your room."

YOU THINK YOUR SO SPECIAL NOW
BUT YOUR NOT!!!

Tyler wanted to point out that Eric had written "your" instead of "you're," but he didn't. "I'm not special," he wrote back. Eric pushed the note off his desk without reading it.

Tyler wrote another note. "I'M SORRY, OKAY?!!!"

Eric crumpled the paper and tossed it at the recycle

bin at the front of the room. He missed by more than a foot. Eric never did have a very good hook shot.

"Are you going to pick that up, young man?" asked Mr. Hartman.

"No," said Eric.

"Okay, just checking." Mr. Hartman went back to watching his computer screen. He let the crumpled note stay where it was. A few other boys threw crumpled papers at the bin as well. When they ran out of notepaper, they tore pages from their textbooks.

"Eric!" Tyler spoke out loud instead of writing another note. Eric blocked his ears and moved his desk away. *Great,* thought Tyler. Not only was the world about to end, but now his best friend wasn't talking to him, and he wasn't sure which upset him more.

Later in the morning, Mr. Hartman looked up from his computer screen. He looked right at Tyler. "Hey, you're that kid!"

"What kid?" Tyler asked.

"That kid they've been talking about all over the Internet. Holy cow! This show is all about you and your mom."

"My mom?" Tyler ran to the front of the room.

Yolanda Speaks Out, one of those talk shows that Tyler's mom liked, streamed through a tab in Mr. Hartman's browser. "We've seen it over and over, but let's look at that video again," said Yolanda.

Tyler's mom appeared on the screen, pushing Tyler in front of her. Tyler could hardly believe it. The entire world was watching him! On the *Yolanda* show!

Tyler's mom shook her fist. "If you don't get those microphones away from me, this will be *your* last day on Earth," she shouted. Then she did it backwards. Then she did it again and again in slow motion. It seemed to last for hours.

Yolanda returned to the screen. Behind her was a huge snarling picture of Tyler's mom, looking scarier than any horror-movie monster. "That's what I'm talking about," said Yolanda. "You can't act like that in front of your children. It's bad parenting. Am I right or am I right?"

"You're right, Yolanda," said a woman in the talk-show audience. "Mrs. Sato doesn't respect herself, and she doesn't respect her child. Did you see that bathrobe she was wearing? You just know she's been drinking."

"But that's not what happened," Tyler blurted out. Everyone in class stared at him. "Really," Tyler said. "There were reporters all over our front lawn, and my mom told them to go away. That's all." He was there. He knew what had happened. But looking at the big, scary picture behind Yolanda, even Tyler wasn't sure anymore.

"Too bad it's not up to me," said Yolanda. "I'd take that child away from her. It would be the best thing for him." Her TV audience rose to their feet, cheering and applauding.

Tyler pushed the computer monitor off Mr. Hartman's desk and onto the floor. The screen cracked, popped, and went dark. "Hey!" Mr. Hartman picked up the monitor and pressed all the buttons, but the screen remained blank.

"Are you going to send me to the principal's office?" Tyler asked.

The teacher fell back into his chair. "Nah. I'd have done the same if Yolanda insulted my mother. Why don't you just go to lunch. All of you. Or take an extra recess period. If I'm not here when you get back, just do what you want."

Tyler watched all the other kids race out of the room before Mr. Hartman had a chance to change his mind. "I think I learned something today," Tyler told Mr. Hartman.

"What's that?"

"If a bunch of reporters show up at your house some morning, the best thing to say is nothing at all."

MIDDLE SOLAR SYSTEM:

Two hundred sixty million miles from Earth, the pilot of the silver spaceship finished reviewing results from the Galactic Quinternet.

Dye-Sato was a colorful plant from the marshes of Dee Minor 7. Dice-Ahto was a table game played on Planet Yahtsea. Tie-Sah-Toh was a dance step invented in the Flannel Nebula. But there was no entry for anything called TY SATO.

The pilot called the ship's technician to the bridge. There was obviously something wrong with the ship's translation system.

PLATTE BLUFF, NEVADA:

Tyler ate lunch with John, Brayden, and Lucas. The school had brought in food from Burger Barn because the cafeteria workers never showed up.

Brayden dug into a box of Chik'n-Lik'n Chunks. He chewed each chunk at least ten times. "I want to make this last," he said. "It might be our last lunch ever."

"Second to last," said Lucas between bites from his Barnstorm Burger. "If TY SATO hits Earth, it'll happen tomorrow afternoon."

Tyler frowned into his Green Jean Salad. "I wish people would stop calling it that."

"Sorry, Ty," said Lucas.

"At least you get to be famous for a day," said John.

"Yeah," said Brayden. "The rest of us might not even see middle school."

"I won't either," Tyler reminded them.

Someone wheeled a TV into the cafeteria from the teachers' lounge. It was tuned to the news. Tyler recognized the building behind the reporter's back. "That looks like our school."

"It *is* our school," said Lucas. "Didn't you see all the news vans outside?"

"How does it feel to be friends with *the* Tyler Sato?" the reporter asked some kid Tyler had never seen before.

"Ty's a great guy," said the kid. "We hang out all the time. He has a killer asteroid named after him, but I'm still proud to call him my best friend."

A boy at the next table pointed at the screen. "Hey, everybody! If we say we're Ty's friends, we can get on TV too!"

"Race you to the news vans," someone else said. A mob of kids Tyler hardly knew all rushed outside, pretending to be his friends.

Tyler's real friends stayed at the table, except Eric Parker. He sat at another table and glared. Tyler couldn't believe Eric was acting that way just because Tyler didn't invite him to the pizza and star-naming party. Only a ten-year-old could get so upset about something like that.

"Want to come over after school?" John asked.

"We have soccer practice," Tyler reminded him.

Tyler's friends looked at him as if he'd lost his mind. "Come on," said Lucas. "You don't really think Mr. Boughis will have soccer practice today."

Tyler shrugged. "It's such a crazy day. Who knows?"

MIDDLE SOLAR SYSTEM:

Two hundred fifty million miles from Earth, the Mrendarian captain accepted another quantum call from her father-parent. The ambassador's impatience came through in the tone of his voice, in the folds around his eyes, and in the posture of his body in the holographic display. "What is taking so long, M'Frozza? I was sure that by now you would have dispatched this pointless challenge and returned home in victory."

"Home?" asked M'Frozza. "Do you really wish me to go there?"

"You know what I mean," the ambassador snapped. "Certainly I don't want you on Mrendaria right now, but I need you back here with me. I need to keep three eyes on you at all times to know that you are safe. This is a difficult time for our people, and we can't afford any of our enemies taking advantage of our weakness."

"Which is exactly why I can't refuse any challenges right now," the captain stated. "Wouldn't our enemies find that suspicious?"

The ambassador made a sound that mixed a grumble with the rippling of his face-tentacles. "Just watch out for yourself, Daughter Child, and don't take any unnecessary risks."

"Agreed," said M'Frozza, although she twisted a pair of nervous tentacles behind her back as she said it.

TOKYO, JAPAN:

Twenty-five hours before the most important event in human history, Daiki and Tomoko walked together through the residential neighborhood where the Shindo family lived. Houses and apartment buildings crowded together on narrow streets that had no names. According to the news, riots had broken out in major cities around the world. Some countries had even deployed soldiers and combat tanks to keep the peace! But the news people weren't reporting about quiet areas like Daiki's, where most people were staying home and the only sign of trouble was a black smudge in the southern sky—something in Shinjuku was burning, but too far away for any fire engines to be heard.

Daiki stopped at a vending machine for a can of hot cocoa. He offered some to Tomoko, but she shook her head. "Chocolate makes me hyper, and other kinds of caffeine too, which is a shame because I really like green tea, and what's wrong with being a little hyper sometimes?" This quick rambling speech seemed like a question and even came with a very short pause, but Tomoko started talking again before Daiki could form a thought. "You'd think that being on the edge would be an advantage in a judo match, but Obaa-chan says directed action comes from a calm mind and my mind isn't calm even without the caffeine."

"So . . . that's a no? You don't want a sip of cocoa?"

Tomoko shrugged. "The world's ending tomorrow anyway, so why not." She put the hot can to her lips, drained it, and handed back the empty container. "Look! A river!"

Daiki searched around for a recycling bin before following his friend. He caught up to Tomoko in the middle of a footbridge. She had stopped to peer over the railing at a river of yellowish-brownish water. "That's the Kandagawa," he told her.

"It's so sad!"

Daiki frowned. "Who's sad?"

"The river. You just know it used to be wild and free before people built concrete banks to tell it where to flow, and drains and dams to keep it from flooding. We've taken this beautiful thing of nature and made it controlled and artificial. The river is sad, and that makes me sad too."

"I've never known anybody who could feel sorry for a river."

"That's because you've never known me." Tomoko stood and watched the river intently for a very long time.

Daiki had to wonder whether she saw something different than just flowing water and the occasional floating twig or leaf. "You should see it when it's full of cherry blossom petals," he told her.

"Daiki-san?" Her voice was almost a whisper.

"*Hai?*"

"What do you think the river will do when we're not around to tell it where to go anymore?"

It was such a strange question that Daiki thought he must have misheard her. "I'm sorry, what?"

"When TY SATO hits Earth, we'll have fires, earthquakes, a cloud of dust that blocks out the sun, a new Ice Age, and the end of human civilization as we know it—but the river will still be here. What will happen when people aren't around to tell the river what to do anymore? Kandagawa-sama may be sad now because it can't change direction or spread out over the streets, but do you think the river will miss humans at all after we've gone extinct?"

Daiki put his hands on Tomoko's shoulders and turned

her away from the railing. "Tomoko-san, it's a river. It has no feelings."

She nodded. "Of course you're right. I was just thinking. I do that sometimes when I'm bored and there's nothing to do, and I'm waiting, and do you think the hospital would mind if we went to see Obaa-chan before visiting hours officially start?"

"We should wait," said Daiki. "Maybe we could watch some *Hunter-Elf Zeita* videos or play a game."

"Oh! We can look for Takeda-sensei at the arcade! He's a worthy opponent and also an effective teacher. He was even kind enough to let me win!"

"Mori-sama banished Takeda-sama from the arcade."

Tomoko blinked in confusion. "But why would a grand master like Takeda-sensei be forbidden from competition?"

Daiki told Tomoko about the magazine cover, about Jun's tantrum, and about the broken machine—although he chose not to tell her that he'd been the one who'd found the magazine and brought it to the arcade in the first place.

As Daiki spoke, Tomoko's eyes widened, her mouth hung open, and she began to shake. "This is horrible! I can't allow Takeda-sensei to be punished for defending my honor."

"I don't think that's why—"

"There could be no other reason for Takeda-sensei to attack a machine." Tomoko raised her right fist to the sky. "As you are my witness, Daiki-kun, I will avenge this injustice and return Takeda-sensei to his proper place in the world of arcade gaming!"

Daiki sighed. "How is it that everyone around here knows how to make a dramatic speech except for me?"

MIDDLE SOLAR SYSTEM:

Two hundred twenty-five million miles from Earth, the pilot of the silver spaceship was angry enough to blow jets of steam from his first, third, and fifth nose-holes. The ship's technician had taken the translation system apart. Pieces were scattered all over the bridge, and now the fool couldn't put the machine back together again.

The pilot would have called the technician an idiot, but the pilot spoke only Northern Mrendarian, while the technician spoke only Southern Mrendarian. Without a working translation system, they couldn't understand each other at all.

TOKYO, JAPAN:

Daiki and Tomoko pushed through a crowded street jammed with stalled traffic and angry pedestrians. Police officers with bullhorns asked people to return to their homes, but nobody seemed to be listening. Missionaries handed out pamphlets and raised signs that read "the

world ends tomorrow, and this time we mean it!" and "TY SATO is coming! Repent!"

The Pack-Punch Video Arcade was closed.

Daiki peered through the glass door. The overhead lights were out and the neon gateway was dark, but the game machines still flashed through their glowing demo screens. "I've never seen this place closed before."

"We have to get in," said Tomoko.

"Can you judo kick the door open?"

Tomoko snorted. "Don't be silly. Judo is the subtle art of using an opponent's strength to one's own advantage. How am I supposed to do that against an inanimate object?"

"Sorry. What do you suggest?"

"We must think like warriors. What would Hunter-Elf Zeita do in a situation like this?"

"Jump into a tree and start firing magic arrows from her longbow," said Daiki.

"Yes, I see." Tomoko looked around the busy retail street. "Nothing but streetlight poles here. Also, I'm entirely out of magic arrows. And longbows."

"Mori-sama probably isn't in there anyway." Daiki leaned against the glass doors and slid down to a sitting position on the sidewalk. "This is a useless quest."

"There is no such thing, Daiki-san. When I visit Obaa-chan in the hospital today, I want to be able to tell her that I did something good and noble with my time. That will make her feel better until the asteroid wipes us out. Somehow we need to find Mori-sama and convince him to allow his best player back into the arena. Then we need to find Takeda-sensei and have him play against me again, and this time let him know it's okay to play his best and beat me. Then everything will be as it was before—until civilization comes to a fiery end."

"I wish you'd stop saying things like that," Daiki complained.

A cinderblock smashed through the window of an electronics store farther down the block. A gang of teenagers scrambled out of the building with their arms loaded with cameras, phones, and laptops.

Daiki jumped to his feet. "Where are the police?"

"Busy." Tomoko nodded at an officer who seemed

to have joined the missionaries in their somber march around the train station. The officer held a hastily hand-written sign that read "Have a nice doomsday!"

One of the teenagers pointed their way. "Hey, look! An arcade! I've always wanted my own *Time Crisis* arcade game!" The rest of the gang followed him with their bats, crowbars, and tire irons ready to attack the glass storefront.

"Yet another instance where magic arrows would come in handy," Tomoko pointed out. "It's too bad life isn't more like *Hunter-Elf Zeita*."

"We should get out of here," said Daiki.

"I agree," said Tomoko. "I may be a judo champion, but only a crazy person would stand between that gang and their looting."

As if summoned by magic words, a round-bodied figure stepped out of the crowd and glared at the approaching teens. He adjusted the bandana on his forehead, cracked his knuckles, and growled through gritted teeth. It was Jun Takeda, and he was as angry as a raging dragon. "Hashimoto-san," he rasped at the leader of the gang.

The gang leader narrowed his eyes. "Takeda-san!"

"You know each other?" asked Daiki.

"Hashimoto Fumio-san goes to my high school," said Jun. "He's the captain of the chess club."

Fumio grinned. "Even chess-club geeks have a right to rampage at the end of the world. What do you say, Takeda-san? Would you care to join us?"

"You shouldn't steal things that don't belong to you," Jun stated.

Fumio laughed. "Come on, Takeda-san. Live a little. What are they going to do, throw us in jail for the rest of our lives? That's, like, less than a day!"

"Leave the Pack-Punch Arcade alone," Jun ordered. "Your fighting and violence aren't welcome in this place of . . . fighting . . . and violence."

Tomoko whispered to Daiki, "That almost made sense."

"He has a way with words," Daiki agreed.

"I heard you were banished from this place," Fumio said to Jun.

"The arcade isn't a place. The arcade is a bug that digs under your skin and swims through your veins. I don't need to be inside the arcade because the arcade is inside of me. Even when I'm not playing *Tekno-Fight Xtreme* on the screen, I'm still playing it right up here." Jun tapped a finger against the side of his head. "Now stand back before I hit the special combination that calls lightning down from the sky!"

"He's completely lost his mind," Daiki whispered to Tomoko. "We have to stop him before he gets hurt."

"Too late!" Tomoko exclaimed. Jun Takeda, with his pudgy hands clenched into pudgy fists, was charging at full speed at the other teen. "What a battle this is going to be! Takeda-sensei has the berserk rage of a video gamer while Hashimoto-sama has the patience and sharp tactical mind of a chess player. There's no telling who will win!"

Five feet from his target, Jun stopped running. "Time out," he sputtered between labored breaths. He reached into his pocket for his asthma inhaler and took two puffs. "Okay, time in."

Fumio slapped Jun across the face.

Jun blinked. "Hey! That stung!"

"Then have another!" Fumio slapped him again.

"Ow!"

"Want more?" Fumio slapped him again.

"Ow! Now cut that out!"

Tomoko sighed. "This isn't the grand battle I expected."

"Takeda-sama!" Daiki called out. "Your nose is bleeding!"

"It is?" Jun rubbed under his nostrils and took a long look at the bright red fluid on his fingers. His face went pale, his eyes rolled up into his head, and he fell forward in a faint.

Fumio screamed as the much larger boy landed on top of him. "I give up! I'll leave the arcade alone! Just

114

somebody get him off me!" The other members of Fumio's chess club gang dropped their stolen goods and ran away.

"Victory!" Tomoko exclaimed. "Takeda-sensei, champion of the Pack-Punch Video Arcade, has saved the day! Justice has returned to the world and our work here is done—until tomorrow, when the entire planet crumbles into a pile of dust."

"Stop saying things like that!" Daiki shouted.

12

Twenty-four hours before the most important event in human history, Tyler changed into his soccer jersey and cleats. Only a few kids from the soccer team had shown up for practice, but others had eagerly joined for the day—all because of a new kicking drill Mr. Boughis had invented. It was just like the old kicking drill, except the goalie was called a Missile Defense System and the ball was called TY SATO.

Some kids lined up to take a turn as the Missile Defense System. The rest lined up to kick the crap out of TY SATO. Eric Parker pushed his way to the front of that line. "Take that, TY SATO! Heeyah!" He booted the ball past the Missile Defense System and into the goal.

Tyler felt like his insides were about to explode. First his dad had just about moved into the observatory. Then his mom had gotten slammed by Yolanda on national TV. His sister hated him, he'd lost his best friend, and now his name was being kicked around the soccer field.

So he grabbed the ball and ran.

"Hey!" shouted Mr. Boughis. "Where are you going with TY SATO?"

Tyler left the field and dodged past the reporters. He ducked between their satellite trucks and kept going. Downtown Platte Bluff was just a cluster of stores and the main campus of the Platte Bluff Institute of Science. Tyler found a bench to sit on while he hugged the soccer ball to his chest.

He lost track of time. He noticed that people all around him were shouting, but he didn't care. Tyler had his own problems. Except people weren't shouting in pain or anger. They were all saying things like "Yahoo!" and "Hooray!"

"What's going on?" Tyler asked a woman passing by with an oversized backpack strapped to her shoulders.

"Haven't you heard?" she asked.

Tyler shook his head.

"It's a ship."

Tyler blinked back at her. "What's a ship?"

"TY SATO. It's close enough to see now, and it's not a killer asteroid after all. It's an honest-to-goodness alien spaceship!"

"So my star isn't an asteroid? My star is a space-ship? Wow!"

"They've declared tomorrow an international holiday. TY SATO Day! It'll be the biggest celebration in the history of the world."

"But . . . the spaceship might still be coming to destroy us."

"True," said the woman, "but at least it won't crash into us. An asteroid can't change direction, but a spaceship sure can."

INNER SOLAR SYSTEM:

One hundred sixty million miles from Earth, in the asteroid belt between Jupiter and Mars, the technician on the silver spaceship finished his repairs. There were only three parts he couldn't fit back into the ship's translation system. The technician hid these extra bits in his back pouch and faced the pilot.

"Sir, the garble is all garble. You can garble the garble from now until garble."

The pilot blew steam from all five of his nose-holes. "Garble, garble, garble, idiot!"

"Idiot?" the technician asked. That didn't sound right. Maybe those extra parts were important after all.

TOKYO, JAPAN:

Seventeen hours before the most important event in human history, Daiki sat on a molded plastic seat in a hospital waiting room. His father sat off to his left, draining the last drops from a can of vending-machine coffee. Baby Sakura yawned and kicked as Daiki's mother tried to stroke her to sleep. Riku played a handheld game console, trying to match Daiki's top score on *RoboMaze*.

Tomoko paced back and forth like a caged tiger. "They have to know something by now. So why aren't they telling us? It has to be something bad, that's why!"

"Tomoko-san, please stop!" said Daiki. "You're not doing your great-grandmother any good by getting all worked up like this."

She blinked at him. "You're right, Daiki-san. Of course you're right. If Obaa-chan were out here, she'd tell me to practice my deep-breathing and relaxation techniques." Tomoko took a seat, closed her eyes, and started breathing very slowly.

Riku slammed the game console on the table next to his seat. "Stupid game."

"Hey!" Daiki jumped to his feet. "That's my console!"

"I know. Mine's broken," Riku stated.

Daiki picked up the console and examined it for damage. "No mystery why," said Daiki.

"That's enough!" said their father. "If you boys can't play nicely with that thing, I'll have to take it away."

"Yes, Father." Daiki bowed his head and handed over the game.

"So," said his father. "What button do I press for a restart?"

A doctor stepped into the waiting room. "Miss Tomizawa?" he asked.

Tomoko sprang forward and grabbed the doctor's coat. "Yes? That's me. Tell me what's going on. I'm ready for it."

The doctor cleared his throat. "Miss Tomizawa, your great-grandmother is—"

"Dead?" Tomoko's fingers tightened their grip on the doctor's lapels until Daiki thought the doctor might suffocate. "She's dead, right? You've come to tell me that she's dead? Oh, Obaa-chan, how could you have left me all alone in life!"

"No, Miss Tomizawa," the doctor gasped. "I came to tell you that your great-grandmother is *awake*, and she wants to see you. But you won't have much time with her because—"

"Because she's dying?" Tomoko asked. "Oh no, oh no! This is the worst day of my life! How long does she have, doctor? Hours? Minutes?"

The doctor bristled. "You won't have much time with her because she's scheduled for a stress test in about an hour."

Tomoko screamed in panic. "A stress test? That sounds awful! Will you have to cut her open?"

"We will be testing her reaction to stress," the doctor stated.

"Oh, good," said Tomoko. "Obaa-chan deals well with stress."

"I can't imagine why she would have to." The doctor finally succeeded in prying his coat out of Tomoko's grasp. He gestured toward the door. *"Dozo!"*

Daiki got up to follow them.

"Do you mind if I go in alone?" Tomoko asked him. "You might make her anxious. I think it would be best to expose Obaa-chan only to calming influences, like me."

The doctor coughed.

Tomoko turned on him. "What? Do you think I'm not a calming influence?"

"I did not say that." The doctor coughed again. "I think I may just need a lozenge."

Daiki sat back down. "I'll be here if you need me, Tomoko-chan."

"Arigato, Daiki-kun."

"I hope her great-grandmother is going to be all right," said Daiki's mother as Tomoko and the doctor exited through a set of wooden doors. "From what Tomoko says, she sounds like a very strong woman for her age."

Daiki thought about Tomoko's great-grandmother cracking her stick against Jun Takeda's kneecaps. "Very strong," he agreed. "Tomoko says her great-grandmother was also a judo master, and Tomoko's family has been involved in jujitsu for hundreds of years. They used to run

121

their own school for it, but now it's just Tomoko and her great-grandmother."

"Why?" asked Riku. "What happened to the rest of her family?"

Daiki shook his head. "Something she hasn't wanted to talk about, but it's just been Tomoko and her great-grandmother for a few years now."

"And pretty soon it will just be Tomoko," said Daiki's father.

Daiki and his mother glared at him.

"What?" he asked. "What did I say wrong now?"

Tomoko returned to the waiting room about thirty minutes later. "Well?" asked Daiki.

Tomoko shook her head. "She looked so pale. And her skin! And her eyes! And she had this tube running into her arm. But when she grabbed my wrist, she still seemed to have all her strength." She looked down at a fresh bruise on her arm. "I guess that's a good thing. And she told me she was sorry."

"For what?" asked Daiki.

Tomoko shrugged. "Something about priorities and the way that I was raised. I'm sure she was talking about how I'm so lazy and unfocused—but I know that already. She's been telling me that for years!"

"Will she be all right?" asked Daiki's mother.

"They'll be running tests all day. The doctor said we

should leave and come back later." In a whisper she added, "For some reason, I think he just wants to be rid of me!"

INNER SOLAR SYSTEM:

Ninety-five million miles from Earth, the Mrendarian captain slid around a corner on the ship and nearly collided with the technician. He was pondering an electronic component held in one tentacle and an adjustment tool held in another.

"What is wrong, Technician?" Captain M'Frozza asked.

"The pilot does not understand me."

"Ah!" the captain popped three of her nose-holes indignantly. "I know just how you feel. He is a cranky fusspot, and he won't stop complaining for even a half pulse! First it was the navigation beacons, then it was the toilets, and now he's probably on to something else. Does he not realize that we are on an important mission? You are absolutely right—his problem is a lack of understanding. I will take that up with Father-Parent when we return to the embassy."

The technician looked at her and blinked one eye after another after another. "Actually, the pilot does not understand me because the translator system is offline, and neither of us have a language implant like you do."

"Oh," said the captain. "Well, in that case, carry on!"

13

PLATTE BLUFF, NEVADA:

Eight hours before the most important event in human history, Tyler got dressed for school. Then he remembered that it was TY SATO Day, and figured he'd probably get to stay home. After all, the entire world was celebrating a day named after something that was named after him!

Tyler called his friends to wish them a happy TY SATO Day and to tell them where to drop off their TY SATO Day presents, but he wasn't fooling anybody. Even Brayden knew the day wasn't really about Tyler, but it also wasn't really about the alien spaceship that shared Tyler's name. Mostly it seemed to be about people getting over all the stupid stuff they'd done the day before, when everyone thought the world might end.

Brayden said both his parents had quit their jobs. Brayden's father had called his boss a nasty name on the way out, so now he couldn't even ask for his old job back.

Lucas said his parents had taken all the money from their checking account. They'd gone shopping and spent every penny they had. They'd bought a new car, new clothes, and expensive toys for Lucas and his brothers. Now that the world wasn't ending, they had to take it all back.

John's father had gone into the desert on a vision quest to seek advice from his spirit guides. "Is that a Shoshone tradition?" Tyler asked.

"It's Lakota, I think," said John. "Dad wanted to be covered, just in case." It sounded cool to Tyler, except that John's father hadn't brought any food or his mobile phone, and he still hadn't returned with any wisdom from the spirit world.

As for Eric, Tyler didn't know what his best friend's parents had done because Eric hung up on him seven times in a row.

Tyler's dad had come home from the observatory when Tyler was in school to shower and sleep. He said he had a surprise for Tyler, but no gift could have been better than having his father home again. It felt like he'd been away for months!

"It's an exciting time to be an astronomer," said Tyler's dad over a plate of scrambled eggs and veggie bacon. "People are going to spend a lot more time looking at the stars now that we know there's intelligent life up there."

"Tell me about my spaceship," said Tyler.

"Your spaceship?"

"It's still named after me, right?"

"You'll have to argue with the aliens about that." He tousled Tyler's hair. "The ship is shaped like a wedge of pie, if that pie were as wide across as a football field. It's coated with reflective metal, which is why we could see it from so far away."

"When will it get here?"

"That's hard to say, kiddo. The ship's been traveling at more than nine million miles an hour, so it should reach Earth this afternoon, but we don't know whether the aliens will stop for a visit or even say hello. For all we know, they could buzz right past us and keep on going."

"Have the aliens said anything?" Tyler asked. "Do we know if they're friendly?"

"I wouldn't know anything about that, kiddo. My job has been to watch the ship. Other people have been trying to listen to it."

Tyler's mom came into the kitchen wearing diamond earrings and her best dress. Tyler wished he could send a picture to the TV stations. Then everyone would know his mom was only scary sometimes.

"Aren't you ready yet?" she asked. "They'll be here any minute."

"Who?" asked Tyler.

She looked at Tyler's dad. "Didn't you tell him?"

"I wanted it to be a surprise."

"Go, go, go," Tyler's mom told him. "Wash your face, comb your hair, and change that shirt. Wear the blue one, I think— No, the green."

"All right." Tyler ran to the bathroom and pulled on the door. It was locked, of course. "Come on, Amanda! Today is TY SATO Day and I'm Ty Sato. You have to let me have a turn in the bathroom on TY SATO Day."

"I don't have to let you do anything."

"Mom!" Tyler shouted. "Make Amanda give me a turn in the bathroom!"

"Don't be such a baby," his big sister said through the door. "There'll be a bathroom you can use on the plane."

"Plane?" he asked. "What plane?"

The doorbell rang.

Tyler wondered if Eric had come to apologize for being such a jerk. He didn't have to forgive him, but he probably would. It was TY SATO Day, and Tyler was in a good mood. He opened the door. Two soldiers stood on the front porch—real soldiers with green uniforms and flat black hats.

"Sato family?" asked the first soldier.

Tyler nodded.

"We're here to escort you to the airport."

"I just . . . um . . . bathroom," Tyler babbled. "I mean,

I'm just waiting for the bathroom, *sir*."

The soldiers laughed and one of them told Tyler, "At ease, soldier."

"I'll tell Mom and Dad you're here," Tyler said. "We'll be ready as quick as we can."

"I'd hope so," said one of the soldiers. "The President of the United States doesn't like to be kept waiting."

INNER SOLAR SYSTEM:

Sixty-five million miles from Earth, the pilot of the silver spaceship met with Captain M'Frozza. "Captain, I know you don't care about the appalling lack of navigation beacons in this system, but do you have any idea how the natives wish us to approach their planet? I've detected quite a number of artificial satellites in orbit but no welcome center, tourist facilities, or lodging floats of any kind."

"I don't know, Pilot."

"It seems rude of them not to supply better instructions."

"Just put us in a stable orbit and I'll do the rest."

The pilot hissed steam through his nose-holes. "Perhaps I can find some information from their broadcasts. Our translation system was not faulty after all."

"That is good to hear," said the captain. "Have you determined what a TY SATO might be?"

"Among residents of Earth, 'Ty Sato' can have several

meanings. It can either be a large asteroid or the nickname they've given our vessel. It also seems to be the name of a child living in one of their desert regions."

"A child?" The Mrendarian girl blinked her three eyes in unison.

"Here is an image of him with his mother-parent." The pilot projected an image from one of the Earth broadcasts.

Captain M'Frozza whistled through her nose-holes. "That wild hair! That twisted face! I've never seen such a frightening creature!"

"We should leave this system," said the pilot.

"No, Pilot. We must continue. The honor of Mrendaria is at stake." She looked at the image of the Earth child's mother-parent again and shivered so hard that her tentacles flailed around like whips. "I believe I am going to have nightmares!"

TOKYO, JAPAN:

Five hours before the most important event in human history, Daiki woke to some loud throat-clearing in the middle of the night. Tomoko stood over his bedroll with a big cardboard box in her arms. "Daiki-kun! Are you awake?"

"Barely." Daiki rubbed his eyes and yawned.

"Good. I was hoping you'd be awake because I didn't want to wake you." Tomoko dropped the box with a thud that shook the tatami floor. "I went home for some of my things. My frivolous things, as Obaa-chan calls them."

"That's nice." Daiki wondered when Tomoko would come to the point, and if that point would be worth ruining his good night's sleep.

"They're yours now," she stated.

Daiki blinked. "What's mine?"

"All my frivolous things. Obaa-chan always wanted me to throw them away, but I think it's better to have someone else appreciate them."

Daiki rolled over and peered into the box. Inside was a treasure trove of *Hunter-Elf Zeita* merchandise. "You're giving this to me?"

"Yeah, see? Have a look!" Tomoko began pulling items from the box. "Here's my video collection, an almost complete set of *UFO-Catcher* plush dolls, a soundtrack from the first season, super-deformed figurines, a foldable plastic longbow, and a whole bunch of magazines and posters. The posters still have sticky-tape on the backs because I was in a hurry, but you should be able to peel them off."

Daiki shook his head. "Tomoko-chan, I can't accept these things. They're important to you and you're going to want them back. Is that a genuine animation cel?"

Tomoko removed a transparent plastic sheet from the box. Two characters from the show were hand painted on it. "It's Zeita and Anti-Zeita from episode thirty-eight.

Autographed by the voice actress too. I always meant to have it framed."

Daiki took the cel and handled it with careful hands. "I guess I could take just this, if you were going to throw it out anyway, but as for the rest of it— Is that a collector's edition Zeita pin?"

Tomoko nodded. "I have three of them."

"Okay, I'll just take the cel and the pins. And the posters would look good on my walls. And I'd like to read the magazines, but I'm giving them back when I'm finished."

"I won't take them back. And, oh! I almost forgot." Tomoko removed the colorful Zeita keychain from her keys and dropped it into the box. "That's for you too."

"But that's your good-luck charm!" Daiki exclaimed.

"Obaa-chan doesn't believe in luck," Tomoko told him. "She calls it my most frivolous thing of all."

HOUSTON, TEXAS:

The soldiers took Tyler's family to a Humvee. The Humvee took them to an airplane. The airplane took them all the way to Houston. Each seat on the plane had a phone embedded behind the headrest, so Amanda spent the whole trip blabbing to her boyfriend of the week back home.

Tyler had never been to Texas before. Actually, he'd been outside of Nevada only a few times in his life. As the plane landed, three hours before the most important event in human history, Tyler pressed his nose against the window to get a good view of Houston from the air. "It was nice of the president to meet us halfway instead of making us fly all the way to Washington, D.C."

His sister rolled her eyes and finally detached the phone from the side of her face. "You think the president cares about making life easier for you? You're such an idiot."

"Amanda," said their mom sternly.

Tyler's sister shrugged and returned to her phone call.

"Do you know what's in Houston?" Tyler's dad asked.

"Oil wells?" Tyler guessed. "Tex-Mex chili? Cowboys?"

"How about this?" His dad pretended to speak into a radio. "Houston? Come in, Houston. Houston, we've got a problem."

"Truck drivers?" Tyler asked.

His dad laughed. "Not unless they're truck drivers from outer space."

"Oh." Tyler nodded. "NASA. The space agency."

More soldiers met them at the airport. They took Tyler and his family by helicopter to the Johnson Space Center. Tyler didn't know what it was like there on a normal day, but on TY SATO Day, large crowds rushed among several buildings and down long hallways from one security checkpoint to the next. Most of the men and women wore NASA identification badges on their belts or hanging from cords around their necks, but Tyler also noticed visitor badges with flags from countries around the world.

Tyler's family waited in a VIP lounge for a few minutes until a bald man in a dirt brown suit burst through the door, trailed by a woman with gray streaks in her dark hair. "Now who are these people?" the man asked with a squint in Tyler's direction.

"Ty Sato and family," the woman replied. "The president wanted to meet them."

"What? But you said—oh." The man sighed. "Let's get this over with." He put on an obviously fake smile, strode forward, and held his hand out for a handshake. He spoke fast, like his words were racing each other out of his mouth. "I'm Dan O'Hare, NASA administrator. I'm the one in charge of this whole dog and pony show. And this is Deputy Administrator Wanda Drake. I can't tell you what an honor it is for us to meet the *original* Ty Sato and assorted relatives."

"*'Assorted relatives'?*" Amanda huffed.

Tyler's mother and father glanced at each other, trying to decide between them who would be the first to shake Mr. O'Hare's hand. In their moment of hesitation, the NASA administrator pulled his hand away and retreated toward the exit. "As you can imagine, I'm very busy today, but Deputy Drake will take care of you until the president has a free moment and—oh!" Mr. O'Hare turned to face them again but continued walking backward. "Have you folks eaten lunch?"

"No," said Tyler.

"Then you're in luck. It's Meatloaf Week in our cafeteria. Just imagine, five kinds of meatloaf!"

"But we're vegetarians!" Tyler just managed to get words out as the NASA administrator completed his escape.

"'*Assorted relatives*'?" Amanda asked again.

"I really must apologize for Mr. O'Hare." Deputy Drake's slow Southern drawl was a refreshing change from the administrator's high-speed patter. "As you might imagine, he has a lot on his mind today, and I made the mistake of telling him that Ty Sato had arrived a bit earlier than we'd expected. He must have thought I meant TY SATO, the one from space."

"I understand," Tyler told her. "People get us confused all the time."

Over lunch in the astronaut cafeteria, Deputy Drake told them stories about when she'd been a mission commander on the space shuttle and International Space Station. Tyler was fascinated, and even Amanda listened intently as she picked at her meatless meatloaf muffins. Deputy Drake was in the middle of describing her first spacewalk when her phone buzzed. "The president is waiting for you," she announced.

"Does the president really know who we are?" Tyler asked.

"He's been briefed."

"Wow," said Tyler. "Nobody has ever been briefed about me before. He hasn't seen my latest report card, has he?"

Deputy Drake laughed. "I wouldn't worry about that. Your father discovered TY SATO because he was searching the heavens for your star. You have had a special connection with this spaceship from the beginning, so it only makes sense for you to be here when it arrives."

They bypassed four security checkpoints on their way to an enormous room containing row after row of long tables. It looked a bit like the cafeteria, but without a salad bar. Technicians at the tables all faced an enormous video screen at the front of the room as they fiddled with their computers, phones, and paperwork. Many of the tables seemed to be reserved for other space agencies from around the world. Tyler could see flags from China, Russia, India, a whole bunch he didn't recognize, and— "Hey! That table's all people from Japan! Does Japan have its own NASA?"

"They call it JAXA," said Deputy Drake. "The Japanese have done some amazing work with very thin sails that unfold to catch the solar wind. In the future, solar sails may be more efficient than rockets for reaching the outer planets of our solar system."

"Origami in space!" Tyler's mother exclaimed. "See, kids? Those little paper cranes I make can be used to explore other worlds!"

Amanda made one of her embarrassed look-away hair flips and froze at the end with her eyes wide and jaw hung open. "That's him!" she shrieked.

Tyler followed Amanda's pointing finger to the back of

the room, where the President of the United States stood with his hands clasped in front of him. The president looked even taller than Tyler had expected. On the president's left stood NASA Administrator O'Hare, who spoke as quickly as ever while gesturing at the president like a madman. On the president's right stood a uniformed soldier with more medals and decorations than anyone Tyler had ever seen. The decorated soldier eyed Mr. O'Hare's windmilling arms intently, and Tyler had no doubt in the man's ability to defend the President from any unintentional backhands to the face.

Deputy Drake waved to catch the administrator's eye. Mr. O'Hare said one more thing to the president before jerking his head and neck in a "get over here" gesture that made the NASA administrator look like he was shaking the water from his left ear after a dip in the pool. The decorated soldier tensed his hands in response.

"Mr. President," said Mr. O'Hare, "I'd like you to meet the Sato family."

"But don't mind me," said Amanda. "I'm just an '*assorted relative.*'"

"Have you really been briefed about me?" Tyler wanted to know.

"Indeed I have." The president shook their hands. "Dr. Sato, Mrs. Sato, Amanda Sato, and young Tyler. I envy you, young man."

Tyler blinked. "You . . . envy me? Sir?"

The president smiled. "If I do a good job, they might name an aircraft carrier after me someday. But you've got an alien spaceship named after you already."

"I just hope the aliens aren't mad when they find out," said Tyler.

The president laughed. "Tyler, why don't you stand over here between me and the Secretary of Defense." He indicated the decorated soldier. "I always feel better when I have at least one person between us—no offense, General Slagowski."

"None taken, Mr. President," said the general.

Tyler was almost too dazed to speak. "Yes, sure, all right. So I'll stand right here, then? Thank you, Mr. President!"

Tyler heard his sister whisper to his mom, "It's not fair. Ty's a dork. The president isn't supposed to like him so much."

"Amanda, hush," said his mom.

Tyler stuck his tongue out at his sister when the president wasn't looking.

"What's happening now?" Tyler's dad asked.

"We're broadcasting messages of peace in all the languages of Earth," said Mr. O'Hare. "We're also playing music from countries around the world."

Tyler's dad nodded. "So the aliens hear the best of our cultures."

"That's the idea," said the president. "They're also picking up the worst of our television shows, but that's beyond our control."

General Slagowski's frowny face collected some additional shadows. "They know too much about us, and we know too little about them. We must be careful, Mr. President."

"We will be, General."

As the technicians shuffled their papers and made their phone calls, people kept coming by to let the president know they were ready for him. They were ready if he wanted to make a speech on TV. They were ready if he wanted to consult with other world leaders. They were even ready if he wanted to launch nuclear missiles at TY SATO. "Thanks," said the president. "I'll let you know."

While everyone else rushed madly around the room, the president stayed calm and mostly just spoke with

Tyler about his school. Tyler told him about his classes, the soccer team, and everything else. He even told the president about how Eric Parker wasn't talking to him.

"I remember being ten years old, like Eric," said the president. "It's not an easy age. As an eleven-year-old, you'll have to be patient and understanding."

"Maybe you're right," said Tyler.

"Of course I'm right," said the President with a wink. "If I hadn't gotten sidetracked by a career in politics, I would have made an excellent school guidance counselor."

INNER SOLAR SYSTEM:

Nineteen million miles from Earth, the silver spaceship's technician rang the door chime on Captain M'Frozza's cabin. "Enter!" came the girl's voice from inside.

Technician N'Gatu opened the door and slid inside on a jet of green slime. "You wanted to see me, Captain?"

"Yes, Technician. I have something important to ask, and I don't want R'Turvo to know."

"I have no problem with keeping secrets from him."

"Good." Her face-tentacles waved in a smile pattern. "On the planet we are approaching, they might not have yet discovered quantum band technology."

"But you said they invited you here for a challenge," N'Gatu stated. "They'd need to use quantum bands for that. Electromagnetic broadcasts would take ages to reach

another system, and nobody else in the Galaxy would be listening for them."

"Ah, yes." M'Frozza laughed nervously. "Of course you are right. But . . . what if these people prefer to use electromagnetic broadcasts? Would we have any way to contact them?"

"It would not be difficult. We have all the necessary parts in our waste reclamation system already."

"That would be great! And then . . . could you patch the transmitter into the ship's quantum console? Only don't tell the pilot, or my father-parent, or anyone else?"

N'Gatu sighed. "The residents of this system did not actually contact you for a challenge, did they?"

"No," said M'Frozza quietly. "They did not."

"I suppose that as I am a mere technician, that detail doesn't really concern me and I should just do as I am instructed. I will build you a transmitter and make it work like a quantum hail, as you request."

"And you will keep my secret?" M'Frozza sealed her nostril-flaps to hold in her breath.

N'Gatu bowed his head. "As I said, I am a mere technician. If I accused our planet's captain of deception, who would believe me?"

M'Frozza wrapped her arm-tentacles around N'Gatu in a grateful hug. "Thank you, Technician! Thank you, thank you!"

"You are welcome," he said, pushing her away. *"We'll just have to make sure nobody is using the toilet and the radio at the same time, or one of them will get a whole lot of feedback!"*

TOKYO, JAPAN:

Minutes before the most important event in human history, Daiki and his family gathered around the television. The room was crowded with uncles, aunts, grandparents, cousins, and some people Daiki had never even met before. It was a family celebration because the spaceship was named after their American relative, but Daiki still felt anxious about what the aliens might do. Katsuro and his family were there as well, since they hadn't had the chance to buy a new television yet.

Katsuro nudged his arm. "Hey, Daiki-kun, where's that girlfriend of yours?"

Daiki pointed to a window. "Out there, and she's not my girlfriend."

Katsuro stepped over and gawked out at the courtyard where Tomoko was doing a set of foot-sweeping exercises. "That's the girl who beat Takeda-sama at the arcade! Tomizawa Tomiko! What is she doing at your house?"

Daiki shrugged. "Judo drills."

Katsuro shook his head in amazement. "An alien

spaceship is one thing, but *this* is truly unbelievable—Daiki-kun's girlfriend is a judo superstar!"

"Tomoko-chan is not my girlfriend."

Katsuro grinned. "Tomoko-*chan*? I believe you've just proven my point."

Daiki groaned into his hands.

"Daiki-kun!" his mother called. She held a tray containing a pitcher of water and a plate of seaweed-wrapped rice balls. "Bring these *omusubi* out to your friend. She's been kicking the air for over an hour now, and she must be getting awfully dehydrated."

"Yes, Mother," said Daiki, happy for an excuse to get away from the crowd. Outside, he placed the tray on the ground as close to Tomoko's waving arms and swinging legs as he could safely get. "Tomoko-chan? Aren't you hungry? Thirsty? Tired?"

Tomoko stopped her movements and turned to him, red faced and sweaty. "Sorry, Daiki-kun. I can't really talk right now. I've got a lot of practicing to catch up on, just like Obaa-chan would have wanted."

"Your great-grandmother wouldn't want you to kill yourself. Why don't you take a break?"

"Well . . . maybe for a minute or so." She stepped forward to gulp down water and handfuls of food. "Mmm! *Arigato,* Daiki-kun."

"You know, my whole family is inside watching the

spaceship. You should join us."

Tomoko shook her head. "Can't. Gotta practice. No more fun for me. No more games, and no more episodes of *Hunter-Elf Zeita*. I need to change my priorities like Obaa-chan said." She stepped away and started her work-out routine again from the beginning.

"Tomoko-chan?" Daiki called. "Tomoko-chan!"

She did not respond. Daiki shook his head and went back inside.

INNER SOLAR SYSTEM:

Less than a million miles away, the silver spaceship fired its thrusters and prepared to enter into an orbit around Earth.

15

"Get ready," said the president. "In a few moments we will all witness the most important event in human history."

"We will?" Tyler asked.

The president gave him a thin-lipped smile. "We're about to make contact with beings from another world. I can't promise that it will be the *best* moment in human history, but it will certainly be a moment when human history becomes part of something much larger than our own little world and almost certainly older than our own civilization. That seems pretty important, at least to me."

The giant screen displayed a close-up of TY SATO as it flew past the International Space Station. It really did look like a silver slice of pie, just like Tyler's dad had said. The technicians jumped around and gave each other high fives. So many people were shouting at once that Tyler could hardly hear what anyone was saying.

Next to him, General Slagowski leaned over and spoke to the president. "Sir, you'd be safer in the bunker. It's not too late to get you down there."

"I prefer to stay where the action is, General," said the president. "Don't you agree, Tyler?"

All Tyler could do was nod.

Tyler watched an electronic map of Earth at the front of the room. A white dot showed the alien spaceship trailing a wavy line across the Pacific Ocean. *Ships in orbit must move pretty fast,* Tyler thought, because this one crossed the ocean in just a few minutes.

"Remember, Mr. President, the missiles are armed and standing by," said General Slagowski. His fingers twitched and sweat ran down his face. Tyler was glad this man couldn't fire any nuclear missiles without the president's permission—or at least, Tyler hoped not.

"We have an incoming broadcast from the alien ship!" one of the technicians shouted. Everyone became really quiet, really fast.

"Who gets to speak to the aliens?" Tyler whispered.

"That was a tough decision." The president put a hand on Tyler's shoulder. "The International Academy of Astronautics brought a proposal to the United Nations. They decided it was between NASA and the Russian space agency to work it out, so Mr. O'Hare met with the head of Roscosmos and they flipped a coin—and that's why Mr. O'Hare will be the voice of our planet."

Tyler felt his eyes bug out. "Because you won a coin toss?"

"No," said Mr. O'Hare. "Because I lost." He took a seat in front of a larger and more elaborate computer than anyone else seemed to have. The speaker crackled and everyone—the technicians, the president, the secretary of defense, and Tyler's family—leaned forward to hear better. Nobody took a breath.

A gruff and grumpy voice boomed from the console. "Hello? Hello? This is Pilot R'Turvo of Mrendarian Diplomatic Yacht M4949-R1, the ship you charmingly refer to as TY SATO. May I speak to the being in charge of planetary assistance?"

"They speak English!" one of the technicians exclaimed.

"They must have learned it from our broadcasts," said another. "Either that they're using some kind of two-way translation system. My theory is that such a system would establish and define localized language zones and act as a real-time filter for any spoken—"

"Johnson, hush!" Mr. O'Hare shouted. "Nobody wants to hear your doctoral thesis right now."

"Yes, sir," squeaked the technician.

Mr. O'Hare held his finger over his microphone's mute button, which was flashing red to show that the microphone was off. He took a calming breath, tapped the mute button, and spoke into the microphone. "TY SATO, this is Houston. How may we help you?"

"Mr. Houston, I wish to file a complaint about your navigation beacons. Specifically, there aren't any. How dare you issue a challenge to our captain and then not provide us with the beacons we needed to reach your planet at mid-drive speed!"

Mr. O'Hare's eyebrows bunched up like a pair of confused caterpillars. He tapped the mute button again and turned to Deputy Drake. "Navigation beacons?"

The deputy administrator shrugged.

Mr. O'Hare pressed the mute button again. "Sorry for your inconvenience, TY SATO. We'll . . . have those navigation beacons installed as soon as we can."

"You'd better. Also it seems your holographic interface is offline, allowing only this inadequate audio transmission. What sort of operation is your planet running?"

"Again, I am sorry. Now, you said something about a challenge?"

"Don't pretend ignorance, Mr. Houston. Our world's captain will discuss the matter directly with your world's captain."

Mr. O'Hare pressed the mute button again. "It sounds like they're demanding to go over my head."

"I don't like this," said General Slagowski. "Our world's

captain? Why would they be asking for somebody with a military rank unless they're about to ask for Earth's unconditional surrender?"

"English isn't their first language," the president reminded him. "I may not be a captain, but I do have some experience talking with my fellow heads of state. May I?"

Mr. O'Hare jumped out of his seat and allowed the president to take over at the fancy console. The president collected his thoughts for a moment before he pressed the flashing mute button. "Hello, TY SATO. This is the President of the United States. On behalf of Planet Earth, I welcome you in the spirit of peace."

"You sound old," said a new voice from the alien ship. It was the voice of a young girl. "You sound even older than our cranky old pilot," she said.

"Are you . . . the captain of your world?" asked the president.

"Let me speak to somebody my age," said the alien girl. "Don't you have any kids there?"

Everyone turned to look at Tyler, who was by far the youngest person in the control room. The president muted the microphone and waved Tyler over.

"You want *me* to talk to her?" Tyler asked.

Amanda rolled her eyes. "Yeah, that figures. Out of seven billion people on Earth, the aliens only want to talk to you."

Tyler felt as if his legs were made of Jell-O as he walked to the communications console, aware that everyone was watching him. He heard one of the technicians whisper, "Oh, sure. The most important event in *human history* and they're asking to speak to some kid."

Tyler reached the console and took a seat. His finger on the flashing mute button felt like it weighed a million pounds. "Um, hello?"

"Hi there," said the alien girl. "I am M'Frozza, Captain of the Mrendarian Galaxy Games team. Who's this?"

"I'm Tyler Sato."

The radio made a squeaking hiss. Tyler couldn't tell if that horrible sound came from the equipment or from M'Frozza. "Tyler Sato? The child with the scary-looking mother-parent? I've seen your image on your planet's broadcasts!"

Tyler saw his mom's face turn bright red. Who could have guessed that *Yolanda Speaks Out* had viewers in space? "Mom wasn't at her best that day," Tyler told M'Frozza.

"Oh. I understand. You should see my father-parent in the dawn hour before he's lathered his tentacles."

Tyler felt a shiver in his spine and quickly pressed the mute button. "She has tentacles. I'm talking to an octopus from space."

"Don't let that get to you," the president told him.

"Take a deep breath and try to keep her talking. You're doing a great job, Tyler."

"Thanks, Mr. President." Tyler unmuted the microphone and tried to think of what a person might say to an octopus from space. "So, M'Frozza . . . what brings you to Earth?"

"Is this a private connection, Tyler Sato? There is nobody else listening in?"

Tyler looked around at the huge room full of people hanging on every word of their conversation. He also figured that most of the world's population would be watching at home on TV. "There may be a few other people around," he told M'Frozza.

"Aw, *smazzroot!* I need to talk to you in private. Can you come up?"

"Come up?"

"Yeah. As the Captain of Earth you must have a ship. It would be extremely suspicious if you did not have your own transportation."

Tyler frowned. Something in M'Frozza's voice sounded strange, like she also had somebody listening in on her end. *Maybe that grumpy pilot guy,* Tyler figured. *And what was that part about him being the Captain of Earth?*

"Hold on, M'Frozza." Tyler pressed the mute button and looked over at Mr. O'Hare. "Sir, could I borrow a space shuttle or something?"

Administrator O'Hare's eyes bugged out. "You want to *borrow* a space shuttle? Are you out of your mind? You're not even old enough to borrow your dad's car keys!"

"We can't let this alien make a potential hostage out of one of our citizens," stated the secretary of defense. "We should demand that this Captain M'Frozza come down to Earth instead, turn herself over to military jurisdiction, and surrender her ship for our inspection."

Mr. O'Hare narrowed his eyes. "Maybe you'd also like to declare war on her entire species while you're at it? See, this is why you're not speaking to aliens on behalf of our planet."

"Neither are you anymore," the general pointed out.

"Gentlemen!" the president exclaimed. "Have you already forgotten that this is supposed to be the greatest event in human history? This is our one opportunity to demonstrate our humanity and make a good first impression to the rest of the universe."

The general and Mr. O'Hare both looked away like naughty children being scolded by a parent. "Sorry, Mr. President," they both mumbled.

"Apology accepted. Tyler, you have the full cooperation of NASA and the United States government."

"And the Russian government as well," countered a woman at the table of tri-colored Russian flags.

"And the People's Republic of China," added a man at

a table of Chinese flags. "We'll get you into space some-how—if it's okay with your parents, of course."

Tyler gave his parents a pleading look.

"What an amazing opportunity to advance our knowledge of extraterrestrial life," his dad exclaimed. "Of course you have to go."

Tyler's mother met this statement a knife-edged glare. "You want to shoot my baby into space? Are you nuts?"

"Of course not!" Tyler's dad staggered backward and blinked rapidly, as if he'd been hit by an invisible punch. "I mean, technically yes, Tyler would be shot into space, but he'd come back. Probably. Every advancement in human knowledge comes with a risk—"

"We have to talk about this," Tyler's mom insisted.

Tyler's dad sighed. "We'll talk, but do we have to do it in front of the president?"

Tyler's mom pointed to the door. "Hallway. Outside. Now."

Tyler watched anxiously as his parents made their way into the hall. Whenever Tyler's mom and dad left a room with two opinions, Tyler could count on them returning with only one—but he had no idea which one would win out.

"You're not going anywhere," Amanda told him smugly. "When I was your age, Mom wouldn't let me go to a sleepover at Mary Beth Waumbaugh's house—and she only lived right across the street!"

The alien girl's voice came back on the speakers. "Hello? Captain Tyler? Captain Tyler of Earth? Are you still there?"

"Keep her talking," Mr. O'Hare urged.

"About what?" asked Tyler.

"Anything! Just make sure she stays with us."

Tyler forced his teeth to stop biting his lower lip. His nervous fingers pressed the mute button. "So, um, M'Frozza . . . seen any good movies lately?"

"Actually, I have!" M'Frozza exclaimed, and by the time Tyler's parents returned to the control room, the Mrendarian girl was gushing about the best Earth program she'd watched during her trip across the Solar System. "Then the man said the first fifty callers would receive an attachment for cleaning drapes and a lifetime supply of bags! I don't know what drapes are, but everyone in the audience stood up and cheered."

"That's one of my favorite shows, too," Tyler lied. He just didn't have the heart to tell the alien girl that she'd wasted an entire hour watching a vacuum-cleaner infomercial. M'Frozza started to describe another scene where a woman used the machine to suck spaghetti sauce from a carpet, but Tyler was only half-listening. His parents were close enough now for Tyler to see the deep scowl on his dad's face. It wasn't looking good for Tyler's trip into space.

"Something about that Earth woman reminded me of my own mother-parent," M'Frozza said wistfully.

Tyler's mom stopped, mid-stride, to listen.

"I know it's silly, but I think about her all the time," said M'Frozza. "My father-parent, too. Even halfway across the Galaxy, my family is always with me."

Tyler's dad dropped heavily into the seat next to him. "Can you hold on another moment, M'Frozza?" Tyler asked the alien girl.

"Okay, sure." M'Frozza made a soft buzzing noise that might have been the Mrendarian version of humming to pass the time.

Tyler hit the mute button and gave his dad one last pleading look. "Well?"

Dr. Sato shook his head. "Sorry, kiddo, your mother has a good point about the danger—"

"Wait." Before anyone could stop her, Tyler's mom turned off the mute button and spoke into the microphone. "M'Frozza? This is Mrs. Sato, Tyler's mother."

"Oh! Hello, ma'am," came the alien girl's surprised voice.

"I understand you're many light-years from home," said Tyler's mom. "I'm sure your parents must miss you very much when you're so far away."

"I know they do, ma'am," M'Frozza agreed. "Mother-

Parent, Father-Parent, Other-Parent, Spawn-Parent, Egg-Parent, Mud-Parent, Straw-Parent—even my dear departed water-parent is probably watching over me in spirit."

"That's . . . a lot of parents," said Tyler's mom. "And they're all fine with you being here?"

"Oh, yes," said M'Frozza. "I am the captain of my world, and this meeting has to be between me and a captain from your world. Between me and Tyler Sato."

Tyler's mom gave Tyler's dad a look, and Tyler's dad nodded back at her. All the while, Tyler held his breath and waited. He could hardly believe the next words his mother spoke into the microphone. "If your parents could let you come halfway across the galaxy to speak to our son, I suppose we can let Tyler out of our sight for long enough to meet you."

"Thank you, ma'am," said M'Frozza.

Tyler's mom gave him such a hard hug that Tyler thought his ribs might break. His brain was in too much shock for him to be embarrassed, even when the hug was followed by a round of kisses on the top of his head. He was going into space to meet with aliens!

The entire control room erupted in cheers and applause—except for Amanda, who stomped her feet and pouted. "I can't even tell you how unfair this is!" she exclaimed.

16

KIRUNA, SWEDEN:

For the first possible flight from Earth, a private jet brought Tyler and his family to Kiruna, Sweden. An old airport there had recently reopened as the European launch site of Falcon Spacelines, a company that eccentric billionaire Stephen Falconer founded to bring wealthy tourists on joyrides into orbit. "Tickets on the *Falcon One* are usually a million dollars and up," their pilot told them. "I hope you've brought your checkbook!"

The plane was met on the tarmac by a man whose bright yellow turtleneck sweater clashed with the spikes of rust red hair on his head and beard. As Tyler's family stepped down the metal stairway, the bearded man offered to help carry their luggage into the spaceport.

"Tip him a dollar," Tyler's mother whispered as she pressed a wrinkled bill into Tyler's hand.

Tyler offered him the money but the man just

laughed. "No thanks, mate. I already have more por-
traits of George Washington than I know what to
do with."

"I don't understand," said Tyler's
mother. "Who turns down money?"

"Someone who doesn't need any,"
said Tyler's father. "Stephen Falconer,
I presume?"

"Guilty as charged," said the
multibillionaire with a wink.

Amanda shrieked. "I can't believe it's really you! I love your
lip gloss soooo much!"

Mr. Falconer rubbed a finger

across his lower lip. "I didn't think I was wearing any."

"No, I meant Falcon Fashions Kiss-Goo Number 5." She dug a short jar of goop from one of her pockets. "Could you autograph it for me?"

"Amanda," Mrs. Sato snapped.

"We really appreciate your help, Mr. Falconer," said Tyler's dad. "Tell me, how can your company have a rocket ready so much faster than all the governments of the world put together?"

Mr. Falconer laughed. "I could tell you that Falcon Spacelines doesn't have as much red tape as NASA and fewer forms that need to be filled out on canary yellow paper. Or I could be truthful and say that we already had the *Falcon One* fueled and ready to go for a client of ours. Amy Thrush is so disappointed that you're bumping her from her flight."

Amanda shrieked so loud that Tyler felt his skull vibrate from the sound. "Amy

Thrush? The lead singer of Traveling Jones? That Amy Thrush?"

"Yes," said Mr. Falconer, rubbing his ears.

"She's, like, my favorite singer of all time! Why don't we send her to meet the aliens instead of my dumb brother?"

"Because I'm the one they asked for," Tyler shot back.

"Mr. Falconer?" Tyler's mother asked. "Is your spacecraft safe?"

"Mrs. Sato, I'd trust my own life to the *Falcon One*. In fact I already have, more than a dozen times. We fly higher and faster than any of our private-sector competitors. We can buzz the International Space Station, surf a wave of orbital debris, play a little satellite pinball, and have your son home in time for dinner."

"But can you dock with an alien spaceship?" asked Tyler.

Mr. Falconer's wide green eyes twinkled with excitement. "We'll find out, won't we?"

Before the flight, Tyler watched a short video about the *Falcon One* and some of the most important parts of space travel: how to wear a spacesuit, how to eat astronaut food, and how to use a zero-gravity bathroom. Tyler didn't like the space toilet's Velcro straps or vacuum hoses, but at least Amanda wouldn't be jumping into *this* bathroom when he needed it most.

After a quick medical checkup, Tyler rejoined his family in the spaceport terminal. They were the only ones there except for a grumpy woman with a pink Mohawk, who occupied a seat by the viewing window. Tyler figured that she had to be Amy Thrush because of the way she kept looking over and snarling at him.

Tyler's mom and dad had tears in their eyes and, to his surprise, so did Amanda. "I know I give you a hard time, but I think you're very brave to do this," she said. "If you don't come back, I'll tell everyone what a great brother you were."

"What if I do come back?" Tyler asked.

She shrugged. "We'll worry about that if it happens."

Tyler hugged his family good-bye, then stepped through the gate that led to the *Falcon One*. "Welcome aboard the Falcon Spacelines flagship space plane, *Falcon One*," said a familiar voice. "I, Stephen Falconer, will be your pilot, navigator, and steward. The space plane will be carried by a mothercraft to an altitude of sixteen kilometers—that's 52,000 feet to you, Yank. At that point we will detach and continue, under our own power, into orbit. Our destination will be a rendezvous with the Mrendarian spaceship TY SATO. You will find an assortment of magazines and comic books in the media compartment in front of you as well as the best movies Falcon Studios has to offer. Now sit back, put your feet up, and enjoy the ride!"

The trip started like an ordinary flight in a very small jet airplane with Tyler as the only passenger. When they were so high that Tyler could look out the window and see the horizon curve like part of a thin blue circle, Mr. Falconer's voice came back over the intercom. "The captain has turned on the fasten-seatbelt light, the grab-your-armrests-like-your-life-depended-on-it light, and the squint-your-eyes-shut-and-pray light. Biting your tongue is optional. *Falcon One* will detach from the mothercraft in fifteen seconds. Rocket thrust will begin ten seconds after that. Have a nice day!"

There was a loud clunk, then a sudden sinking feeling in Tyler's stomach. This was followed, ten seconds later, by a thrust that would make the world's biggest roller coaster feel like a gentle merry-go-round. The *Falcon One* rattled and shook. Comic books flew out of the cabinet and the engine roared so loudly that Tyler could barely hear himself scream.

"Don't throw up," said Mr. Falconer. He repeated it over and over. "Don't throw up, don't throw up, don't throw up," all the way into orbit.

"Okay!" Tyler shouted. "I didn't throw up!"

"Actually, I was talking to myself," said the billionaire

pilot. "I always forget to turn the intercom off during that part."

LOW EARTH ORBIT:

Tyler spent the next couple hours floating around the passenger cabin, talking by radio to his family, and staring out the window at Earth—not a picture of Earth or a map of Earth, but the actual Earth itself! If his vision were a whole lot better, he'd have been able to spot his house as the space plane passed overhead, his school, all his friends looking up at the sky, Eric Parker, Eric's house, the blacktop basketball court in Eric's driveway, and the faded *X* of chalk at the end of the driveway.

Mr. Falconer poked his head into the passenger cabin. "Nice view, eh? We call it space at sixty-two miles up, but that's like sticking your big toe outside your own front door and saying you're in the wilderness."

"It's still pretty cool," said Tyler.

"Oh, it's very cool." Mr. Falconer drifted to the window. "Being up here changes you. That's why it should be more than just a handful of elites who get to see Earth from this distance." He tapped a finger against the window to indicate two parts of the world below. "Do you see any lines between this little bit of the world and that little bit over there?"

Tyler shook his head.

"Exactly my point." Mr. Falconer drifted back to the cockpit, leaving Tyler alone with his thoughts.

A few minutes later, Mr. Falconer's voice crackled over the intercom. "Take a look out the starboard window, Tyler. That little speck is your fair-dinkum alien spacecraft!"

"Really?" Tyler pressed his nose against the glass. He thought he could make out a pinpoint of light above the blue arc of Earth's horizon. Finally, TY SATO, seen through his own eyes!

"I need to fire the thrusters to draw closer and match its orbit. You'll want to be strapped in for this part."

Tyler made a clumsy trip back to his seat and worked himself back into the safety straps. TY SATO slowly grew larger in the window until its silvery metal surface blocked Tyler's view of the Earth. A set of robotic arms reached out from *Falcon One* to the alien ship, and the passenger cabin shuddered as the ships came together. Through the window, Tyler watched a flexible tube bridge the gap between *Falcon One's* airlock and a similar opening in TY SATO.

While he waited, Tyler spoke by radio to reporters on Earth. He was ten minutes into the third interview before he realized that this reporter was located in Japan. Strangely, it didn't seem much different from talking from orbit to a reporter from the United States. "Being up here changes you" is what Mr. Falconer had said. Tyler thought that maybe it was happening to him already.

"I have someone here who wants to speak to you," said the reporter.

"Okay," said Tyler.

A boy's voice crackled over the radio. "Hello, Cousin Tyler-kun!"

Tyler blinked. "Cousin Daiki?"

"All Japan wishes you luck."

"Thanks, Daiki. I wouldn't be here at all if you hadn't named a spaceship after me."

Daiki said something that the reporter translated into English: "For your next birthday, that will be hard to top."

Tyler had always thought that he and his Japanese cousin could never really be friends because they lived in different parts of the world and spoke different languages. Now, none of that seemed to matter. They spoke through a translator about everything that had happened in the last week, and it felt like they had always been close.

"What should I do when I meet the aliens?" Tyler asked.

"Give a dramatic speech," said Daiki.

"Like what?"

"I don't know, but if you have a choice between

something dramatic and something not dramatic, go with the dramatic one."

"Gee, thanks, Daiki-kun."

"*Gambatte*, Cousin Tyler-kun."

"I'll do my best," Tyler agreed.

Mr. Falconer came out of the cockpit again. "It's time. The gauges say there's pressure on the other side of the airlock, so at least we don't need to worry about explosive decompression."

Tyler blinked. "Explosive what?"

"Like I said, it's something we *don't* have to worry about, and that spacesuit you're wearing should protect against any corrosives in their atmosphere. Once we attach the headpiece, this oxygen recycler will let you breathe." He pulled a huge metal cylinder from a compartment on the wall.

Tyler's eyes bugged out. "Do I need to wear that thing on my back? It looks like it weighs as much as I do!"

"No worries, mate. You're in microgravity. It'll be no different from scuba diving off the Great Barrier Reef."

"I've never gone scuba diving off the Great Barrier Reef," Tyler told him.

"Really? Then never mind. It's really not much like scuba diving at all. I just have no better way to describe it." Mr. Falconer tightened and adjusted Tyler's space-suit and breathing equipment until he was satisfied that everything was working perfectly.

"This is really uncomfortable," Tyler squeaked. "Aargh! I've got Mickey Mouse's voice, and my breathing sounds like Darth Vader's!"

"Darth Mickey Syndrome, eh? That's perfectly normal around these parts. Trust me, you're better off breathing through this mask than not breathing at all. Now if you get into trouble over there, just press this button to radio me and I'll be through that airlock faster than you can say *nanu-nanu*." He made a gesture with his hand that Tyler guessed was probably from an old-time TV show, or maybe one that only played in Australia.

"*Nanu-nanu,*" Tyler repeated, trying his best to repro-duce the hand signal. He didn't like to think about all the hundreds of things that could go wrong in an alien space-ship, but he did like the idea of being able to radio for help. "Thanks for all your help, Mr. Falconer."

"That's what I'm here for: taxi service, tech support, and bodyguard duty. Now off with you, before the aliens die of boredom from waiting around for you."

"Okay." Tyler pulled himself into the airlock door. "Just don't go anywhere, Mr. Falconer. I might need a ride home."

Tyler floated through the airlock, down the tube, and into the alien ship.

He instantly fell hard onto the floor. The space plane didn't have any gravity, but the alien ship sure did. The aliens must have brought it with them. The metal breathing tank that had been awkward but weightless on the space plane now held Tyler to the deck like a shellside-down turtle. Tyler flailed his arms and legs but couldn't even roll back into the airlock to escape.

Tyler desperately unclicked the straps and squirmed away from the metal cylinder. The mask tore from his face, and he took in a surprised gasp of alien air. It smelled like spicy mustard. Tyler pressed the button to send a radio signal to the *Falcon One*. "Hello! Mr. Falconer! My mask came off and I think I've been poisoned. *Nanu-nanu! Nanu-nanu!*"

There was no response from Mr. Falconer. Something in TY SATO seemed to be blocking the radio signal. The only thing Tyler heard each time he pressed the radio button was the sound of a flushing toilet from deeper inside the alien ship.

A few quick, mustardy breaths proved to Tyler that the air had enough oxygen, even for a hyperventilating eleven-year-old. He tried to stand, but the floor was covered in slippery green slime. Tyler fell three times before giving up.

He was sitting cross-legged in the slime when a round door irised open in a nearby wall.

A five-foot-tall purple creature slid through on a ring of tentacles where she should have had feet. There were more tentacles coming out of her shoulders, and shorter tentacles on the side of her head instead of ears. The tentacles flailed around as she watched Tyler with all three of her eyes.

"M'Frozza?" Tyler asked. He'd been expecting her to look like a space octopus, but she was nothing at all like he'd imagined. She was more like a space squid than a space octopus.

"Hello, Tyler Sato. We have much to discuss. What took you so long?"

LOW EARTH ORBIT:

Tyler wondered what he should say to the purple alien girl. Something cool? Something historic? What he ended up saying was, "Gee, you don't look like an octopus at all."

"Thanks," she said. "What's an octopus?"

"It's an Earth creature with eight tentacles. But you have one, two, three . . ."

"Twenty-eight." She wriggled them around like snakes. "Ten foot-tentacles, eight arm-tentacles, six face-tentacles, and four that aren't any of your business."

"Oh." Tyler tried to think of something else to say. "You've sure got a nice spaceship."

"This old thing?" She made a strange bubbling sound. "It's my father-parent's diplomatic yacht that I've borrowed. Would you like to see the rest of it?"

"Sure!"

She spun around on her foot-tentacles and slid across

the floor like a figure skater. Tyler tried to follow, but he slipped on the green slime that covered the floor. He waved his arms but couldn't keep his balance. He fell and landed on his back.

M'Frozza stood over him. "Are you unhurt, Tyler Sato?"

"Yeah, I'm fine." He tried to stand, but slipped and fell on his face.

"You're not much of an athlete, are you?"

Tyler thought about the one time he scored the winning goal in a soccer game—a winning goal for the other team, kicked into his own team's net by accident. "Not really," he told her.

"Then you will have to pretend. Everyone on my home planet believes that you are the greatest child athlete on Earth. They believe we are here because you have invited me to a challenge."

Tyler gasped. "Why would they think that?"

"Because that is what I have told them." She made that odd bubbling sound again. Tyler guessed that was the way she laughed.

Tyler managed to stand, and M'Frozza let him hold one of her arm-tentacles. It wasn't slimy like he expected. It was sticky like dried maple syrup. When M'Frozza slid across the floor, this time Tyler slid with her.

M'Frozza showed him the engine room, air pumps,

and recreation lounge. Then they visited the kitchen. An adult of M'Frozza's people was banging on one of the food machines with a metal pipe. At least Tyler assumed he was an adult, since he was a foot taller than M'Frozza and had gray spots on his tentacles.

"Tyler Sato, this is Technician N'Gatu," said M'Frozza.

"Pleased to meet you," Tyler said.

N'Gatu waved his face-tentacles. "The pleasure is mine. I'd rub tentacles with you, but I'm up to my gleezers in machine oil."

"Oh, that's all right," said Tyler. "I have to say, you speak English very well."

"English?" asked N'Gatu.

M'Frozza interposed herself between them. "Such a joke! Of course Captain Tyler knows that the ship has an automatic translation system."

"Oh, right," said Tyler. "I was joking."

"Don't be upset that I didn't laugh," said N'Gatu. "Jokes often don't translate well over this ship's outdated translation system. Or am I supposed to be pretending that you have a language implant? You would have one, if you really were a great Galaxy Games player like the captain is pretending you are."

Tyler had no idea what N'Gatu was talking about so he just nodded.

"I'm sorry," N'Gatu apologized to M'Frozza. "I'm really bad at being sneaky."

M'Frozza thought for a moment. "If anybody asks"—she looked toward another section of the ship—"we can explain that Captain Tyler has refused an implant so far because his people are shy and solitary. I've told R'Turvo that already."

"Good." N'Gatu nodded hard enough to send his face-tentacles flying in all directions. "Let me write that down."

M'Frozza took Tyler's arm with her tentacle and pulled him across the slime-slicked floor. "Take care, Technician. We will leave you to the important work of fixing the freen juicer."

"It was nice to meet you!" Tyler called out as the kitchen door irised shut behind them.

"I apologize for the awkwardness," said M'Frozza. "N'Gatu is the person I trust most with my secrets, but even for a technician he's not very bright."

"Is the secret that I'm not a Galaxy Games captain?" asked Tyler. "If it is, that's a really good secret because I don't even know what the Galaxy Games are!"

"Yes, I know! We will remedy that situation as soon as—"

A door irised open, and another adult Mrendarian skated through on wriggling foot-tentacles. He was even bigger than N'Gatu, and a darker shade of purple. "So! This is the Earth child who has challenged the honor of Mrendaria?" He snapped an arm-tentacle at Tyler, who nearly slipped and fell. "This must be a joke," the alien scoffed. "You can barely stand!"

"Pilot," said M'Frozza, "this is Tyler Sato. Tyler Sato, this is our pilot, R'Turvo."

"It's a pleasure," said Tyler.

"No," said R'Turvo. "There's no pleasure here, only outrage. Your species doesn't deserve to share a galaxy with Mrendaria. I can't imagine why M'Frozza would lower herself to even consider your challenge."

"That's for me to decide," said M'Frozza. She made a whistling sound, and steam shot out of the holes on her face where her nose should have been. "You forget your place, Pilot. You are my father-parent's servant, but you are not my father-parent."

R'Turvo lowered his head. "As you say, Captain M'Frozza."

"Come this way, Tyler Sato." M'Frozza pulled him along with her down the hallway. "You can present the terms of your challenge to me in my quarters."

"All right," said Tyler, though he still wasn't sure what challenge she meant. R'Turvo puffed steam at Tyler from his nose-holes. Tyler was glad to be away from him.

M'Frozza's quarters had stumps to sit on and a pool

of sludge that might have been her bed. Another door led to an alcove that might have been a bathroom, except that Tyler thought he heard the faint sound of music from inside. *The room was cozy,* Tyler thought, *in an alien, mustard-smelling kind of way.*

M'Frozza sucked air into her nose-holes. "Tyler Sato, I must ask a favor."

"All right." Tyler leaned forward to hear what she had to say.

"There is a disease on my home planet of Mrendaria."

Tyler leaned way back away from her. "A disease, you say?"

M'Frozza blew steam from her nose-holes. "I am not contagious, Tyler Sato. I'm not one of the sick. I was on Homabaru-Three with my father-parent when the disease struck. But the rest of my team can't leave Mrendaria until we find a cure."

"That's terrible," said Tyler.

"The disease is not so bad. Many will suffer, but we do not expect deaths. Our main problem is that the rest of my Galaxy Games team is stuck under quarantine."

"There's that phrase again," said Tyler. "What are the Galaxy Games?"

"The Galaxy Games are the universally accepted rule-set for interplanetary sports," M'Frozza explained. "All major conflicts between worlds are settled by teams of children in arenas across the Galaxy."

"Wait, hold on," said Tyler. "If the games are so important, why don't adults play them?"

"In some planetary cultures, adults don't play games—but children always do. For the Galaxy Games to be a true galactic standard, all the teams have to be in the same range of maturity. You would not take on an adult Mrendarian like R'Turvo, and I certainly would never challenge your mother-parent." She seemed to shudder at the idea.

Tyler did not like where this was going. "So your people think there's some kind of conflict between our worlds? And you and I have to battle it out until there's a winner?"

"No, not a conflict, Tyler Sato. They believe there is a challenge for our slot in the Galaxy Games Tournament."

"Wait, time out," said Tyler. "There's a tournament?"

M'Frozza nodded. "The Galaxy Games Tournament is the most important competition in the universe, but this time the Mrendarian team won't be able to even show up! If our team has to forfeit, we will be forever shamed. Other worlds will stop trading with us, and we might never be allowed to compete again. I can't let that happen, Tyler Sato. That is why you must challenge me to a game, defeat me, and take an Earth team to the Galaxy Games Tournament to represent both our worlds."

MRENDARIAN EMBASSY, PLANET HOMABARU-THREE:

"Incoming quantum," the chief bureaucrat announced.

The ambassador sank wearily into his chair and flicked a speck of slime from one of his arm-tentacles. *"Another trade mission, no doubt. Take a message, B'Groo."*

"It's from Earth, sir. From M'Frozza."

The ambassador's three eyes instantly popped open. *"Route it into my ready room."*

"Of course, sir." The chief bureaucrat tapped a sequence of buttons. By the time the ambassador could slide into his private office, the image of his daughter-child was already on the holographic display. Next to her stood a horrible-looking creature with two arms, two legs, and not a single tentacle. The creature's fleshy-lipped mouth was entirely unprotected by any sort of filter. Its twin oval-shaped eyes sat under thin brows of hair. Between the eyes and mouth, a central bulge held the creature's nose-holes—but there were only two of them, and they stubbornly refrained from flapping open and shut like proper Mrendarian nose-holes did. The ambassador had met dozens of vile-looking aliens in his line of work, but a creature this hideous was impossible to forget.

"Father-Parent," said M'Frozza, with a respectful bow.

The Earth creature gawked out from the display. *"That's your dad? Yikes! And you thought my mother was scary!"*

M'Frozza gave the Earth creature a nudge with one of

her arm-tentacles. "Father-Parent," she said again, "I'd like to introduce Captain Tyler of Earth."

The ambassador puffed steam from his nose-holes. "We've already met."

M'Frozza scrunched up her face-tentacles. "I'm sorry, Father-Parent, I must have misheard. Did you say you'd already met Captain Tyler?"

"I'd think I would have remembered that," the Earth boy added.

The ambassador forced himself to study the Earth boy's expression. He looked as honestly surprised as M'Frozza, but the ambassador wasn't fooled. "You dare to issue a challenge to my daughter-child after all the trouble you caused me back on Mrendaria?"

"Really, you have me confused with somebody else," the Earth boy insisted.

The ambassador puffed out another blast of steam. "And now you imply that I am the one who is confused? Such audacity! However, this discussion is irrelevant, as I'm sure M'Frozza has successfully defended our planet's honor with a victory in your challenge game."

"There is no dishonor in losing a well-fought battle," M'Frozza stated quietly, almost in a whisper.

The ambassador roared and flailed his tentacles. In response, the Earth creature jumped backward, slid on a patch of slime, and fell flat on his back. "Daughter-Child! Am I to understand that you lost your challenge to a creature who seems unable to remain upright on its own feet?"

M'Frozza helped the Earth boy to stand again. "Father-Parent, Tyler Sato is one of the most accomplished child-athletes I have ever met. I stood no chance against his keen strategic mind."

The Earth creature's cheeks turned red. "That's nice of you to say."

"This contest means nothing without the sanction of the Galaxy Games Commission," the ambassador snapped.

"Actually, we do have a Galaxy Games Commissioner on board," said M'Frozza.

"You do?" asked the ambassador.

"We do?" asked the Earth boy.

M'Frozza stepped back from the holo and rummaged through her effects cabinet until she found a small glass jar filled with a swirling black mist. A pair of glowing red lights appeared from the depths of the mist. M'Frozza spoke to the jar. "Honored Commissioner, I humbly present you with the official scoring sheet from my Challenge Season game against Tyler Sato, Captain of Earth."

The commissioner's red eyes flickered like fireflies inside the jar. "There was no prior sanction to this challenge," the commissioner noted. "And the game itself was not witnessed."

The ambassador watched the Earth boy's jaw fall open

when the commissioner spoke, as if the boy had never heard of a gas-based life form before.

"Challenge Season rules allow for certification after the fact if both captains attest to the conditions and results of the game," M'Frozza stated.

"This is true," said the commissioner. Its eyes flared bright for a moment before fading back into embers. "M'Frozza of Mrendaria, did you come to Earth territory of your own free will, knowing a challenge might be offered?"

"I did," said M'Frozza. "I came here freely and lost a fair contest against Captain Tyler Sato."

The mist swirled in the commissioner's jar. "Tyler Sato of Earth, your world was previously unrecognized by the commission. However, your victory over a tournament-class opponent has demonstrated great personal ability. Do you accept the rights and responsibilities accorded to Galaxy Games captains, and do you agree to bind your world to the schedules of the tournament and all stipulations in the Galaxy Games Covenant?"

"I'm talking to a jar," the Earth boy muttered. "I'm talking to a jar with laser eyes and little flashes of lightning."

"Tyler Sato!" the commissioner snapped.

"What? Oh, yes, whatever you say, Mr. Jar."

"Then I hereby accept and affirm the results of this scoring sheet. Planet Earth now occupies Galaxy Games Tournament slot Gizmo-Three, formerly held by Planet

Mrendaria, formerly held by the Ossmendian Empire, formerly held by the Commission Trust."

"Thank you," the Earth boy sputtered.

The commissioner continued, "The Ossmendian Empire will be notified that their oath of fealty has been released. As such, they are no longer bound to support Planet Mrendaria in matters of gaming, trade, or diplomacy. Ambassador, are you able to bind your world in a new oath of fealty?"

The Mrendarian ambassador let out a hiss of steam. "Tyler Sato of Earth, on behalf of the Mrendarian Ruling Council, I have no choice but to accept your team as our proxy in the upcoming tournament." The words left a bitter taste all along his oral groove. "For your sake, I hope you do not let us down."

"That makes two of us, sir." The Earth creature's face had become pale and sickly, and the ambassador disconnected the quantum link to avoid seeing Planet Mrendaria's new human champion spew fluids or lose consciousness.

"This will be a problem." The ambassador drummed his tentacles in thought. "B'Groo! Connect me with a representative from the Ossmendian Empire right away!"

LOW EARTH ORBIT:

Tyler kept staring at the holographic display after M'Frozza ended the transmission. The image of the Mrendarian ambassador blinked into a single speck that faded away like a distant star. "So . . . that's it?" he asked.

"That's it," said M'Frozza. She placed the commissioner's jar back into her closet.

Tyler gave the closet door a suspicious glare. "What was that cloudy thing in the jar?"

"That was a commissioner," M'Frozza explained. "They serve as referees and administrators for the Galaxy Games. But do not worry, the commissioner cannot hear us now." She gave her arm-tentacles a thoughtful thumping against the desk. "Tyler Sato, are you sure you have never been to Mrendaria?"

Tyler stared at this alien girl who casually zipped from world to world while Earth's most accomplished astronauts hadn't yet made it any farther than their own moon. He pretended to give the question a serious consideration. "Mrendaria . . . Mrendaria . . . no, I'm pretty sure I've never been there."

The alien girl nodded. "Then Father-Parent must have mistaken you for somebody else. I've been watching your planet's toilet-frequency video broadcasts and it's often difficult to tell you apart from each other—um, no offense."

"None taken. So what happens now? I don't know what a Gizmo-Three slot is. I don't know how to be a Galaxy Games captain. I don't even have a team!"

"There is time before the start of the tournament for you to learn and prepare, and I'm sure Father-Parent will allow me to stay long enough to help train your team. It will provide a good excuse for me to avoid returning to Mrendaria."

Tyler's head spun as he recalled everything M'Frozza had told him about her home planet, all the other civilized worlds in the Galaxy, and the sports contests that kept them from tearing each other apart. Was it really such a good idea for Tyler to bring Earth into that whole mess? "Maybe this was all a big mistake," he told the alien girl.

M'Frozza narrowed all three of her eyes. "Was it a big mistake for me to trust in you, Tyler Sato? Was it a big mistake for me to travel across the Galaxy to tell you a secret that nobody outside my home world can ever know? Was it a mistake to name you Captain of Earth and Champion of Mrendaria?"

"Yes, exactly," said Tyler, relieved that she understood what he meant. "Is it too late to go back and pretend all that never happened?"

The alien girl's face-tentacles tangled and untangled as she thought. "I am sorry, Tyler Sato. This is a situation that both our worlds must live with now."

TOKYO, JAPAN:

Three weeks after Earth's first contact with aliens—the most important event in human history—Tomoko pulled Daiki by the wrist along a crowded sidewalk. Businesses were open again, and every shop displayed signs and banners to celebrate Earth's entry into the Galaxy Games Tournament. "Where are you taking me?" Daiki asked.

"You'll see," said Tomoko. "It's a surprise!" They navigated a wide arc around a knot of people at a convenience store that was giving away Tyler Sato commemorative posters.

Daiki pulled Tomoko to a stop. "That's my cousin," he proudly announced to the crowd. A good number of them wore shirts with pictures of Tyler, M'Frozza, or the TY SATO spaceship. Daiki pointed to his own face. "Can't you see the family resemblance?"

A woman tilted her head and squinted. "I guess if you

had purple skin and a few tentacles, you probably would look a bit like M'Frozza the Mrendarian."

"No, not her! My cousin is Tyler Sato! Captain Tyler!"

Tomoko pulled him away. "We don't have time for this. Come on!"

An even larger crowd on their way to the many celebrations taking place around Tokyo jammed the entrance to the train station.

"I hear there are ice sculptures at the Meiji Shrine," Daiki told Tomoko. "Is that where you're taking me?"

"You'll see."

"It's just that my family is leaving for America next week and I want to show Cousin Tyler-kun a picture of himself made of ice."

Tomoko frowned. "I could have been made of ice."

"What?"

"I mean, how hard could it be to beat up something made entirely of slime and tentacles? I could have done it. Then they would've put me on a T-shirt, and you wouldn't be going away."

"Tyler would still be my cousin," said Daiki.

"Whatever." Tomoko pushed through the mob to create a path for Daiki and herself. "*Sumimasen, sumimasen, sumimasen.* Hey! 'Excuse me' means get out of our way, people!"

They passed the station and kept going. "So we're

not going by train," Daiki noted. "Is it a judo exhibition? Something your great-grandmother wanted you to do?"

"Something like that. It turns out Obaa-chan wanted me to have more fun, more of a life. *That's* what she meant about changing my priorities."

"She told you this?" Daiki asked.

"Yes."

"Does that mean she's feeling better?"

"Yes, yes, yes!"

Daiki thought he knew exactly where Tomoko was leading him, and he became certain when they passed the electronics store with the smashed-out window. The glass had been replaced by plywood, with a cartoon picture of a construction worker bowing apologetically. "We are sorry for the mess" read the sign. "Our shop will be cleaned up and open again as soon as possible."

Farther down the street, the neon archway of the Pack-Punch Video Arcade flashed welcomingly.

Tomoko led Daiki into the arcade, where they found a huge crowd surrounding the *Tekno-Fight Xtreme* machines. "Good," said Tomoko. "We're not too late!"

"Too late for what?" asked Daiki. They pushed their way to the front of the crowd, where Riku stood watching something in shock. "Big Brother! What are you doing here?"

Riku turned toward them. "Oh, Daiki-kun. Where else would I be? Takeda-sempai has a lot of training to catch up on now that he's been unbanished."

"Good for Takeda-sensei," said Tomoko.

Daiki blinked. "Takeda-sama's been unbanished? How did that happen?"

"Mori-sama had no choice once he heard about Takeda-sempai's heroic defense of the arcade."

The overhead speakers crackled. "I would not use the word 'heroic,' " said Mr. Mori. "However, a review of the video footage showed a loyalty that should be rewarded."

"I wish I could have been there to see the battle." Riku sighed. "Takeda-sempai says he defeated a giant and his entire gang, which is more than your judo girlfriend has ever done."

"She's not—aw, forget it." Daiki tried to get a view of the game that everyone was crowded around, but too many people blocked his way. "What's happening now?"

"It's a royal rumble," Mr. Mori's voice announced from above. "The daring defender of the Pack-Punch is taking on the ancient white-haired queen, and she's really good!"

Tomoko clasped her hands in excitement.

"Ancient white-haired queen? It couldn't be—" Daiki pushed his way to the game machine and saw Jun Takeda working his controls at a frantic speed. Next to him stood a short woman with white hair and a cane that rested against the machine as she played.

"Fight on, Obaa-chan!" Tomoko cheered.

Tomoko's great-grandmother and Jun were both playing Nekomecha, the cat robot, in an arena that looked like a traditional Japanese bathhouse. Nekomecha hated water, so the two cat robots stood at either edge of the screen and fired missiles at each other across a steaming pool. Suddenly, Tomoko's great-grandmother made her master move. Her Nekomecha kicked a bar of soap, which skipped across the pool like a skimming stone across a pond. The soap landed at the feet of Jun's Nekomecha.

"No way!" shouted Jun. He jerked the stick back and forth as his Nekomecha slipped and danced around trying to regain its footing. It landed with a splash in the middle of the pool, sending sparks from its cat-shaped metal head. The Nekomecha's life-bar went black, and its glowing red eyes faded out.

"Game over!" shouted Tomoko's great-grandmother.

"Darn!" Jun brought his foot back to kick the machine, but looked up at the ceiling and seemed to reconsider. "Best two games out of three? Nobody ever beats Jun Takeda two games out of three."

"That *was* our second game," the old woman reminded him. "Tomoko-chan!"

"I'm right here, Obaa-chan."

"Ah, so you are. This is a good game for you, Tomoko-chan. It encourages fast reflexes and strategy. You will be allowed to play it, but only after you've done your homework and judo drills."

Tomoko nodded respectfully. "Thank you, Obaa-chan."

The old woman looked around the rest of the arcade. "I don't know yet about these other games, but I will try them all. Young man!"

Daiki jumped. The old woman was pointing her cane directly at him. "Ma'am?"

"Would you care to challenge me to a session of *Time Crisis III*?"

"Maybe later," said Daiki.

"Watch this," Tomoko whispered to Daiki. She turned to her great-grandmother. "Obaa-chan? Daiki and I were going to watch a new episode of *Hunter-Elf Zeita*. Would that be all right?"

The old woman's eyes sparkled. "Is that the show about the elf who fights dragons with her magical quiver of arrows?"

"Yes," said Daiki.

The old woman grinned. "Sounds like fun. Let's go!"

MANHATTAN, NEW YORK:

Six weeks after Earth's first contact with aliens, Tyler Sato stood in front of the United Nations General Assembly.

The wooden box under his feet only just allowed him to reach the microphone and to see over the edge of the gigantic marble podium. Representatives from every nation on Earth sat in rows of curved tables, and behind them stretched a gallery and packed upper balcony of Very Important People.

All of them were staring intently back at him.

Tyler cleared his throat. A translucent screen at the edge of his podium was supposed to scroll a brilliant speech written by the president's own speechwriters. All Tyler had to do was read the words, wait for his standing ovation to end, and walk off the stage. The display had worked perfectly when Tyler had practiced over and over in the empty room a few hours before, but now the screen was blank.

Tyler cleared his throat again. "Hey! How's everyone doing today?"

Some of the representatives pressed earphones farther into their ears to hear Tyler's words translated into a dozen different languages by a team of real-time translators.

Beads of sweat formed on Tyler's forehead. Finally, thankfully, words appeared on the screen, but Tyler's relief turned to panic as he started reading. Somebody had mistakenly loaded the French version of his speech instead of the English version!

"*Mess-dames et Messy-oars* . . . um, okay. Look, you already have copies of the speech I was going to give, so let's pretend I just gave it. And let's pretend it was totally awesome."

The auditorium was quiet for a moment. Then the ambassador from India stood and began clapping. Others joined in until the walls shook from the enthusiastic applause.

The noise eventually died down, and Tyler felt like a complete fake. First he'd pretended to beat M'Frozza at a Galaxy Games challenge and now he'd just pretended to give a speech to the United Nations. He almost expected the UN guards to converge on the podium and throw him in jail for lying. "Thank you, everyone. You're all so good at playing Let's Pretend . . . or is it disrespectful for me to say that? Whatever. The resolution you're voting on today will help me fill my team roster with thirty-six kids who will represent all of Earth in the Galaxy Games Tournament. Every nation gets to nominate a few child athletes, and I'll pick the final team with help from my advisor from Planet Mrendaria." Tyler looked up at the gallery and was easily able to pick out the three Mrendarians. Standing between the pilot and technician, M'Frozza waved her tentacles at him.

Tyler tried to remember some of his speech. "You know all that stuff I was supposed to say about our Galaxy

Games team bringing the world closer together? Well, actually, I think we're already closer because of what we've been through. We survived the end of the world—or what we all thought was the end of the world—and we shared a first contact with aliens!" Tyler waited through another round of applause that was louder than ever. He felt much better about himself now, and maybe he didn't need a written speech after all. Also, he really did feel more connected with the world, which gave him an idea about what to say next.

"It's like me and my cousins from Tokyo." Tyler scanned the gallery crowd for his family, but they were harder to find than the purple aliens. "Daiki? Are you out there?"

On the right side of the gallery, a Japanese boy stood and waved his hand. "*Hai!*"

"Can you come down here?" Tyler asked.

Daiki shook his head so violently, Tyler worried it might come off.

"Please?" asked Tyler. "It feels weird being up here all by myself."

Daiki made his way from the gallery to the front of the room, escorted by UN security guards. He and Tyler were barely able to stand together on the wooden box behind the podium. "This is my cousin Daiki," said Tyler. "My cousin is from far away and we don't understand each other well yet, but I think he's really cool. His family is staying with us for the rest of the school year, and we're having a lot of fun. I'm teaching him English, and he goes to school with me. It almost makes up for not being able to play basketball in Eric Parker's driveway anymore." He pointed directly into the nearest TV camera. "That's right, Eric. I know you're at home watching this, and I don't care at all that you're not speaking to me, so there!"

When Tyler paused to catch his breath, the ambassador from Cameroon stood and applauded. Representatives from other countries joined in, possibly to be polite.

"Hooray!" Daiki joined in. Tyler wondered whether his cousin would be cheering as loudly if he understood that he'd just been compared to a driveway.

PLATTE BLUFF, NEVADA:

Nine weeks after Earth's first contact with aliens, Tyler's father and Daiki's mother shared a pot of green tea on the living room couch as they looked at old photo albums from Japan. Every minute or so, Mrs. Shindo slid her gaze to baby Sakura, who was asleep in her carrier next to the coffee table. "Everything is different for us now, but Sakura will never know a world without aliens in it. She'll grow up thinking it's completely normal for her cousin Tyler to be zipping across the galaxy with his team."

"True enough," said Dr. Sato. "Hey, remember our family ski trip to Hokkaido?"

Mrs. Shindo laughed at the page of photographs. "You had such big ears, even when you were a boy."

Dr. Sato frowned. "At least I didn't break my ankle on the bunny slope."

"The ankle got better, but your ears are as big as ever!"

They laughed and groaned through several more pages until they were interrupted by the doorbell. "Tyler, can you get that?" Dr. Sato called, loud enough for his voice to carry upstairs. "Tyler? Amanda? I know you're home!"

There was no answer but the continuing pulse of Amanda's stereo on the other side of the ceiling.

Dr. Sato got up to open the door and found a five-foot-tall purple squidlike alien standing on the front stoop. "Hello, M'Frozza," said Dr. Sato.

"Hello, Mr. Captain Tyler's Father-Parent," the Mrendarian girl burbled. "Is Captain Tyler here?"

"He's upstairs with his cousin. Go right up."

"Thank you, Mr. Captain Tyler's Father-Parent, sir."

"Can she climb stairs on those . . . feet?" Mrs. Shindo asked in Japanese.

"My foot-tentacles are quite versatile," M'Frozza replied, also in Japanese.

"Oh!" Mrs. Shindo exclaimed in surprise. "You speak my language!"

M'Frozza tapped the side of her head with one of her arm-tentacles. "I have a language implant, issued by the Galaxy Gaming Commission. Captain Tyler will get one as well, once his roster is approved."

"Then he'll be able to understand Daiki better," said Dr. Sato.

"Only if that device translates from video-game language," Mrs. Shindo joked.

"If that is a language, the implant will translate," M'Frozza promised. "I am here to assist in the roster selection process. Has Captain Tyler received his player-candidate dossiers yet?"

"Tyler did say he was expecting a delivery from the United Nations today." Dr. Sato poked his head outside and looked around for an envelope from FedEx or UPS. "I don't see anything yet but we'll keep an eye out."

"Thank you, Mr. Captain Tyler's Father-Parent. And thank you as well, Mrs. Captain Tyler's Father-Parent's Sister-Sibling." M'Frozza made a respectful bow to the adults, then climbed the stairs exactly like an ordinary human would have—if that ordinary human happened to be balancing on the back of a ten-legged slime-coated octopus.

Mrs. Shindo put a hand over her mouth. "It's too

much, *Otooto*. I'm too old to adjust to things like this!"

Dr. Sato fanned his sister's face with one of the photo albums, causing a random picture to fall out.

Mrs. Shindo looked at it and smiled. "Oh, that ugly yellow sweater! You hated that sweater so much, but every time you'd leave it somewhere on purpose, it would just get returned to our house!"

"That sweater was far too memorable," said Dr. Sato. "Once a neighbor saw me in it, they associated it with me forever."

A few photo-album pages later, the doorbell rang again. Mrs. Shindo looked up from pictures of a family visit to the giant Buddha statue in Kamakura. "Another alien?" Her whole body tensed up as if she were getting ready to jump under the table to hide.

"Not likely," Dr. Sato assured her. "That must be Tyler-kun's delivery." Dr. Sato opened the door, expecting to see a delivery person with a computerized clipboard. Instead, he found a short woman with freckled skin the color of sandpaper. Her mop of bushy brown hair looked like it had been sculpted into place by gardening tools, and reminded Dr. Sato that he needed to return his neighbor's hedge clippers. The woman's silky black suit held a plastic badge in its jacket pocket, identifying her as Section Chief Marwa Jelassi of UNOOSA, the United Nations Office for Outer Space Affairs. "Could you please direct us to Tyler Sato?" she asked.

"Us?" asked Dr. Sato.

Section Chief Jelassi gave a shrill whistle through her teeth. At the curb, four blue-helmeted United Nations soldiers emerged from a Humvee and unpacked a large wooden crate with carrying-poles slotted through iron mountings. Across the street, another personnel carrier disgorged ten United States Marines who assembled in a formation behind the first set of soldiers.

"Why does 'us' always mean 'me and my soldiers'?" Dr. Sato wondered aloud.

"This wouldn't have been my first choice either," Section Chief Jelassi admitted. "The truth is that in order to operate in most countries, international security agents need to be comfortably outnumbered by local forces. That way it doesn't look like we're trying to take over."

Dr. Sato examined the gigantic box and its well-armed escorts. "Right, then, this all looks to be in order. Tyler's room is up the stairs, second door on the right."

"Thank you." Section Chief Jelassi stepped into the foyer, but stopped when she noticed the pairs of shoes neatly laid out against the wall. "Should we remove our shoes as well?"

Dr. Sato considered this. "Normally I would say yes, but today the stairs are coated in Mrendarian tentacle slime. You may need the extra traction."

The first of the Marines stepped forward to scrape a

bit of mustardy-smelling slime with one finger. "Pattern Delta!" he shouted, and immediately, an additional pair of UN soldiers and four Marines appeared at the top of the stairs with ropes to hoist the crate up the slick steps.

Dr. Sato gawked at them. "How did they get inside my house?"

"Helicopters," said Section Chief Jelassi.

"But—"

"Helicopters to the roof," she clarified as she tossed Dr. Sato a roll of fifty-dollar bills. "This should cover the damages."

Dr. Sato shook his head and rejoined his sister on the living room couch.

"You acted like that was entirely normal," Mrs. Shindo noted.

Dr. Sato sighed. "For good or bad, this is normal for us from now on. Would you care for a fresh pot of tea, *Nee-chan*?"

"Please."

Upstairs, Amanda peeked out from her room and rolled her eyes at all the uniformed men and women in the hallway. "Hey, squirt! Tell your personal army to stop stomping around so much. I'm trying to expose Cousin Riku to some good American music in here."

"Really?" Tyler asked. "It sounded to me like you're listening to Amy Thrush."

"Ha-ha. I'll have you know that 'Tyler Sato Jacked My Ride' is her most amazing song ever. It's about how unfair life can be when a certain little runt gets whatever he wants. I can totally identify!"

Tyler grumbled under his breath while the wooden crate was delivered to his room, where it took up most of the available floor space. Section Chief Jelassi presented Tyler with a crowbar as she introduced herself. "I am Marwa Jelassi of Tunisia, chief of the new Interplanetary Games Section of UNOOSA, empowered by the nations of Earth to deliver these player-candidate dossiers for your consideration."

"Thank you, I guess." Tyler turned the crowbar over in his hands. "Chief . . . Jelassi, was it? This is my cousin Daiki, and this is M'Frozza the Mrendarian."

Daiki bowed his head and M'Frozza waved her face-tentacles.

"Lovely to meet you all," said the section chief. "Captain Tyler, from now on I will be your primary contact with the United Nations. All of your team's activities will be coordinated through my office so you can concentrate on just playing the game."

"Um, sure," Tyler told her. "So are you the one I'd complain to about the soldiers?"

Section Chief Jelassi sighed and removed another wad of bills from her pocket. "What did they break now?"

"Oh, nothing. We've just had soldiers like those up and down our street for a month now, and I was wondering, is that really necessary?"

Section Chief Jelassi's expression seemed sympathetic. Her head nodded a little bit while her hair bobbed up and down a lot. "Sorry, Tyler. You're picking a team of kids to visit other worlds, and that's important to a lot of people. Some want to stop you, and others are a little too eager to help you. If we don't keep the public away, they may try to bribe you, or threaten you, or influence you in some other way."

"Like on the *terebi*," said Daiki, demonstrating his new mastery of the English language.

Tyler rolled his eyes.

"The . . . what?" asked the section chief.

"The television," Tyler translated. "Someone found out which shows I like. Now half the commercials are from parents who want me to pick their kids for the Galaxy Games team."

"Brad can run! Brad can jump! Brad can skate!" Daiki hopped onto the bed and jumped up and down, mimicking one of the commercials. He added a comment in Japanese that had M'Frozza convulsing in her odd burbling laughter.

"Good one!" the Mrendarian girl exclaimed.

Tyler frowned. He could hardly wait for the language

implant that would finally let him understand all the clever things his cousin couldn't say in English.

Section Chief Jelassi opened the door to the hallway. "I will remain outside this room until you have finalized your roster selections. Then I will take care of informing the appropriate parties. Each government will be responsible for making a public announcement or keeping the information private, as they prefer."

"Thanks," said Tyler, glad that someone else would have to tell thirty-six kids they were on the team, and hundreds of others that they were not.

Once the section chief had gone out into the hall, Tyler stuck the crowbar into the side of the crate. It took all of his strength, plus Daiki's and M'Frozza's, to pry open the box. A flood of Styrofoam peanuts gushed out, along with dozens of canvas bags with national flags sewn onto them.

Tyler opened one of the bags and pulled out a stack of folders, each with the name of an athlete printed on the front. "This batch is from the Republic of Moldova. I don't even know where that is!"

"In Eastern Europe between Romania and Ukraine," said M'Frozza.

Tyler blinked at her.

"I have been studying your planet's governments," the Mrendarian girl explained. "It did not take long. There are fewer than two hundred of them, after all."

Tyler sat at his desk and started reading. Each folder contained pictures, statistics, personal histories, and an essay on why each player-candidate wanted to be on the team. "These kids are amazing. All of them! They're better than me at everything. Why would they ever accept me as their captain?"

"Because you defeated me," said M'Frozza.

Tyler frowned. "Well, not really." He got up and grabbed another stack of folders. "The Kingdom of Swaziland? That place can't be real. It sounds like some kind of fairytale kingdom."

"It's between South Africa and Mozambique," said M'Frozza.

Tyler sighed. "I should have paid more attention during our world geography unit."

While Tyler and M'Frozza discussed the player-candidates from Swaziland, Daiki shuffled through the dossiers from Japan. He wasn't surprised to find one for Tomoko Tomizawa—she was one of the nation's top young judo stars, after all. Tomoko's face looked confident and happy in her picture, and not angry or upset like she'd been at the airport. "Obaa-chan wants me to have more fun," she'd told him. "How am I supposed to have fun all by myself?"

"You'll figure it out," Daiki had said. "This trip is important to my family, Tomoko-chan. Mother has seen my uncle only a couple times since he went away for college in America."

Tomoko narrowed her eyes to an intense glare. "So you're saying people in your family who go to America tend to never come back? Thanks, that makes me feel so much better. When you see Tyler Sato, tell him that I'll never forgive him for taking my best friend away from me." She'd turned her back and that was the last he'd heard from her.

When he was sure Tyler and M'Frozza weren't looking, Daiki moved Tomoko's dossier to the top of the stack and drew a big star next to her name. If he could get her onto the team, maybe that would make her happy again.

LOS ANGELES, CALIFORNIA:

Twelve weeks after Earth's first contact with aliens, the *Yolanda Speaks Out* studio buzzed with excitement as the show returned from a commercial break. Yolanda Jones danced in her chair until her show's catchy theme song died down. "All right, get pumped! This week Yolanda is speaking out about all the reasons why the Galaxy Games Tournament might be the *worst* thing to ever happen to our planet. We started on Monday with a whole show about the horrible parenting skills of Tyler Sato's mother, Naomi."

Behind Yolanda, a gigantic video screen displayed the

now-famous clip of Mrs. Sato, dressed in a pink flowered bathrobe, with wild hair and an angry snarl. Mrs. Sato pumped her fist and shouted, "If you don't get those microphones away from me, this will be *your* last day on Earth!"

Yolanda's audience hooted and shook their fists in outrage and disapproval.

Yolanda shook her head sadly. "So much anger. So much rage. You just know that'll make Tyler Sato freeze up under the pressure of a big game. And won't we all be embarrassed when that happens? On Tuesday we revealed that many of the choices on the Earth team's roster were actually dictated by alien influences."

A recording of M'Frozza the Mrendarian appeared on the giant screen behind the talk-show host. M'Frozza's nose-holes popped and whistled in outrage as Yolanda's offscreen voice accused her of having too much power over Tyler Sato. "No, Yolanda Jones, I don't see it that way at all," M'Frozza replied. "It was entirely proper for me to be present when Captain Tyler made his roster selections. As the Earth team's strategic advisor, I am required—"

"But what about the fact that all thirty-six kids chosen were from outside the United States? Was that Tyler's choice or yours? Miss M'Frozza, what exactly does your species have against the United States of America?"

"This interview is over!" M'Frozza shouted.

Yolanda's live audience booed and hissed. Someone

started a chant of "Aliens go home! Aliens go home! Aliens go home!"

Yolanda waved her arms to quiet her audience, but her face held a wide grin. "It sounds like a lot of you are upset about aliens on Earth, and so is our next guest. He is a five-term US senator who recently introduced a bill to have the solar system declared an alien-free zone. In the past few months, he has become a prominent leader in a global Seclusionist movement. Ladies and gentlemen, please welcome Senator Thomas Archer!"

The white-haired senator stepped onto the stage, accompanied by patriotic music. He took a seat next to Yolanda's desk. "Thank you, Miss Jones, but I'd like to correct you on one point: I don't consider myself a leader in the Seclusionist movement. The movement is led by ordinary citizens—factory workers, farmers, doctors, teachers, plumbers, mothers, and fathers—who all believe that our children deserve to live in a world free from alien influences. They are my leaders, and I am their humble follower."

"Of course, Senator," said Yolanda. "Now as we all know, Earth's participation in the Galaxy Games is being organized through the United Nations. Why does this disturb your fellow Seclusionists so much?"

"We see it as part of a disturbing trend, Miss Jones. Our president foolishly gave too many of our country's rights to the United Nations. The United Nations then gave up those rights to alien life forms. Just this week a trade delegation of ice slugs took up residence in the asteroid belt, and a group of living rocks set up a trade mission on the moon. Think of it—our own personal moon, which had proudly flown the American flag exclusively for more than forty years, now hosts some weird alien flag from some weird alien planet filled with weird aliens." Senator Archer pounded the interview desk and waited through a wave of boos from the live audience. "My friends, I share your disgust. If things continue this way, aliens will soon control and dominate our world without any of us firing a single shot in self-defense."

Another chant of "Aliens go home!" rippled through the audience.

"But can't we all just be friends?" asked Yolanda. "Tyler Sato and M'Frozza seem to get along pretty well, don't they?"

"That's a big lie told by the pro-alien lobby," said Senator Archer. "These folks think we can all be friends after Tyler Sato proved that humans are physically and tactically superior to Mrendarians? Mark my words: It's only a matter of time before Tyler and M'Frozza are at each other's throats like the natural enemies they are."

"Natural enemies?" Yolanda raised her left eyebrow. "I'm not sure I follow you, Senator."

"Well, obviously they were never meant to be friends. He's *Japanese* and she's *sushi*!"

Back in Platte Bluff, Dr. Sato turned off the show in disgust. "Ugh! What an ignorant buffoon."

"But what if he's right?" asked Mrs. Sato. "Not about M'Frozza," she said quickly upon seeing her husband's shocked expression. "She seems nice enough, but there's a whole galaxy of other aliens we know nothing about. Some of them might be nasty Earth-conquering monsters, and we're inviting them over for a playdate with our only son!"

"We can't back out now," Dr. Sato stated. "The entire world is counting on Tyler to lead our team. Besides, it's a sports tournament, not a war zone."

"I've been to college football games," Mrs. Sato reminded him. "That's closer to war than I ever want to be again."

GUANGZHOU, CHINA:

Three months after Earth's first contact with aliens, Ling-Wa Bei slung a heavy black bag across her shoulder. She snuck through the busy gym as quickly as she could, past girls practicing floor routines, vaulting, and the balance beam. Ling wished she could chalk her hands for one last spin around the uneven bars, but there wasn't time. Her bus would arrive in just a few minutes.

Ling's red leather boots squeaked with every step. Her best friend's parents had sent them, along with a note that read, "Happy twelfth birthday." Ling had only just turned eleven, and she needed two extra pairs of socks to make the boots fit, but it was the thought that mattered. Her own parents had certainly never sent her any birthday presents.

The other girls spotted Ling and gathered around.

"What's the big secret, Ling? Where are you going?"

"Away. For a while. But I'll be back," Ling promised.

"It's the Galaxy Games, right?" asked Hu. "I knew they would choose you. And now you're off to space with Tyler Sato!"

"Ooooooooh!" the other girls chorused.

"Quiet, please." Ling looked around anxiously. "Master Wan will hear you."

"He doesn't know?"

Ling shook her head.

"Then hurry," urged Hu. "Master Wan will be back at any moment."

Ling nodded and ran to the south exit. The other girls cheered as she charged through the door. Their smiles faded when they all saw Master Wan standing outside. He held his arms crossed, and his breath formed a mist around his angry face in the pre-dawn chill.

The other girls scattered back to their practice stations. The door closed, and Ling could not see them anymore. Master Wan loomed over her. "Where are you going with that bag, Miss Bei?"

Ling swallowed a lump in her throat. "M-m-master Wan, I've been ch-chosen for the Galaxy Games."

"Well, they can't have you!" Master Wan punched the metal door. "I was the first to see your potential.

I molded you into the gymnast you are today. You are mine!"

Ling shook her head. "I am sorry, Master Wan. You have been kind to me, but I have to see the world. I have to see the universe!"

"A girl who quits this program can never return. Think about that, Miss Bei. If you leave now, you will lose your shot at the Olympics. Is that what you want?" Master Wan put an arm around her shoulders. "Come inside, Miss Bei. Your place is here."

Ling almost went with him, but just then, a warm wind blasted out of the twilight. She and Master Wan looked up to see a flying orange shark swoop over the rooftops of Guangzhou.

"That must be my bus." Ling pushed away from her coach. "So long, Master Wan."

SÃO PAULO, BRAZIL:

The Brazilian Youth Team trailed by one goal going into the final minute of the game. The goalie for the visiting German team punted the soccer ball toward midfield. Luiz Rafael Vila Lobos took it on the head. The ball landed at the feet of his teammate Matheus.

Matheus passed the ball back. "Take it, Weez. Show them why you're going to the Galaxy Games."

Weez grunted in agreement and kicked the ball from

foot to foot. At the corners of his vision he saw two German kids race at him. At the last possible moment, Weez pushed forward. The two middle fielders collided in a tangle of arms and legs.

The stadium crowd rose to their feet as Weez wove a zigzag path to the goal. Nobody on the German team could touch him. They tried to channel him toward the sideline, but Weez broke into the open field.

"Ten seconds left!" called the center referee.

Weez dodged the last German defender and faced a goal guarded by Felix Hoffmann, possibly the best young goalie in all of Europe. *And no wonder,* thought Weez. Felix was big. Not just big for his age, but just plain big. Not just tall, but wide. Felix was not just a goalie, but also an unmovable force of nature.

Weez's eyes locked with Felix's from fifteen feet away. Time seemed to stop for a moment. Then Weez saw Felix smile.

I'll wipe that grin off your face, Weez thought. He lined up his shot and traced the path of the ball in his mind: from his foot to the lower left corner of the goal. He gave the ball his hardest kick ever.

Felix shifted, dived, and caught the ball at the line. He was not just big, but also fast!

The referee blew his whistle three times to signal the end of the second half. "Game over! Germany wins!"

The stadium erupted in disappointed groans as Weez stood dumbfounded.

Felix ran over to him with the ball under his arm. "Good shot," he said in German. Weez's language implant fed a Portuguese translation directly into his brain. Weez winced and remembered how the alien doctor had said the implant would hurt when he used it, at least until his brain got used to it.

"Good block," said Weez in Portuguese.

Felix grinned. "You got two other shots past me. You should be happy."

"I can't be happy right now, not when I just lost the game."

The other boy laughed. "Relax, Luiz. This game means nothing. The real game starts when that bus whisks us off to the Galaxy Games. Then we'll be on the same team. You, me, and the amazing Tyler Sato!"

Weez frowned. Sure, he'd made the Earth team roster, but there was no guarantee he'd be chosen to go into space. Not unless he could beat out other players like Felix Hoffmann.

TOKYO, JAPAN:

From the outdoor stage, Tomoko Tomizawa watched her own face on the big screens above Shibuya Square.

Thousands of people had packed into the streets to see her off, as if she were a movie star or pop-music idol. With all those people watching, Tomoko felt super-embarrassed by the vibrant purple hair dye her great-grandmother had talked her into.

The man with the microphone waited for an answer.

"I'm sorry. What was the question?" Tomoko asked.

"What do you say to Seclusionists who want to keep Earth free from alien influences?"

"Oh." Tomoko frowned. "That's politics, isn't it?"

People in the crowd laughed. They thought Tomoko had made a joke, she realized. Really, she just wasn't used to anyone asking her such important questions. Until being picked for the Galaxy Games, she'd been just an ordinary girl who loved shopping, singing along with the radio, watching *Hunter-Elf Zeita* episodes, and winning national judo tournaments. Her biggest problem was that Daiki, her best and only friend, had gone off to America for the rest of the school year to visit his suddenly famous cousin.

For months she had hated Tyler Sato for taking Daiki away, and in less than an hour she would be face-to-face with him. Tyler Sato. *The* Tyler Sato. The Japanese American boy who defeated a Mrendarian warrior with his bare hands. Okay, sure, his victory had earned Earth a spot in the Galaxy Games Tournament. And yes, he was giving Tomoko and other kids a chance to tour the universe. But other than that, Tomoko found it hard to see what was so great about him. She could have done the same thing, and probably even better.

"Earth to Tomoko-chan," said the man with the microphone.

"Um . . . sorry. The question again?" asked Tomoko.

"Seclusionists," said the man. "What do you think of them?"

"Oh, right." Tomoko thought for a moment. "The Seclusionists don't want anyone to leave Earth. So, that's fine, I guess. They don't have to go. But they shouldn't try to stop kids like me from playing against other kids on another world. It's a free galaxy, you know."

The crowd cheered her answer, except the group on her left side. They booed and held up signs in Japanese and English. Tomoko could hear their hateful chants over the rest of the crowd: "Earth is for humans, space is for freaks! Earth is for humans, space is for freaks! Earth is for—"

"Tomizawa Tomoko!" The microphone man shouted her name loud enough to drown out the Seclusionists. "Before your bus arrives, will you demonstrate your judo skills for us?"

"What? Now? Here? But I'm not—"

"Ready?" The man raised a red and white fan over his head. "Ninja battle, go!"

As the fan fell, three men in black ninja costumes slid down cables onto the platform. Tomoko dropped into a crouch. She hadn't expected this. Otherwise she might have worn her judo uniform instead of sweats and a pink *Hunter-Elf Zeita* T-shirt.

The first ninja ran at her. Tomoko planted her feet and leaned her right shoulder forward. The man's own weight and speed pushed him over her body and into the air. He landed on his back with his arms out, slapping the platform.

So he knows how to land safely, Tomoko thought with relief. *At least I don't have to worry about hurting anyone.*

"That's one down!" shouted the man with the microphone.

The second ninja ran at her. This time Tomoko fell backward as he approached and kicked upward. Her foot caught his stomach and sent him flying. He went easily, and Tomoko realized that he wasn't trying to defeat her—he was trying his best to make her look good for the cameras.

"That's two down!" shouted the man with the microphone.

Tomoko hopped back onto her feet. The last ninja approached slowly with his arms out. He tried to grapple her. Tomoko swept her leg under his feet and pushed him over onto his back.

"And that's three down! Tomoko-chan is the winner!"

The three ninjas bowed to her and the crowd cheered—even the Seclusionists.

This must be how Tyler Sato felt, Tomoko thought, except that he'd *earned* his victory against the Mrendarian Galaxy Games captain, while these ninjas had given her an easy win.

MEXICO CITY, MEXICO:

There were too many people and not enough privacy. That's what El Gatito decided as he searched the outdoor market for a place to put on his mask.

"A *luchador* is more than just a masked wrestler. A *luchador's* mask is his soul and personality. That's why a *luchador* is never seen without his mask." El Jaguar had said that, and El Jaguar should know. El Jaguar was the greatest *luchador* of all.

Correction, the boy thought. *El Jaguar was the greatest luchador on Earth, but El Gatito would be the greatest luchador in space!*

"Get your *luchador* dolls!" called one of the merchants. "Your favorite masked wrestlers are here: El Jaguar, El

219

Hijo del Dragón, Diablo Rojo, and any others you could name!"

The boy stopped. "Do you have a doll of El Gatito Grande?"

"Who?" asked the merchant.

"El Gatito, the most legendary kid *luchador* of the twenty-first century!"

"Oh, right, the boy who made the Galaxy Games team." He dug through his boxes and pulled out a doll with a blue cat-eared mask. "Here is a doll of El Gatito."

The boy stared at the doll. "That is not El Gatito. El Gatito would be insulted by this doll. El Gatito has big muscles like these!" The boy flexed his skinny arms.

"You look familiar," said the merchant. "Have I seen you before?"

The boy put his arms across his face so the man wouldn't figure out who he was. "You must be mistaken. But . . . could you point out a place where I might quickly change into a mask?"

The merchant pointed to a nearby alley.

"Gracias, Señor! If you see a bus from outer space, tell them El Gatito—who is someone other than myself—will be ready as quickly as he can."

"I'll tell them," said the merchant.

In the alley, the boy took a blue leather mask from his

bag and slipped it over his head. It wrapped all the way around and laced up in the back. Two points stuck up on top like cat ears. He then changed into a skin-tight white costume, added a thick brown belt, and finished his costume with a bright red cape.

"Now El Gatito Grande is ready to fight!" He tackled a trash barrel as if it were another masked wrestler and threw it down the alley. "Look out, aliens! Here comes El Gatito!"

He reached down to grab his bag and noticed his reflection in a puddle. El Gatito froze. "Oh, no! Is that a smudge on El Gatito's mask? El Gatito can't wear a dirty mask to meet the great Tyler Sato!" He splashed puddle water onto his head and rubbed it as hard as he could.

Ten minutes later, El Gatito charged out of the alley. His mask was dripping wet but much cleaner. "Now El Gatito Grande is ready to— Hey. Why is everybody staring into the sky?"

"A shark," said the merchant, still looking up. "An orange shark with black fins. Made of metal. Flying through the air."

"Where?"

"It's gone now. Back into the sky."

"*Dios mío!*" El Gatito kicked at the ground. "You were supposed to tell them to wait!"

20

Tyler Sato couldn't concentrate on his school work. As Mrs. Hogan droned on about math, all he could think about was the space-bus that would be coming for him directly after class. The bus would whisk Tyler away to Earth's high-tech Galaxy Games Complex, under construction at a former Olympics venue in Greece. There he would meet his team in person for the first time—and probably for the last time as well. As much as Tyler wanted to visit other worlds, the team would do better with someone more athletic as their captain. With someone more honest as their captain. With *someone other than Tyler Sato* as their captain. Quitting the team was the mature, eleven-year-old thing to do.

"Tyler Sato! Are you paying attention?" asked Mrs. Hogan.

"Yes," said Tyler, but of course that was a lie. It didn't help that Tyler's cousin Daiki, who had learned a decent amount of English in the past two months, suddenly insisted on speaking to him only in Japanese. Tyler's new language implant still needed some adjustment, so each translation twanged his neurons like a harp player with thorn-covered fingers.

"Tell the teacher I need to use the bathroom," Daiki whispered in Japanese, and a fresh spike of pain bounced around the inside of Tyler's skull.

"Tell her yourself," Tyler shot back. "You know how to say that in English. That was the first thing you learned!"

"There are subtle shades of meaning that only a native speaker can convey," Daiki explained.

"What subtle shades?" asked Tyler. "You need to use the bathroom. On a scale of one to ten, how badly do you need to go?"

"About a three."

"So, all right. You don't need a Japanese-to-English translator to tell her that."

"Tyler? Daiki?" Mrs. Hogan shot the two boys a stern glance from the front of the room. "Do you have something to share with the class?"

Daiki stood and cleared his throat. "Mrs. Hogan-sensei, I need the bathroom pass, please. I have to do a number three."

While the class laughed, Tyler dropped his face into his hands. "Okay, maybe you *do* need a translator."

At lunch, it seemed like the entire school filed past Tyler's table to wish him luck. "It's just orientation and training," Tyler repeated over and over, like a robot version of himself. *And I'll be home way before the end of it,* he added silently. Tyler couldn't stand to look any other kid or teacher directly in the eye, and he figured that would be the way things had to be from now on. Once he quit the team, he'd be too ashamed to look anyone in the eye for the rest of his life.

"Dude, you totally don't look as happy as you probably have to feel," said Brayden in typical Brayden style.

"Yeah, what's up?" asked Lucas. "There's nothing dull about orientation and training when it's orientation and training to play against kids *from the other side of the galaxy*! With your own team of international all-stars!"

"Yeah, I guess." Tyler shuffled his feet and avoided his friends' eyes even more than anyone else's.

"Go kick some alien butts for us, okay?" asked Lucas.

"If they have butts, I'll kick them," Tyler promised.

"Even if they don't have butts, find something on them that *looks* like a butt," said Brayden. "Use your imagination and squint if you have to."

"Okay."

Brayden squinted and unsquinted his eyes to demonstrate. "Now my elbow looks like an elbow—and now my elbow looks like a butt! Sort of. But don't kick it for reals 'cuz I was only showing you an example."

Daiki tapped Tyler on the shoulder and made a painful Japanese exclamation. "Look! Even Eric Parker is coming over to wish you good luck!"

Tyler forced his head to turn toward Eric's usual table. His former best friend, who hadn't said a single word to him in months, really was shuffling over to Tyler's lunch table. Could Eric have finally given up on his pizza party grudge?

Eric kept walking until he stood directly in front of Tyler.

"Hi, Eric," said Tyler.

"Hi, Tyler," said Eric. "I saw on the news that you have a translator thing in your head now."

Tyler put a finger to the side of his head and felt the inch-long incision line. "The language implant that lets me speak and understand other languages? What about it?"

"I thought it was interesting, that's all." Eric rocked back and forth on the heels of his sneakers. "When I found out about it, I went on the Internet and learned how to say that you're a jerk in five languages. *Tyler Sato is a jerk, Tyler Sato is a jerk, Tyler Sato is a jerk,*

Tyler Sato is a delicious meat-filled pastry, Tyler Sato is a jerk!"

Tyler winced through the five-way translation. "Thanks a lot. You know, that fourth one doesn't mean what you think it does."

"Oh, so now you think you know more than the Internet?" Eric demanded. "That makes you a mega-super-ultra jerk!" He turned and stomped back to his table.

"Why are you smiling, Tyler-kun?" Daiki asked.

"Because Eric's talking to me again instead of ignoring me. That's real progress. Maybe we'll be playing hoops in his driveway again someday, just like old times."

"Forget him, Tyler," said Lucas between bites of potato puff. "The entire galaxy is your driveway now."

Tyler's grin disappeared. "I can't swish a thirty-footer from an *X* of chalk anywhere else. I'm pretty sure of it." If only the Galaxy Games Tournament could all take place in Eric Parker's driveway, Tyler wouldn't have to quit the team.

Twenty minutes before the school day officially ended, Principal Johansson made an announcement over the PA system. "Tyler Sato, report to the parking lot. Your buslike thing has arrived."

"We'll see you next month, Tyler," said Mrs. Hogan. "And don't think that being an interstellar sports star will get you out of your homework obligations."

"Of course not, Mrs. Hogan." Tyler got up and swept his books into his NFL backpack.

Daiki stood as well.

"Do you have to go 'number three' again, Daiki?" Mrs. Hogan asked with a slight smirk.

Daiki spoke in Japanese. "I have something important to tell my cousin before he leaves. I think I've done something really bad and he needs to know."

The language implant buzzed inside Tyler's skull. *That translation couldn't be right*, he thought. Tyler was the one who had lied to the entire world about being such a great athlete. Daiki couldn't have done anything as bad as that. He tried to look at his cousin for a clue, but Daiki was unreadable.

"What did he say?" asked Mrs. Hogan.

Tyler gave her a fake smile. "He wants to be my honor guard, to escort me to the bus. Please, Mrs. Hogan? It would mean a lot to him."

Mrs. Hogan waved her hand. "Fine, fine, but come right back, okay?"

"Okay, Mrs. Hogan-sensei," said Daiki.

Daiki bit his lip and clenched his hands as they walked together through the empty school hallway. Tyler held his forehead, ready for a new wave of pain. From Daiki's expression, Tyler imagined his cousin was about to say something that could hurt, whether in

English or Japanese. "Spill it, Daiki-kun."

Daiki took a long breath in and out. "Cousin Tyler-kun, do you remember choosing a girl from Japan to be on your Galaxy Games team?"

"The judo champion?" asked Tyler. "Tomoko something?"

"Tomoko Tomizawa," said Daiki.

"Yeah, I remember. The Japanese nominating committee put her on top of the pile with a star by her name. Somebody must have really been impressed by her."

"No, I was the one who put her on the top of the pile," Daiki confessed. "And I made the star."

"You?" Tyler thought back to the afternoon when he'd made his picks. "You did say you'd seen her a couple times, and she was really good," he said.

"I have seen her more than a couple times. Tomoko-chan was my friend back in Tokyo."

Tyler stopped short in surprise. "Oh." He started walking again, taking extra-long steps to catch up to his cousin. "Why didn't you ever tell me you had a girlfriend back in Japan?"

"She's not my girlfriend," said Daiki. "But she *was* a very good friend. Then I left to visit America and Tomoko got really mad about it. I haven't really spoken to her since then. She's sort of like my very own Eric Parker."

Tyler thought about that for a few moments. "Okay, so she's mad at you."

"Worse than that," said Daiki. "She's mad at *you* for taking me away from her. I am sorry, Cousin Tyler-kun. It will not be easy for you to be on a team with her."

"All the people who are mad at me should form a club," Tyler grumbled. "They could call themselves the Tyler Haters International Association. Eric, Tomoko, Senator Archer, the Seclusionists—even John Moon hasn't forgiven me for going through the United Nations to put my team together. As if it's my fault the Western Shoshone Nation doesn't have a seat on the General Assembly!"

Tyler pushed open the door to the parking lot and found a zoo of reporters, camera operators, and at least three helicopters. In other words, the usual after-school crowd.

A reporter lunged forward and stuck a microphone in Daiki's face. "Tyler Sato! How does it feel to finally have your team in training?"

"I'm Tyler." Tyler waved his hand. "Over here."

The reporter turned her head and blinked. "Really? I thought for sure you'd be taller."

Tyler gave his cousin a sideways glance. Daiki had gotten a haircut recently and maybe he did look a bit more like Tyler than he had before, but he couldn't possibly look more like Tyler than Tyler himself.

A group of police officers formed into a line and pushed the reporters back with plastic riot shields. "Clear the path! This boy has places to go and aliens to meet!" A red-faced police captain put a hand on Daiki's shoulder. "It's okay, son. These jackals won't bother you while my troop is on duty."

Tyler shouted, "Hey! Excuse me! I'm Tyler Sato, not him."

"Oh, sorry about that." The police captain's face got three shades redder than it had been before. "I just figured you'd be taller."

"Taller than what?" Tyler demanded. "Taller than Daiki?"

"That must be your bus." Daiki pointed through the gap in the reporters to an orange metal shark with black fins.

Tyler grinned at the sight of the interstellar space bus, part of the fleet that Earth's leaders had leased from the Ossmendian Empire and fitted with human-style seats. The bus looked dangerous and cool, but as Tyler viewed the strange symbols printed on the side of the bus, his language implant created English words that seemed to float in the air like subtitles in a foreign movie: "Property of Horizon Nursery School #4749, New Ossmendia III." It would probably be best if he didn't tell anyone about that part.

"I sure wouldn't be able to ride on an alien bus like that," said Daiki. "I had a panic attack on just a regular plane from Japan."

"It has gravity systems," said Tyler. "M'Frozza says that if you close your eyes, it doesn't feel like you're moving at all."

Daiki shook his head. "I would still know. Have a safe trip, Cousin Tyler-kun."

"I will," said Tyler. "And I'll say hi to your girlfriend for you."

"She's not my girlfriend!" Daiki shouted.

Tyler stomped through the crowd of microphone-waving reporters until he reached an even larger crowd of well-wishers and fans. He could tell they were fans from their homemade signs:

GOOD LUCK, TYLER!
WE LOVE YOU, TYLER!
EARTH KIDS RULE!

Everyone wanted to shake Tyler's hand or slap him on the back and tell him how great he was. It made Tyler feel worse than before. He wondered if they'd still be cheering if they knew he wasn't actually the greatest sports hero of all time. If they knew M'Frozza had been trying to pass her planet's tournament slot to any other world she could find, like it was a bad case of cooties on the playground.

The bus driver honked the horn to hurry Tyler along—or at least Tyler thought it was the horn. It sounded more like somebody strangling a goat. *MEEEEH-EEEEH! MEEEEH-EEEEH-EEEEEH-EEEEEH!*

Tyler scanned the crowd for his parents and sister but they were probably still at home, packing, so they could join him at the training complex while he settled in. A door hissed open in the side of the shark and Tyler scrambled inside. "Um, hello. I'm Tyler Sato," he told the six-armed yellow puff-ball at the wheel.

"*Squeeje duka mekh farrah!*" the puff-ball shouted through a mouth shaped like a megaphone. A spike of pain stabbed the left side of Tyler's head as his language implant pushed an English translation into his brain: "Move to the back of the bus!"

"Yes . . . sir? Ma'am? Um . . . thing?"

"*Hoot squeeje!*" the puff-ball replied. "Just move!"

Other kids were already on the bus, staring at him with awe. "*Nosso capitão!*" shouted a boy with dark copper skin and a bright green Brazilian soccer shirt. Tyler remembered him from his dossier picture. He had a long name that Tyler couldn't quite remember, but the boy

232

went by the nickname of Weez. "Our captain!" buzzed the language implant.

"Tyler Sato," whispered a Chinese girl, who then blushed and looked away. Tyler tried to remember whether her name was Ming or Ping. No, it was *Ling*, short for Ling-Wa Bei. Ling was a gymnast, and certainly had the build of a gymnast—small and thin, like a much younger child. Tyler knew Ling had to be stronger than she looked, but her image wasn't helped by the pastel barrettes pinning back her hair or her gigantic red leather boots that didn't quite reach the floor of the bus.

"In Wirklichkeit ist er viel kleiner als im Fernsehen!" said a boy with ruddy cheeks, wild blond hair, and friendly eyes. Tyler thought his words sounded like German, which would make him Felix Hoffmann, a soccer goalie who played against some much older boys. "He looks so much shorter than on TV!" came the translation.

The kids shouted in several languages at once. Then, along with Tyler, they all grabbed their heads in pain. "Synchronized headaches," groaned Tyler. "We really are a team!"

"I'm glad you survived that scary crowd," said Ling.

"Those people aren't scary," Tyler told her. "Those are our fans."

"Not them. Over there." Ling pointed to the other side of the bus at a larger, angrier group of people. They were

shaking their fists and making ugly faces. Some also held
handmade signs.

ALIENS GO HOME!
EARTH IS FOR HUMANS!
CAPTAIN TY IS A TRAITOR!

"Seclusionists?" asked Tyler.

One woman threw a rock. It shattered like a snowball
against the bus window. Others started throwing rocks as
well. They pushed forward, and there were so many of
them that the police couldn't stop them.

A girl with purple hair spoke quickly in Japanese.
She had to be Daiki's friend, Tomoko Tomizawa, the judo
champion. Tyler's language implant buzzed with a translation that included Tomoko's snarky tone: "They're trying to block the bus. What are you going to do about it,
great and powerful Tyler Sato?"

The puff-ball driver opened the door to let a soldier
push somebody else aboard. It was a boy who fell awkwardly to the floor of the bus. When he stood up, Tyler
realized it was his cousin Daiki. "Don't worry, Tyler, you're
safe now," the soldier told Daiki as the door closed again.

"But I'm not Tyler!" Daiki shouted. He pounded his

fists on the door. "Let me out! Somebody let me out! I'm not supposed to be here!"

"*Squeeje duka mekh farrah!*" the puff-ball shouted.

Daiki didn't need a language implant to know that the alien wanted him to move away from the door. He jumped back and fell into the seat next to a shocked Tomoko Tomizawa. "Er, hi, Tomoko-chan," he said to her. "I like what you've done with your hair."

The crowds and landscape fell away as the space-bus rose into the clouds.

21

MEXICO CITY, MEXICO:

The Galaxy Games bus backtracked to pick up a player who had been missed before, a boy who called himself El Gatito Grande. Tyler figured the name had to mean something more in Spanish than just "The Great Kitten," because that would be an extremely silly thing for a person to be called.

El Gatito wore a crazy costume that included a red cape and a blue cat-eared mask that covered his entire head, just like in his dossier pictures. Instead of a real name and real biography, the dossier had explained that masked Mexican wrestlers were mysterious and secretive about their true identities. When Tyler had reviewed the file back in his bedroom, El Gatito had been an obvious pick for the team. Only superheroes wore masks and hid their true names, and who wouldn't want to play on a sports team with a superhero? But in person, El Gatito seemed more like a superhero's scrawny underage sidekick who needed to be rescued at least three times in every episode.

The puff-ball swiveled its head around at the new kid and made clucking noises, which the language implant turned into a complaint about being behind schedule.

"It was not El Gatito's fault that you could not wait for him," said the masked boy defiantly. He took the seat directly in front of Tomoko.

The bus took off into the sky, weaving around a church spire on its way out of Mexico City. El Gatito bounced up and down in his seat. Tomoko resumed her angry glare at Tyler. Tyler resumed his worried watch over Daiki. Daiki resumed closing his eyes, pressing his knees into his chest, and praying for his safety.

El Gatito leaned over to Felix Hoffmann. "El Gatito detects an awkward silence," he whispered. "Is there an awkward silence on this bus?"

"Ja." Felix nodded.

"I knew it! El Gatito is never wrong about these things." He made a self-satisfied smile and leaned back in his seat.

Tomoko very slowly turned her attention from Tyler to the back of El Gatito's mask. Her fingers twitched as if she were losing a battle against some primal Japanese-girl instinct. Somewhere over the Atlantic Ocean, she gave in. "Aww . . . *Neko-kun ga kawaii, ne,*" Tomoko exclaimed as she scratched the top of El Gatito's mask. "Kitty-cats are so cute!"

"El Gatito is not cute," the masked boy corrected her. "El Gatito is fierce!" He held up his hands as if they had claws and made a hissing sound.

Tomoko giggled.

Tyler let out a relieved breath. El Gatito still hadn't proven to be a superhero and Tomoko still hated Tyler's guts, but at least the two of them were canceling each other out for a while. If Tyler could send Daiki home with the bus after they arrived in Greece, and if he could work up enough nerve to quit the team, the day could still work out like he'd planned.

Weez moved over to the seat next to Tyler's. "Hello, Captain Sir," he said in Portuguese. "It's such an honor that you chose me for your team!"

"Thanks, Weez." Tyler tried to remember a few details from the Brazilian boy's dossier. "You said in your essay that you'd lost your little brother a couple years ago. I felt bad about that. Picking you for the team was the least I could do for you."

"Actually," Weez lowered his voice to a whisper, " 'lost' is only the official word."

Tyler squirmed in his seat. The Brazilian boy's wide-open eyes were making him very uncomfortable. "What's the unofficial word?" Tyler asked.

"He was *abducted*," Weez whispered. He gave their puff-ball driver a suspicious glance before adding, "Abducted by *aliens*. And I think that one might know more than he's telling."

"Okay." Tyler nodded politely and wondered why the dossier hadn't said anything about his Brazilian soccer player being completely insane. That might have been useful information. "It's nice to finally meet you, Weez. If you need me for anything, I'll be sitting . . . over there."

Tyler got up and moved next to Felix Hoffmann.

"*Guten tag,* Tyler Sato." The giant-sized Felix offered one of his giant-sized hands.

Tyler took it and winced through a finger-crunching handshake. "It's nice to meet you too, Felix. It really impressed me when I read how you were the youngest kid on a soccer team of sixteen- and seventeen-year-olds. You must be an amazing goalie."

Felix's ample stomach jiggled as he laughed. "I wasn't the goalie. I was the team's mascot!"

Tyler blinked. "Mascot?"

"*Ja.* I wore a butterfly costume and danced for the crowds. But I did take over as goalie during one game when my brother got hurt. That's probably what you read about."

"Oh." Tyler nodded. "Did you do all right?"

"I stopped a bunch of shots and we won the game."

Felix grinned. "I'm big for my age and I have good reflexes, but the six-foot cardboard butterfly wings also helped cover the goal."

Tyler felt a little better about himself. It would be embarrassing when everyone found out exactly how he'd beaten M'Frozza, but at least he hadn't been wearing a butterfly costume at the time.

"Enough talk about my work as a butterfly goaltender," said Felix. "Tell me, Tyler Sato, how does it feel to be the best kid athlete on Earth?"

Tyler winced as he still did whenever anybody asked him that question, even three months after he'd "defeated" M'Frozza. "I'm not the best kid athlete on Earth."

"But of course you are," Felix insisted. "Everyone in the world knows how you bested the Mrendarian Galaxy Games champion in one-on-one competition."

"That's not quite true," Tomoko jumped in. "Nobody knows exactly what Sato-sensei did to win that challenge."

Tyler frowned. His language implant allowed him to feel the sarcasm in the overly-respectful honorific Tomoko had used to turn his name into an insult. The others seemed to have picked up on it as well.

"He's never said a word about it in all those interviews he's done," Tomoko continued. "So how about it, Captain? What exactly was your winning takedown move against M'Frozza the Mrendarian?"

El Gatito jumped up and down in his seat. "Ooooh, yes! Was it a pile driver of justice or a headlock of righteousness? Tell us all about it!"

The other kids all looked at Tyler, waiting to hear the details of his victory. "I got lucky," Tyler told them. That was all he had ever told anyone, and if it had been a good enough answer for interviewers from *Sports Illustrated* and *60 Minutes*, it would have to be good enough for his teammates, at least for now. He would make the real answer part of his big announcement when he got to Greece.

ELLINIKO, GREECE:

The bus swooped out of the clouds, revealing the ground below. El Gatito Grande pressed his masked face against the window. "Is that Greece already? Hooray! El Gatito has never been to the Greece! El Gatito has never been *anywhere!*"

"Neither have I," said Ling. "Greece was where the Olympic Games started, thousands of years ago. I have always dreamed of coming here."

"Really?" asked Weez. "Did your dreams include a flying orange shark driven by an oversized dust bunny?"

Ling shook her head emphatically.

Weez slumped back into his seat. "Darn. I was hoping you might have ESP or precognitive abilities. It's so hard to find people who can accurately predict future events these days!"

Daiki hugged his knees and rocked back and forth in his seat. He jumped as his mobile phone beeped twice. "I have a signal again! Finally, I can make a call!"

"You should call Tyler Sato. If he can't help you, nobody can!" Felix proclaimed. Because he was talking directly to Daiki, and since Daiki had no implant of his own, the German soccer player's language implant made his words come out in Japanese. "Oh, wait, he's already here. Never mind."

Daiki dialed his phone and spoke quickly into it. "Hello, Mother? No need to pick me up from Cousin Tyler-kun's school today. Why not? Because I'm in Greece, that's why not! And yes, the Parthenon does look particularly lovely today."

"It certainly does," El Gatito agreed as the ancient landmark whizzed past the window.

Daiki put his phone away and resumed rocking back and forth.

"Don't worry, Cousin. We'll send you home as soon as we can," Tyler promised.

"You'd better." Tomoko pointed a finger at Tyler's face. "You're responsible for this. You've turned poor Daiki-kun into a trembling ball of nerves."

"Me?" asked Tyler. "I'm not the one who threw him onto a flying shark bound for another continent."

Tomoko crossed her arms. "That happened because

he looks like you. And Daiki's family is only in America because of you. And I'm not having any fun because of you. And Obaa-chan wants me to have fun, so I'm going to end up disappointing her because of you. And there are no salty snacks being served on this flight, which I'm sure is all because of you as well!"

Tyler didn't know what to say after that, or if Tomoko really wanted him to speak at all.

"Excuse El Gatito," said the boy in the mask, addressing Tomoko. "El Gatito could not help but overhear that you are not having fun. El Gatito feels bad because he is having such a huge amount of fun. Maybe it'll get better for you when the training starts, yes?"

Tomoko's scowl contorted as she looked at El Gatito. Finally, her face broke out in a wide grin. "Awww! Those cat ears are just too cute!"

"No, no, no!" El Gatito poked the right ear with his finger. "El Gatito's ears are mean and intimidating, like a tiger's. Grrr!"

The bus lurched downward toward a cluster of large buildings on the horizon, causing Daiki to shriek and dig his fingernails into the seat.

"Galaxy Games Complex, straight ahead," Felix announced. "Indoor and outdoor arenas fit for interstellar competition, including an entire kayak slalom course! When the construction is done, this is going to be the most advanced sports complex ever built on Earth, with a Galaxy Games village that can hold dozens of different alien species."

"I know," said Weez. "I have blueprints on my bedroom wall back home, right between my UFO Believer's Club poster and a map of the Milky Way galaxy."

The bus glided over a road and touched down. A few minutes later it passed through the security gate and rolled past stadiums, arenas, and construction cranes, just like any ordinary shark-shaped bus would have. "Look at all those news vans," said Felix. "If we make this much news for a training session, imagine how many reporters will show up for actual games."

"There are networks here from China," said Ling, pointing.

"Then you'd better change those boots before you embarrass yourself back home," Tomoko told her.

Ling looked down at her feet. "What's wrong with my boots?"

Tomoko rolled her eyes. "Oh, where to start! If you're going to share a team with me, you'll need to develop a better fashion sense. Good boots make you look like a pop idol. Your boots make you look like a construction worker who just stepped in a bucket of red paint."

Ling swung her feet back and forth. "They were a gift from my friend's family."

"Really?" asked Tomoko. "Did they keep the receipt?"

The bus pulled into a lot with six other shark-shaped buses, all with names from various nursery schools in the Ossmendian Empire. It made Tyler wonder how big the elementary school buses from Ossmendia were, and whether the Earth team would have to play against Ossmendia in the tournament. He sure hoped not.

"Looks like we're the last ones to arrive," said Felix.

"Which, El Gatito would like to point out, is not El Gatito's fault," said El Gatito.

Through the bus windows they could see kids from dozens of countries playing catch, kicking soccer balls, and waiting for the orientation to begin. Tyler and the others blinked through the pain of their language implants going into overdrive.

"Is that Tyler Sato?" somebody asked in Greek.

"I think so," another boy replied in French. "He looks much taller on TV."

"This is all very nice, but when do we eat?" somebody asked in Russian.

Tyler thought back to what Stephen Falconer had said about people being changed forever when they saw Earth without boundaries. Looking at this group of kids from all over the world, all of them understanding what everybody else was saying, Tyler felt like he was seeing Earth without boundaries all over again. The team really did represent the entire planet.

It would make it that much harder for him to quit the team.

"Achee dukatah!" shouted their puff-ball driver. "Everybody off!"

"Can you bring my cousin back to Platte Bluff now?" Tyler asked.

"Eechaka takka chooh!" said the driver. "I am not a taxi service!"

"What? What did he, or maybe she, say?" asked Daiki.

"She, or maybe he, said we're stuck with you," said Tyler.

"Joy." Daiki joined Tyler and his teammates as they filed off the bus, directly into the path of a large purple creature with many squidlike tentacles.

"A Mrendarian!" Felix exclaimed.

Weez jumped forward with a photograph he'd pulled from his pocket. "Excuse me, sir! Have you seen this boy? His name is Gustavo. He'd be three years older by now, so imagine him as a handsome six-year-old version of me. He could be a slave or a medical experiment—or maybe he's being kept as a pet!"

The alien folded its tentacles over each other and glowered down at Weez with all three of its eyes.

"This isn't a Mrendarian you want to mess with," Tyler whispered to Weez. "This is R'Turvo, the pilot from Captain

M'Frozza's ship. He's got . . . a bit of an attitude."

R'Turvo made a harsh cracking sound that may have been a clearing of his throat. "I have never seen a group of children disembark from a transport vehicle in such a dangerous and chaotic manner."

"Sorry," said Ling.

"Simple apologies will not suffice. Your Galaxy Games team will hold my home world's former slot in the tournament and represent us, so your sloppiness reflects badly on the entire Mrendarian race. I must insist that the six of you conduct a disembarkation drill before you can join the others."

"We don't have time," said Tyler. "The other players are going inside now."

"You will join them once you've proven that you can safely board and disembark from your transport vehicle."

"You don't understand," said Felix. "This is Tyler Sato! He's the one who defeated—"

"Get back onto the transport vehicle!" R'Turvo snapped.

Tyler and the others scrambled back onto the bus.

"Fukhatah kableem zich akakoh," said the puff-ball driver. "My shift ended ten throbs ago." He (or maybe she) powered down the driving console and rolled away from the bus like a beach ball in the wind.

"You will now disembark like professional athletes,"

said R'Turvo. "One at a time, in a calm and pleasant manner."

"Excuse me." Daiki tapped the side of his head. "My brain has no language translator thing in it like the rest of you have. What's everyone saying?"

"This alien won't let us go anywhere until we're as calm and pleasant as professional athletes," Tomoko told him.

"That's going to take forever!" Daiki exclaimed.

"One more thing," R'Turvo said. "Whatever you do, keep your appendages away from the emergency recall button as you pass by."

"Emergency recall button?" For the first time, Tyler noticed a flashing blue button on the driving console. It was the only control still active.

"Yes, yes." R'Turvo waved his tentacles impatiently. "In the event of an emergency, that button activates an auto-nav program to bring your vehicle to a pre-programmed safety point. But you'd have to be a complete idiot to press it in a nonemergency situation."

El Gatito stared at the button as if he'd been hypnotized. "Such a pretty shade of blue!"

"Don't even think of it," Tyler told him.

"Disembark—now!" R'Turvo commanded.

They left the bus in a single-file line, more slowly and orderly than before. El Gatito paused for a moment in front of the emergency recall button. Tyler noticed a twitchy motion in the masked boy's hand, but he managed to restrain himself and keep moving.

"How was that, Mr. Alien sir?" asked Felix once they were all assembled in the parking lot again.

"Horrible," R'Turvo stated. "You are supposed to disembark in order, according to your ranking on the team."

Weez clutched his head in dismay. "We have a ranking? Already? Nobody told me that—is it because I'm being cut from the team already?"

"I haven't assigned the rankings yet," said Tyler.

"A Galaxy Games captain is required to maintain a comprehensive system of rank at all times," R'Turvo stated.

"But this is our first day!" said Tyler.

"You will need a ranking system for at least the players on your bus right now," R'Turvo insisted. "Without rankings you will not be able to conduct a proper disembarkation drill or handle any Challenge Season invitations you might receive."

"Challenge Season invitations?" Tyler thought that was a strange thing for the Mrendarian to suggest, since challenges for a slot in the Galaxy Games Tournament could take place only off world—like how M'Frozza had to travel to Earth for Tyler to officially defeat her. "Come on, R'Turvo. I only just met these guys. How can I tell who's better than anyone else?"

"If you ever wish to join your other teammates inside the briefing room, I suggest that you find a way."

"Fine!" Tyler pointed to the others in the order they were standing. "One, two, three, four, five, and Daiki." It surprised Tyler how easy it was to make a snap decision and then wait for his players to tell him how well he'd chosen. Maybe being captain wasn't as tough as he'd thought!

Weez jumped into the air. "Yes! I'm number one! Captain Sato, you won't regret this. I'll work extra hard to win games for us!"

Ling frowned. "I can't be number four. In Chinese culture, that's so unlucky!"

"I'll trade my number five for your number four," Felix offered.

"I'd like that!" said Ling.

"Wait, I didn't say you could trade," said Tyler.

Tomoko grinned. "Hey, Sato-sensei! Since I'm number three, does that mean Felix and Ling have to do whatever I say?"

"No," said Tyler. "I was just picking at random."

"Dance for me, Ling!" Tomoko commanded. "Move those ugly boots and dance, dance, dance!"

"El Gatito will trade numbers with you," the masked boy offered Ling. "El Gatito does not mind starting at the bottom and *proving* that he is the best."

"That makes me number two," Ling noted. "Now I can order Tomoko to dance!"

Tomoko sighed and did a little jig.

"Really," said Tyler, trying again to get everyone to pay attention to him. "The numbers don't mean you can boss each other around. They're only for this drill. Please, Tomoko, you can stop dancing now."

R'Turvo cracked his arm-tentacles, and the seven Earth kids scrambled back onto the bus. Once again, El Gatito paused at the emergency recall button. His hand moved slowly toward the console. "Flashing button . . . El Gatito cannot resist . . . ."

Tyler and Felix grabbed the masked boy and pulled him away from the driving console.

"Gracias," El Gatito told them. "That was close!"

"Try again," said R'Turvo, once they were all seated. "Start with the lowest ranked player and disembark in order, ending with the team captain. The spectator may follow after the team." He indicated Daiki with an arm-tentacle.

El Gatito jumped to his feet. "El Gatito is first this time!"

"Be careful," Weez warned. "Don't mess up the order or we'll be here all day!"

"And don't press that button," Felix added.

This time as the masked boy passed the driving console,

his whole body twitched. Tyler could see beads of sweat running down the boy's leather mask. He spoke in Spanish through clenched teeth. There was only a second's delay until everyone's language implants kicked in, but that was more than enough time for El Gatito's hand to reach out toward the button. "El Gatito . . . is very . . . sorry."

"El Gatito! No!" shouted Tyler as the masked boy's hand mashed down on the emergency recall button. A buzzer sounded, the door snapped shut, and metal covers slid down over the windows. The engine roared to life, and all the players fell to the floor as the bus rocketed forward.

Tomoko grabbed El Gatito by the shoulders. "Why did you do that?"

"It was blue and flashing," the masked boy explained. "How could anyone *not* press a button that's blue and flashing? Do not look at El Gatito like that . . . it was *blue* and *flashing*!"

On the ground far below, R'Turvo the Mrendarian watched the bus until it became a tiny speck in the sky. "Mission accomplished!" he proclaimed.

22

DESTINATION UNKNOWN:

Tyler, Weez, and Ling examined the driving console and tried to figure out how to turn the bus around. Meanwhile, Tomoko and Felix held down El Gatito so he wouldn't be tempted to press any more controls. Daiki just curled himself into a ball on the floor. "Not again, not again, not again," he said over and over.

"Why are all the windows covered?" asked Ling. "We can't see where we're going!"

"It's probably for safety," said Weez. "The bus thinks there's an emergency."

Tyler frowned at the emergency recall button, which had turned from blue to red and was no longer flashing. "Maybe if I press it again?" He tried several times but there was no further effect.

"I'm getting off of this bus, no matter where in the

world it stops next, and I'm not getting back on it again!" proclaimed Daiki.

El Gatito suddenly popped up between Tyler and Weez. "Has anyone tried turning this knob over here?" He twisted the control and the interior lighting dimmed to the intensity of flickering candlelight.

Tyler turned back to Tomoko and Felix. "Why did you let him go?"

"We tried to hold him, but he's so slippery," said Felix.

"Like an eel," Tomoko agreed.

El Gatito gave one of the knobs a quarter turn to the right. With a loud rattling sound, a metal plate slid away from the back window of the bus.

Tomoko ran back and pressed her hands against the glass. "Hey! That's Earth!"

The other kids

pushed in for a view. Earth's oceans, continents, and atmosphere filled the rear window. "Now I've seen the world!" Ling exclaimed in awe.

"This reminds me of an interview I once read from Stephen Falconer," said Weez. "He said seeing the world without boundary lines is a life-changing experience. He was so right!"

"Seeing the world getting smaller and smaller in the rear window, very quickly, is also a life-changing experience," Felix added. "Just not in a good way."

"Turn us around!" shouted Daiki.

"I don't know how!" Tyler shouted back.

"Seriously, Cousin Tyler-kun, turn us around!"

Tomoko put a hand on Daiki's trembling shoulder. "It'll all be okay, Daiki-kun. Just try your best to breathe normally until the oxygen all leaks out and we slowly suffocate to death."

"Are you always such a downer?" Tyler asked her.

"I can comfort my friend any way I want," Tomoko stated.

Tyler took Daiki by the arm. "He may be your friend, but he's my cousin."

Tomoko grabbed Daiki's other arm. "He was my friend first."

"No he wasn't," said Tyler. "He's been my cousin since we were born."

"But he didn't know you very well, did he?" asked Tomoko.

"Can I say something?" asked Daiki.

"No!" shouted both Tyler and Tomoko.

Tomoko gave Daiki's arm a hard yank. "I have more in common with Daiki-kun than you ever will. We're both Japanese."

Tyler pulled Daiki back toward him. "I'm Japanese too."

"You're American and you're a vegetarian," Tomoko retorted. "How can you be Japanese if you don't eat sashimi? And I'll bet you've never even heard of *Hunter-Elf Zeita*."

"Hunter-Elf who?" asked Tyler.

"I rest my case!" Tomoko shouted.

"Can you both let go of my arms now?" Daiki asked. "I feel like a human wishbone."

"Hey, guys!" El Gatito shouted from the front of the bus. "What do you think this button does?" He pressed it, and everyone immediately flew up onto the ceiling of the bus. "Oh! Reverse gravity! How cool!"

"Stop pressing buttons!" everyone shouted at El Gatito in five languages at once.

"But . . . that's what buttons are for," the masked boy explained.

"All right, nobody panic," Tyler told the others.

"R'Turvo said the bus was programmed to bring us to a safety point. It might not be on Earth, but at least it should be safe."

"Being lost in space is not what I'd call safe," said Daiki. He pulled his mobile phone out again. "Hello, Mother? Remember what I said about being in Greece? I can't even see Greece anymore. The entire Earth fits in the back window and now it's drifting to the left. Drifting . . . drifting . . . and it's gone! Have you ever been somewhere where you couldn't see the Earth? I sure haven't!"

"Are you really getting a signal?" Tomoko asked him.

Daiki shook his head sadly and showed her the phone. "No bars. In space, no one can accept your call."

Weez pumped his fist. "Now this is why I joined the Galaxy Games team."

"To end up lost in space in an out-of-control flying bus?" asked Felix.

Weez grinned. "No, to put me that much closer to finding my brother." He peered out the back window as if his missing brother might float past at any moment.

Tyler walked across the ceiling of the bus, carefully stepping over the bags and suitcases that had floated upward with the shift in gravity. The driving console was upside down now, but most of the controls were still in reach. "Maybe we can unblock a few more windows." After a few minutes of trying knobs at random, Tyler managed to slide the metal plate from the front windshield. "Guys? I think I know where we're going."

"It's the moon," said Ling in an awed voice, first in Chinese and then through Tyler's language implant.

"It's so bright!" said Felix.

"It's so beautiful!" said Tomoko.

"It's so coming right at us!" Daiki put his arms out as if he were bracing for an impact.

The moon grew larger until it filled the entire front window. Craters and plains stood out in more and more detail until the entire moonscape slid out of their view toward the bottom of the bus.

"Great," said Daiki. "Now we've lost sight of the moon as well."

"We must be in orbit," said Tyler. "I'll try to uncover the windows in the ceiling—I mean, the floor—I mean, you know what I mean. The ones between us and the moon."

MEEEEH-EEEEH! MEEEEH-EEEEH-EEEEEH-EEEEEH!

"Oh, good!" said El Gatito. "You found the horn! That will be handy if we run into traffic."

Tyler turned another knob. Metal plates slid back from the windows mounted in the floor above their heads, giving a clear view of rocks and craters rushing past at great speed.

"Are we in orbit?" asked Weez.

Tyler shook his head. "I don't think we're high enough to be in orbit."

"We're all going to die!" Daiki exclaimed. "We're going to die on the moon, upside down, in an orange shark-shaped bus! Of all possible ways to die, that's one I've never even heard of!"

Weez pulled a photograph from his pocket and gave it a gentle kiss. "Sorry, Gustavo. I tried my best."

"No, wait, look!" Tomoko pointed to the front window. Sunlight glinted off a glassy, city-sized dome that looked like a giant's overturned soup bowl. "We're saved!"

"We're still on the moon," Daiki reminded her. "It will take a lot more than a big blue bubble for us to be saved."

"Does anyone have a camera?" Weez asked. "*UFO Believers Home Journal* will want some photographic proof of this!"

Tomoko handed him a pink mobile phone with big-eyed cartoon elves all over it.

Weez snapped picture after picture of the moon-bubble as they approached it. Although the dome could have easily held the entire downtown area of Platte Bluff, there were just a few small buildings surrounded by an array of statues. Just before impact, a circular gate opened to allow the bus to pass into the dome's interior.

The ground approached slowly, and the entire bus rocked gently as the four tires touched the surface.

"That wasn't so bad," said Tyler. Then the gravity shifted and they all fell back to the floor, along with a shower of bags, suitcases, and other belongings.

The door creaked open with a rush of air that was lemon-scented but breathable. "El Gatito is still ranked number five out of five, so . . . does that mean El Gatito has to leave first?" The masked boy eyed the door with suspicion.

Tyler shook his head. "I don't care what R'Turvo says, I'm going out first." He stepped along the aisle as the others silently moved out of his way. It might have been a foolish thing for him to volunteer, but he was technically in charge, at least until he had a chance to officially quit the team.

The other players moved behind their captain. "Tyler Sato will protect us," said Felix, which would have made Tyler laugh if he weren't concentrating so hard on maintaining a brave expression. He tried to imagine how a real Galaxy Games captain like M'Frozza would act in a situation like this, if she didn't have slime and tentacles.

Tyler stepped to the open door and looked out. He could see the sun above them, tinted blue and diffused by the dome. Earth was nowhere in sight. "We must be on the dark side," Tyler told the others. "It's not really dark, it just faces away from the Earth so we never get to see it."

"The great Tyler Sato thinks he knows everything," Tomoko scoffed.

"Not everything," said Tyler. "Just what you pick up when your father is a professor of astronomy."

A red carpet stretched from the bus to a building shaped something like a cuckoo clock made from gray lunar rock. On either side of the carpet stood rows of giant stone slabs that looked exactly like the carved moai statues on Easter Island, but as far as Tyler could see, there were no living beings in sight.

Tyler remembered a grainy video he'd seen of early astronauts dropping gently down a ladder to plant an American flag on the moon's surface. "Here's one small step for me and one giant leap for . . . me." Tyler stuck his right foot out, pushed forward, and went flying upward in the low gravity. He flipped twice in the air before landing in a sprawl on the carpet.

Tomoko and Felix sprang toward him. "Captain Sato! Are you all right?"

"Yeah, but watch out for that first step."

Ling was the first to leap off the carpet. She landed on the moon's surface with a cloud of kicked-up dust. "I'm the first Chinese girl on the moon!" she proclaimed. "How do you like my boots now, Tomoko? They may be ugly, but I'll bet they end up in a museum!"

The others joined Ling on the surface. Weez and El Gatito played catch with a moon-rock that would have weighed twenty pounds on Earth. Tomoko and Felix took turns balancing each other, one handed, over their heads. Tyler watched Ling turn somersaults in the air as if she were bouncing on a trampoline. Even Daiki seemed to forget how anxious he'd been about leaving Earth. They were all laughing and joking around so much that they failed to notice that the Easter Island statues were moving, and most of them now scowled in disapproval.

The largest rock statue cleared its throat with a grinding boom. "Ahem!" The dust-covered Earth kids instantly froze—even Ling, who was fifteen feet above the surface in the middle of a spiraling jump.

"Oh . . . hello," said Tyler awkwardly.

"Hello," answered the rock giant.

Wump! added Ling as she flopped onto the ground. She winced and rubbed her right shoulder. "Back on Earth, Master Wan would have scolded me for not sticking my landing."

Daiki tapped Tomoko's shoulder. "Did that giant statue just make a strange grinding sound?"

"No," said Tomoko, "that giant alien just said hello in its native language."

Daiki swallowed hard. "Ah, yes. That is what I was afraid you'd say."

The rocklike aliens watched them with expressions carved in stone—complete with jutting chins, enormous noses, and deep-set eyes. The big-headed creatures had no visible arms or legs and came in a variety of sizes ranging from ten feet tall to more than fifty. Their leader, who could have been hollowed out and used as an office building, moved its thick stone lips to make another stone-grinding speech. "Welcome, Tyler Sato and underlings!"

"Underlings?" asked Tomoko in outrage.

Tyler made a gesture for her to back off. "You know who I am?" he asked the rock giant.

The stony lips moved into a slight smile. "Of course we do. As a Galaxy Games captain, you are the most highly regarded member of your entire species—although I do have to admit, I thought you would be taller."

"That's what I said!" Felix exclaimed.

Tyler frowned. "And who are you?"

"I am Trade Commissioner Rokke of the Ossmendian Empire."

"Oh!" exclaimed Weez. "The Ossmendians! You are the ones who gave us the buses!"

"We were glad to find a use for them," said Commissioner Rokke. "They are a discontinued model, not rugged enough to safely handle Ossmendian toddlers, but perfectly suited for you and your team."

"Thanks." Tyler wondered whether the comparison to Ossmendian toddlers was meant to be an insult. *It probably was,* he thought, but he chose to ignore it. "If your toddlers are that tough, I'd hate to meet your Galaxy Games team."

The Ossmendians chuckled to themselves, and Commissioner Rokke seemed to fight back a secret smile. "Yes, we are quite proud of them. But about the buses, it seems that you haven't yet reprogrammed the emergency recall systems with a location on your planet. Did you fail to read the owner's manual?"

"I guess so," said Tyler.

"Then I must apologize for any inconvenience." Something in the Ossmendian's tone reminded Tyler of the many times when his sister had apologized for something she'd gladly do a dozen more times if she could.

"Don't worry about it," said Ling. She stomped another boot-print into the lunar surface. "We're on the moon!"

"Indeed," said the Ossmendian. "And you have come at a most portentous time. Two of our agents are in your New York City right now, presenting documents to your United Nations General Assembly." The inside of the dome flashed with a message in Ossmendian symbols, and the grin on Rokke's stone face cracked open wide enough to display stone teeth the size of kitchen tables. "It seems our trade mission has just become an official embassy to the nations of Earth."

"Congratulations," said Tomoko. "What does that mean?"

Rokke's teeth banged together in deafening crashes as he spoke. "It means the land under this dome is now recognized as Ossmendian territory under galactic law."

Another Ossmendian began to speak. He was fifteen feet tall and almost ten feet wide, but still looked tiny next to Commissioner Rokke. "Captain Tyler Sato," the smaller Ossmendian proclaimed, "my name is Stonifer. As Captain of the Ossmendian Galaxy Games team, I formally challenge you for your spot in the Galaxy Games Tournament."

"Well, you can't have it," said Tyler.

The young Ossmendian grinned, revealing a mouthful of skateboard-sized teeth. "You're in our territory, so you really don't have a choice." At Stonifer's signal, the ground beneath the dome sank downward in a series of concentric rings, forming the bowl of an enormous artificial crater. Tyler and his teammates found themselves standing with Rokke and Stonifer in the middle of the lowest level, which was as wide across as a football field, while other Ossmendians arranged themselves on the tiers above.

"It's like we're in the middle of a huge stadium!" Ling exclaimed.

"But we're not ready," said Tyler. "We haven't even had our orientation yet!"

"Captain Tyler," said Stonifer, in a formal tone. "The rules of Challenge Season state that you may refuse my invitation to challenge—but if you do, your tournament spot will become ours by forfeit, and your planet will never receive another chance to compete."

23

OSSMENDIAN EMBASSY DOME, THE MOON:

Tyler clenched his fists. "That's not fair! You can't take our spot in the Galaxy Games Tournament. Not when you brought us here against our will!"

"Did we?" Captain Stonifer arched his stone eyebrows. "Were we the ones who pressed the emergency recall button on your transport vehicle?"

"No, that was me!" El Gatito proudly waved his button-pressing finger in the air.

"Well, then, there is your answer."

"The Mrendarians won't let you get away with this," Tyler insisted. "When they find out what you've done, your whole planet will suffer!"

The Ossmendians all laughed as if Tyler had just told the funniest joke ever. "None of this would have been possible without approval from the Mrendarian Ruling Council. Most Mrendarians don't want to pledge allegiance to a planet that cares so little about sports."

"But Earth loves sports!" Felix exclaimed.

Commissioner Rokke glared down at him with disbelieving eyes. "Really? Then why, in the entire history of the Galaxy Games, has nobody from your world ever attended a single tournament game? And before you make up a story about how your great-grand-uncle hopped the Vrindar Express to see Planet Boggarzi push Planet Sphleem to three extended overtime periods, keep in mind that we have access to all the attendance records."

"Of course we've never been to any of your games," Tomoko pointed out. "We don't have any spaceships!"

"That wouldn't stop a real sports fan," Commissioner Rokke insisted.

Tyler felt as if the world were spinning out from under his feet, or maybe that was just the moon's low gravity. "Was R'Turvo was in on this? Is *that* why he insisted on running so many drills past that flashing blue button?"

Trade Commissioner Rokke nodded, which made him look a bit like a giant domino in danger of toppling over. "R'Turvo would have conducted those safety drills for as long as it took until one of you finally pressed that button."

El Gatito nudged Tyler's arm. "So it was a good thing that we got it over with quickly, yes? You should be thanking El Gatito for saving you so much time."

Rokke stifled a yawn. "Are there any more questions before we get to the challenge?"

"Yes!" Weez let the moon's weak gravity carry him forward in a series of kangaroo hops. "Your people must have been to Earth before, right? To a small island in the South Pacific? Rapa Nui? About a thousand years ago?"

"Perhaps." Rokke ground the base of his body into the moon.

Weez grinned. "You must have made a pretty strong impression. The people there spent centuries carving statues in your honor."

"We cannot confirm or deny previous contacts with your species," Rokke stated.

"Of course not," said Weez. "But the evidence speaks for itself. You are creatures of stone, and giant stone structures popped up all over ancient Earth at about the same time—Stonehenge in England, the Great Pyramid of Egypt, the Pyramid of the Sun in Mexico, and more! It's almost as if you were producing a reality show about all the crazy things you could convince our ancestors to build."

Rokke's scowl deepened. "Fine. I'll admit it. You probably would have caught a rerun of *Those Wacky Humans* on a budget-branded quantum eventually, but so what?"

"So," said Weez, "you've been to Earth before, and now you're back. That leads me to a question—a very important question. Possibly the most important question ever."

"What is it?" The Ossmendian's eyes glowed with inner fire and irritability.

Tyler leaned forward, hoping that the Brazilian boy had come up with some loophole to cancel the challenge and get them all safely returned to Earth.

"Be honest." Weez held up the photograph of his brother. "Did you abduct this boy?"

ELLINIKO, GREECE:

M'Frozza paced back and forth, causing her slime trail to thicken and foam. "We cannot start this orientation without Captain Tyler Sato," she insisted.

"I saw his bus land," volunteered a Canadian hockey player named David. "He was talking to a creepy-looking purple squidlike thing in the parking lot, and then he just took off."

"Creepy looking?" M'Frozza shook froth from her tentacles as she spoke. "You think Mrendarians are creepy looking? What about me, do you think I'm creepy looking?"

David shrank back. "Um . . . no, of course not."

M'Frozza's nose-holes popped as she took a series of calming breaths. "There are only three Mrendarians on Earth right now. I'm here, N'Gatu is at a plumbing technology conference, and R'Turvo—" She squinted in thought. "What business would Tyler Sato have with my pilot?"

"Maybe he reminded him about something he'd forgotten back home," suggested an Argentine boy who wore a fringed unitard and went by the name of The Amazing Waldo.

M'Frozza shook her head, spraying flecks of slime in all directions. The human children yelped and jumped away. The lucky ones were able to wipe the slime from their faces or bare arms, while the others had to use fingernails to scrape the blobs from their clothing or hair. "During my time on Earth, I have gotten to know Tyler Sato quite well," M'Frozza told them. "It would be most unlike him to be late or forgetful."

The door opened and another Mrendarian slid into the hall. David pointed and said, "That's him! That's the alien who was talking to Tyler Sato!"

"R'Turvo!" M'Frozza called. "Where is the Earth captain?"

"I cannot say," the Mrendarian pilot told her.

M'Frozza narrowed all three of her eyes. "You cannot say, or you do not know?"

"I cannot say," R'Turvo repeated, and M'Frozza felt a chill go down her spinal support tube. What was the pilot up to?

R'Turvo folded his arm-tentacles across his torso. "Have you not begun your lecture yet? We have a schedule to keep. These Earth children need their basic introduction to the games."

M'Frozza sighed through her nose-holes. "Very well. If you see Tyler Sato or the other missing players, have them sent to this briefing room immediately."

"I will do so . . . if I see them." R'Turvo burbled to himself and slid back out of the room.

Very suspicious, thought M'Frozza, but she didn't have time right then to investigate. "Gather around the platform, humans," she told the Earth players.

The children took their seats around the Mrendarian girl, but left the two closest rows empty.

"The Galaxy Games are scored on a three-by-three grid on which each side is represented by a different symbol, traditionally either a circle or a pair of intersecting lines drawn at a 45-degree angle with respect to the grid. I happen to have brought the scoring sheet from the game I played against Tyler Sato, in which he won your team its spot in the tournament."

The Earth children leaned forward, peering at the paper stuck to M'Frozza's tentacle. They were silent for a long moment until a red-headed Irish rugby player named Conor jumped to his feet. "That's noughts and crosses! Boxin' oxen! X's and O's!"

"Tic-tac-toe," David added.

"Yeah, it's called that too," said Conor. "Do you mean to say that Tyler Sato, our noble captain, the so-called best child athlete in Earth's history, won his greatest battle by putting his O's in three boxes across?"

"No, he did it diagonally." M'Frozza hoisted the page a little higher so Conor could see. "Very sneaky. He caught me entirely off guard."

OSSMENDIAN EMBASSY DOME, THE MOON:

Tyler ripped a page from his roster book and drew a tic-tac-toe board with his pencil. "Do you want to be X's or O's?" he asked the Ossmendian captain.

Stonifer laughed in a booming stonelike voice. "Your handmade scoring sheet will not be required, Captain Tyler." Above their heads the inside of the dome lit up with a three-by-three grid. X's and O's flashed at random in the boxes before withdrawing to opposite sides of the empty game board.

"Tic-tac-toe?" asked Felix in disbelief. "You've come zillions of light-years through space and this is the game you challenge us with?"

"I'd have expected rock-paper-scissors," said Ling.

"No, no," El Gatito told her. "That requires five-fingered hands."

"Oh, yeah," said Ling, glancing at the nearest armless

274

and legless Ossmendian. "These guys have no hands, and they'd probably pick 'rock' every time anyway."

"Your planet's ignorance is astounding," Trade Commissioner Rokke told them. "The logic game that you call tic-tac-toe developed independently in every civilization in the Galaxy. This makes it the perfect basis for a standardized galactic sport, with added rules to incorporate every game, contest, and skill that can possibly be imagined."

"I think we can take them in a game of tic-tac-toe," Felix whispered to Ling, loud enough to be heard by everyone else. "Unless they fall on us while we're filling in our squares."

Stonifer chuckled. "Do you think our omniroots are only good for anchoring us into the ground?"

"Omniroots?" asked Tyler.

The rocky dust around the Ossmendian trembled as six slender metal appendages sprang out of his bottom edge, like triple-jointed insect legs ending in claws. Two of Stonifer's six claws rose up in front of him like hands, while the other four dug into the moon's surface and lifted the alien's bulky stone body off the ground.

"Ah," said Felix. "Omniroots."

"And to answer Captain Tyler's question, Ossmendia will take the O's while Earth will be represented by the X's."

ELLINIKO, GREECE:

Conor raised his hand again. "But tic-tac-toe—or whatever you want to call it—that's just for little kids, innit? If you know the strategy and get first ups, it's impossible to lose."

"Exactly right!" M'Frozza burbled approvingly. "Which is why we add extra rules to make the game more challenging. Each box can have conditions for play, conditions for victory, and conditions for flipping from one mark to the other. The rules change constantly during the game, and negotiating the rules is like a game in itself. An experienced captain will increase his or her or its team's chances of winning, while an inexperienced captain is bound to put his or her or its team at a huge disadvantage. I have been giving lessons to Tyler Sato. As long as he remains your strategic leader, the Earth team should do well."

OSSMENDIAN EMBASSY DOME, THE MOON:

"Time out!" shouted Tomoko. Tyler and Stonifer both stared at her. "Can I call a time out in this game?" she asked.

"The game has not started yet," Stonifer explained wearily. "Take a pulse or two, if you need to devise a strategy. That will give our players a chance to stretch our root joints before the challenge." He and his teammates clattered away together like wobbly, top-heavy insects.

"We're doomed, aren't we?" asked Weez.

Tyler shrugged. "My game against M'Frozza wasn't like this."

"Because you didn't have so many rules?" asked Ling.

"Because she let me win," Tyler confessed.

The other kids stared at him in confusion and disbelief. "El Gatito thinks he understands," said the masked boy. "You are the great Tyler Sato, the most powerful human athlete of all time, and M'Frozza was so intimidated—"

"No, no, no. I'm not the most powerful kid in the world. I haven't spent my life training for the Olympics like Ling. I'm not a national martial arts champion like Tomoko. I'd be a total joke on the soccer field against Weez or Felix. And I wouldn't . . . um . . ." Tyler frowned at El Gatito.

"You wouldn't look this good in a *luchador* mask?" El Gatito suggested.

"No, probably not," Tyler agreed. "You all earned your place on this team, while I just cheated and lied my way onto it."

"I knew it!" Tomoko exclaimed. "The great Tyler Sato is nothing but a fraud! I've been saying that for three months but no one would believe me. The entire world was wrong and I was right! You should quit the team before we all kick you out."

"I was already going to quit," Tyler told her.

"Too late! I'm kicking you out anyway," said Tomoko. "And since we're suddenly leaderless, I'm declaring myself to be the new Galaxy Games Captain of Earth."

"Wait, why you?" asked Felix. "Maybe one of us wants to be the captain."

"I called it first," Tomoko stated.

"Can't we at least take a vote?" Felix persisted.

Tomoko stuck her tongue out at him and pulled down one of her lower eyelids until Felix looked away. "Now that that's settled . . . Tyler-san! Take a seat with Daiki-kun in the stands and try to stay out of our way. Weez-san! You can be my chief tactician. What weaknesses do giant stone children have?"

Weez considered for a moment. "Wind erosion would be the big one over a few thousand years. Or if they fall asleep in a bad neighborhood they might get covered in graffiti."

Tomoko nodded. "Okay, we can work with that. El Gatito! Ling! Check our bus for cans of spray paint."

"Aye aye, Captain Tomoko!" said Ling with a sharp salute.

Tomoko crossed her arms and looked quite pleased with herself. "I have a good feeling about running this team."

24

OSSMENDIAN EMBASSY DOME, THE MOON:

Tyler and Daiki joined Commissioner Rokke in the stadium bleachers. An announcer's stone-scraping voice boomed: "IT'S A BEAUTIFUL DAY UNDER THE CLIMATE-CONTROLLED EMBASSY DOME. YOUR OSSMENDIAN PLANETARY TEAM, LED BY CAPTAIN STONIFER RED-VEIN, IS READY TO CRUSH THEIR WAY BACK INTO THE GALAXY GAMES TOURNAMENT!"

"Yeah!" Commissioner Rokke jumped up and down, starting an alien equivalent of the wave that involved all spectators except Tyler and Daiki.

"ALL LOYAL OSSMENDIAN SUBJECTS, PLEASE RISE FOR THE OSSMENDIAN PLANETARY ANTHEM!" This statement was followed by ten thousand pairs of clawlike root tips clapping along to three minutes of rock-grinding sounds, while the Earth kids winced in pain and held their hands firmly over their ears.

"OUR OPPONENTS ARE FLESHY PRIMITIVES FROM EARTH—YOU MAY KNOW THEM FROM SEVEN HUNDRED SEASONS OF THE TOP-RANKED OSSMENDIAN REALITY SERIES, *THOSE WACKY HUMANS*. AND NOW, AS NEAR AS WE'VE BEEN ABLE TO DETERMINE FROM LISTENING TO THEIR BROADCASTS, THE EARTH PLANETARY ANTHEM!" This was followed by a jingle for Burger Barn.

"Burger Barn, Burger Barn, Burger Barn is great!" sang Daiki with a hand over his heart. "Beef-flavored sandwiches like your great-grandpappy ate!"

Tyler sighed. This wasn't exactly how he'd planned to spend the afternoon, but he felt better as a genuine spectator than as a pretend leader.

"This should be fun," said Daiki. "I hated the flight here and I'm not looking forward to getting back onto that bus, but attending a game on the moon is very cool."

An Ossmendian in a white hat came down the aisle with a tray of gallon-sized cups propped on his chin. "Calcium carbonate!" he called. "Get your freshly dissolved calcium carbonate here!"

"I'll have one," said Commissioner Rokke. Tyler watched in amazement as the Ossmendian took a cup in one of his massive claws, poured the milky white liquid onto the top of his head, and let it soak into his rocky skin.

"You boys want to try some?" the vendor asked Tyler

and Daiki. "Lots of healthy trace minerals in this batch."

"No, thank you," said Tyler.

"I understand completely." The vendor winked one of his stone eyes. "You don't want to spoil your appetite for the quartz rolls and granite lumps, eh?"

On the floor of the crater, Stonifer and his five largest Ossmendian teammates lined up in front of Tomoko and her four players. The rocky aliens clattered against the moon rocks with their metal omniroots. Beeping metal balls floated above the field of play. Tyler wondered what purpose the balls might have in the game.

"Why is Captain Tyler Sato sitting in the stands?" asked Stonifer. The sound system picked up his voice and broadcast it across the entire arena. "Does he mean to offend me, or is he a shameless coward?"

"Can both of those be true?" Tomoko asked.

"Hey!" Tyler exclaimed.

"I'm the captain now so you'd better get used to it," Tomoko told the Ossmendians.

Stonifer and his teammates laughed. "I will accept you as Tyler Sato's stand-in and First Rank of your team, but only because your superior is near enough to correct your mistakes."

Tomoko bristled. "My superior? Him?" She glared out at Tyler. "I don't think so!"

"My First Rank is Chunq." Stonifer nodded at an

Ossmendian player who had a wide base and a coating of green moss. "My Second through Fifth Ranks are Ruffy, Tangh, Yoofis, and Brikk. How is the Earth team ranked?"

Tomoko counted the team members off on her fingers. "My Second is Weez, Third is Ling, Fourth is Felix, and Fifth is El Gatito."

"Are you ready to be crushed into the dust of your own moon?" the Ossmendian captain asked with a gravelly laugh.

El Gatito raised a defiant fist in the air. "We're ready!" he shouted.

"To be crushed into the dust of our own moon?" Ling asked him.

"Yes! No, no, wait." El Gatito reconsidered. "Oh-ho! El Gatito sees what you did there. Of course El Gatito did not mean that his team was ready to be crushed, but that we are just plain ready. See? El Gatito is almost too smart for your trick questions!"

"Almost," Stonifer agreed. "Earth Girl First Rank Tomoko! What is your first move?"

"In tic-tac-toe?" Tomoko looked up at the flashing grid on the inside of the dome above. "I'll put an *X* in the center square, of course."

"EARTH CHALLENGES FOR THE CENTER SQUARE," blared the gravelly voice of the event announcer, translated into various Earth languages by the implants in each human player's head.

Stonifer's rocky tongue scraped against his rocky lips. "Since you picked the square, I get to pick the challenge. Ossmendia proposes a one-on-one wrestling match within a scale-seven circle, with an objective to eject or immobilize an opponent within a period of one hundred throbs."

"Um . . . okay," said Tomoko. There was a long pause.

"No amendments!" shouted Tyler from the stands. He'd learned that much from his strategy lessons with M'Frozza. "Tell him you have no amendments! That'll give you the initiative in picking who gets to compete in the challenge!"

"No amendments," Tomoko stated.

"INITIATIVE TO EARTH," said the announcer.

Stonifer gestured with a metal root tip at Tomoko's teammates. "Well? Which rank are you going to call? Yourself? The boy with the pointy-eared mask? Or maybe the girl with the ugly boots?"

Ling looked down at her feet and sighed.

"First Rank," said Tomoko. "That's me, right? Me and Chunq?"

"FIRST RANKS, TOMOKO TOMIZAWA VERSUS CHUNQ MAYSONREY," the announcer confirmed. "THE

CHALLENGE IS ONE-ON-ONE WRESTLING TO EJECT OR IMMOBILIZE WITHIN ONE HUNDRED THROBS."

In the stands, Tyler groaned in disappointment. "I hope Tomoko is as good as she thinks she is," he told Daiki. "Chunq is a First Rank, so he's probably the strongest player on the Ossmendian team, after their captain. Do you think Tomoko can beat him?"

"I don't know," said Daiki. "I'm pretty sure this is the first time Tomoko's ever wrestled an opponent who has six limbs and stone skin in a circle on the moon."

"Chunq to the circle," Stonifer ordered. Chunq, the first-ranked Ossmendian, clanked into a twenty-foot circle made from a dark powdery dust that stood out from the moon's ordinary gray surface. Tomoko joined him. She made a respectful bow that was not returned.

Tomoko dropped into a ready stance, bouncing on the balls of her feet. In the light gravity of the moon, each bounce sent her two feet into the air. "Now we'll see who the best kid athlete on Earth really is," she said. "Once I beat this rock creature, it'll be my picture on the T-shirts, my name on the banners, and my face all over the news. Tyler Sato? Sorry, never heard of him!"

"BEGIN!" shouted the announcer.

Chunq swung an omniroot that caught Tomoko in her torso as she jumped. She sailed thirty feet outside the circle and landed in a cloud of lunar dust.

"OSSMENDIA WINS THE CHALLENGE!" the announcer declared. Above the arena, a ghostly blue O appeared in the center square of the tic-tac-toe scoreboard. The Ossmendian spectators rocked back and forth in their seats, shaking the ground with their weight.

Tomoko got her feet under her and brushed the moon-dust from her clothes. "Well, that was embarrassing."

"It's okay, Tomoko!" Daiki shouted from the stands. "You can still beat them!" He turned to Tyler and lowered his voice. "She can still beat them, can't she?"

"We just need three X's in a row," said Tyler. "That sure won't be easy once Stonifer accepts his victory in the center square."

The Ossmendian captain raised two claws above his head to silence the crowd. "Ossmendia declines the square," he stated. "We will instead claim initiative in the next phase." The ghostly O disappeared from the scoreboard, and the Ossmendian crowd gnashed their stone teeth in disapproval.

"He turned down the center square?" Daiki asked. "What do you think he's up to?"

Tyler frowned. "Nothing good, I'm sure."

ELLINIKO, GREECE:

"And those are the basic rules for designating play in a given square," M'Frozza finished. "Are there any questions?"

Hands shot up around the briefing room. Before M'Frozza could pick on anyone, red lights flashed and alarm buzzers sounded from all directions. Seconds later, a team of uniformed guards burst through the rear doors, along with Section Chief Marwa Jelassi.

"It's an ambush!" A Somalian cricket player named Basel dropped to the ground and began crawling to the nearest cover.

"This is not an ambush," Chief Jelassi stated.

"See?" asked Basel. "That's what everyone says when they're carrying out an ambush!"

"What's going on?" asked M'Frozza.

"Evacuation," Chief Jelassi told her. "We've just received an anonymous threat. It's probably nothing, but we'll need the team to assemble in the parking lot until we sort this out." She looked around the room. "Wait, where's Captain Tyler?"

"Nobody knows," said The Amazing Waldo in his most theatrical voice.

"Code Red!" the section chief shouted into her radio. "Lock down the complex! Activate the rally points! Conduct a room-by-room search! Come on, people, move it!"

The guards escorted the team outside and verified that an entire busload of players had gone missing, along with the bus itself. The bus driver, a puff-ball-looking alien called a Dardellian, was led away to be interrogated. At the height of the commotion, N'Gatu dropped out of the sky in a Mrendarian shuttlecraft, which was immediately surrounded by heavily armed soldiers.

"Let him through!" M'Frozza snapped. "That's my technician!"

The soldiers warily lowered their rifles long enough for N'Gatu to emerge from his ship with a large box of copper pipes and plumbing supplies. "Looks like you're having some trouble," he said to M'Frozza.

"I am dealing with the situation." Looking around, M'Frozza spotted a third Mrendarian at the far edge of the parking lot. "Pilot R'Turvo!"

The Mrendarian pilot stiffened. "Yes, Captain?" he called back to her.

"The Earth authorities have misplaced Tyler Sato and several others," M'Frozza informed him. "They may be in great danger. We must provide assistance."

R'Turvo sighed through his nostril-holes. "Inform the humans that their players are in a safe place."

M'Frozza's three eyes narrowed to suspicious slits. "Where are they?"

"Safe," R'Turvo repeated. "There is no cause for alarm. These things have been planned at a very high level. Nothing can go wrong and nobody will be hurt."

As the Mrendarian spoke these words, the ground shook from a loud explosion. A second bang followed, then another and another, like a string of firecrackers. Three different buildings in the sports complex suddenly caught fire, sending pillars of black smoke high into the sky.

"Dwogleys!" N'Gatu exclaimed with hushed awe in his voice.

"Ambush for real!" Basel exclaimed, diving to the pavement.

"Casualty report!" Chief Jelassi shouted into her radio.

A reply crackled over the speaker. "All units are accounted for, Chief. The affected areas were empty warehouse space, as far as we can tell."

"Thanks be!" said Chief Jelassi. "Don't let your guard down yet. There may be more to come."

"We need to find a safe place for all the players," said M'Frozza.

"There's no place to hide from Dwogleys," stated N'Gatu. "They exist on every world with intelligent life, and they follow us on our travels around the galaxy."

Chief Jelassi approached the Mrendarians. "Captain M'Frozza! Please translate for me. What is your technician so uptight about?"

"He is worried about Dwogleys," M'Frozza's language implant rendered her words in the section chief's native Tunisian Arabic.

Chief Jelassi confronted N'Gatu. "Who are the Dwogleys?"

"Tell her to please ignore our bumbling technician," R'Turvo told M'Frozza. "His brain cells are clearly beginning to slip away through his skleezer-glands."

"Which makes me particularly open-minded," said N'Gatu proudly. "I know a thing or two about Dwogleys. They say Dwogleys are all around us but can't be detected by the sensory organs of any known species. They say Dwogleys are obsessed with sabotaging the Galaxy Games and advancing their own evil plots. They *say* Dwogleys can enter a person's dreams and plant dangerous ideas or suggestions *without anyone ever knowing.*"

M'Frozza relayed this information to Chief Jelassi, who rolled her eyes and walked away, muttering about how she didn't have time for ghost stories when there were Seclusionists to be found.

"*They* say these things because *they* have wild imaginations," R'Turvo concluded.

"We didn't imagine those explosions," M'Frozza stated. She spun on her slime trail as she puzzled it out. "First the Earth captain goes missing, and now there is an attack on Earth's Galaxy Games Complex. The two events must be related."

"They are not," stated R'Turvo. "The timing of this event is a mere coincidence."

All three of M'Frozza's eyes widened. "You would not be able to say that unless you knew something about this attack, or about the location of Tyler Sato, or both."

R'Turvo twisted his tentacles in discomfort.

"Or about the Dwogleys," N'Gatu added.

"There are no Dwogleys!" R'Turvo snapped.

"Pilot R'Turvo," M'Frozza snapped back. "If you know where Tyler Sato is located, you must tell us. The Earth authorities must be informed. His mother-parent and father-parent will be worried. You must tell us right now!"

R'Turvo popped and clicked his nose-holes in thought for a moment before he nodded. "I will tell you, but only because it is now too late for you to interfere. Captain Tyler is on this planet's moon, engaged in a challenge that was personally arranged by your father-parent. The Earth team will lose its tournament slot to a much stronger and better team. Therefore, this attack has no real meaning or effect."

M'Frozza wriggled her face-tentacles as she took in this information. "N'Gatu?" she asked in a quiet voice.

"What can I do for you, Captain?" asked the technician.

"Fly me to the moon."

OSSMENDIAN EMBASSY DOME, THE MOON:

"Flint caps!" the Ossmendian vendor shouted. "Get your genuine flint caps!"

Directly behind Tyler and Daiki, an eight-foot Ossmendian child bounced up and down in her seat. "Mummy!

Can I have flint caps? Can I, can I, *pleeeeeeeeeeease!*" Tyler and Daiki grabbed their ears in pain at the young child's high-pitched wail.

"Just buy her the caps and save my eardrums," Tyler muttered.

The Ossmendian's mother waved the vendor over. She selected a pair of hollow rocks and carefully fit them over the child's blocky teeth.

"Thank you, Mummy!" the child exclaimed. When her teeth came together, orange sparks flew from her mouth. She laughed and slammed the flint caps together again and again to create a cascade of fireworks from her mouth.

"Time to find some new seats," Tyler told Daiki as the two boys ran to avoid the rain of sparks from the young child's new toy.

Out in the middle of the crater, Stonifer tapped his root tips impatiently. "Pick a square, Earth Girl First Rank Tomoko," he snapped. "Any square will do."

Tomoko stared up at the scoreboard in dismay. On the inside of the dome, the scoreboard showed blue O's in the upper-right and lower-left corners plus all four edge-squares—top, bottom, left, and right. The other three squares, including the center and two corners, remained empty. "You can get three in a row anywhere!"

"I know," Stonifer agreed. "The game is pretty much

over. Still, I would like to play it out. A proper victory is so much more satisfying than a forfeit."

"Hmm."

The announcer cut into the long and painful silence. "WHILE THE EARTH TEAM PONDERS ITS NEXT MOVE, LET'S PLAY ROCK RACE! CAN YOU GUESS WHICH ROCK WILL CROSS THE FINISH LINE FIRST?" The enormous image of three rocks appeared on the dome overhead.

Tyler groaned. "I hate when they play gimmick games at a sporting event."

"The rock in the middle looks more aerodynamic," said Daiki. "Go, rock in the middle!"

"They're not even moving!" Tyler exclaimed.

"Of course not," said Daiki. "They're rocks."

"Upper-left corner," Tomoko decided, and the dome shifted back to the scoreboard.

"EARTH CHALLENGES FOR THE UPPER-LEFT CORNER," the announcer declared. "THIS WOULD BLOCK A POSSIBLE DOUBLE-WIN."

"What's a double-win?" asked Felix.

"Three in a row, two different ways," said Yoofis on the Ossmendian side of the field. "That's double disgrace for Earth and a double-sweet victory for Ossmendia. If this were an actual tournament game, it would mean extra points in the standings."

Stonifer scratched his gigantic jutting chin with one

of his metal root tips. "Let's see. I believe I will propose another one-on-one wrestling match. Same rules as before."

"How about it, Earth girl?" asked Chunq. "Are you up for a rematch?"

"Hold that thought." Tomoko jogged toward the circular stands, searching out Tyler and Daiki in their new seats. "Tyler-san?" she asked.

"Yes?" asked Tyler.

Tomoko's voice dropped to a whisper. "Don't tell anyone this, but I'm not very good at team sports. In judo, I'm used to winning or losing just for myself. Here, when I lose, it will be for the entire team."

"No," said Daiki. "It will be for the entire planet."

The blood drained from Tomoko's face. "Don't say that!"

"What do you want me to do about it?" asked Tyler.

Tomoko narrowed her eyes to a squint. "Don't make me say it out loud."

"Say what?" asked Tyler.

Tomoko sighed. "Tyler Sato, I need your help."

"Forget it," Tyler exclaimed. "There's no way I'm wrestling one of those monsters of rock."

"No, not as a player," she said quickly. "I need your help as a fan, as somebody who understands this game. What I need is your advice." Her pleading eyes locked onto Tyler's until he blinked. "Tyler-san, how can I win a wrestling match against Chunq?"

"You can't," Tyler told her.

"Well, that's kind of a rude thing to say." She flipped her purple hair out of her eyes. "Sure he's big, but I'm used to flipping opponents who are larger and stronger than I am."

"Opponents made of solid rock with metal limbs that end in pincerlike root tips?" asked Daiki.

"Well . . . no," Tomoko admitted.

"It wouldn't be possible for you to judo flip an Oss-mendian," Tyler stated. "With the moon's gravity, you weigh only about thirteen pounds here, like a house cat on Earth. If you get anywhere near Chunq—"

"He'll toss me out of the circle like a stuffed doll," she finished glumly.

"That's what happened last time," said Daiki.

"So that's it?" asked Tomoko. "Even Felix isn't big enough to stand up to a living boulder. We have no chance!"

"You do have one chance." Tyler pointed into the arena at El Gatito.

Tomoko shielded her eyes. "I won't let you distract me again with cat-boy cuteness."

"No, really, think about it," said Tyler. "You remember how you and Felix together couldn't keep El Gatito pinned to the floor of the bus? He's slippery like an eel."

Tomoko's eyes sparkled with hope. "Thank you, Tyler-san. I'm so glad to be captaining a team with you as my number one fan!"

She ran back to relay her choice to Stonifer. "FIFTH RANKS EL GATITO GRANDE VERSUS BRIKK BROKKEL," shouted the announcer.

"Brikk to the circle," Stonifer ordered. Brikk had an extra-thick brow and slight reddish tint. He bowed to his captain and clambered to the circle.

"Think you can beat a giant Easter Island statue?" Tomoko asked El Gatito.

El Gatito watched Brikk paw the ground with his metal omniroots, like a bull about to charge. El Gatito removed the bright red cape from his shoulders and waved it around like a bullfighting *torero*. "The question is not whether El Gatito can beat a giant Easter Island statue. The question is whether a giant Easter Island statue can beat El Gatito, and the answer is no!"

"BEGIN!" the announcer shouted as soon as El Gatito jumped into the circle. Three of the beeping metal balls settled over the match, and a set of flickering symbols and a shrinking red line on the scoreboard seemed to mark the time remaining.

El Gatito waved his cape and shouted, *"Torro! Torro!"*

His arms and legs flailed in the low gravity. Brikk swiped at him with a metal omniroot like a batter going after a fat pitch on the outside corner of home plate. The Ossmendian then seemed surprised when he only made contact with the Earth boy's cape.

"El Gatito is going to need that back," said the Earth boy as the red cloth wrapped around the omniroot and resisted Brikk's attempts to shake it off.

Brikk swung at El Gatito with a second limb, but this time the cat-masked boy grabbed the omniroot as it passed and held tight. "Good move! El Gatito didn't expect you to try the same attack that had failed before. You've obviously played this game before, no?"

Brikk reared up on three of his four remaining omniroots and struck at El Gatito with his fourth. The sound of metal grinding on metal made even the other Ossmendians wince, but El Gatito held on.

"El Gatito won't be tricked into letting go to hold onto his ears. El Gatito eats fingernails off chalkboards for breakfast! No, wait, that didn't make any sense, did it? El Gatito is sorry for the mixed metaphor."

"Stop talking about yourself like you're somebody other than yourself!" Brikk growled.

"Oh, is that what El Gatito was doing? El Gatito didn't even realize."

The red line on the scoreboard was nearly gone. Brikk

danced around, trying to shake El Gatito from his perch before time ran out. He lifted one more omniroot and made a desperate attempt to shake the human boy loose, but El Gatito just moved from one omniroot to another.

Up in the stands, Tyler and Daiki jumped to their feet. "He's really good!" Daiki exclaimed.

"He's harder to shake than a booger from one of your fingers," said Tyler.

"Ewww!" Daiki wrinkled his nose in distaste.

Brikk, precariously balanced on two omniroots, fell backward toward the edge of the black circle. El Gatito jumped off at the last moment and flipped around in the moon's gravity. He landed on his feet just inside of the circle, while Brikk kicked up a cloud of moon dust on the outside of the boundary.

"EARTH WINS THE SQUARE," said the announcer, and a red X appeared in the upper-left corner of the scoreboard. While the other Earth players jumped and flipped in celebration, Tyler watched the stony expression of anger harden on Stonifer's face.

"NOW LET'S CHECK BACK ON OUR ROCK RACE. LOOK! DUE TO SOME SEISMIC ACTIVITY, THE ROCK IN THE MIDDLE HAS EDGED SLIGHTLY AHEAD!"

"Hooray!" Daiki exclaimed.

The image shimmered as a small silver shuttlecraft passed through the dome. It landed on the field, and two familiar Mrendarians stepped out. The smaller one posed like an angry warrior with clenched tentacles, while the larger one looked calmly around and gave a friendly wave to Tyler in the stands.

"LADIES AND GENTLEMEN, PLEASE WELCOME M'FROZZA, THE MRENDARIAN GALAXY GAMES CAPTAIN, AND . . . UM . . . ER—"

"Chief Technician Level Five N'Gatu," stated N'Gatu.

The announcer started again. "PLEASE WELCOME M'FROZZA, THE MRENDARIAN GALAXY GAMES CAPTAIN, AND SOMEBODY UNIMPORTANT!"

The Ossmendian crowd clapped their root tips in tepid applause.

"We're saved!" Tyler exclaimed. "M'Frozza will know how to stop this crazy game!"

M'Frozza glared up at her Ossmendian counterpart. "Hello again, Captain Stonifer. Just what do you think you are doing?"

"Restoring the balance," Stonifer replied. "You won your tournament slot from me, Captain Tyler won it from you, and soon I will take it back for the greater glory of the Ossmendian Empire!"

"You cannot do this," M'Frozza stated.

"The challenge is fully sanctioned and already underway. There is nothing you can do to stop it."

M'Frozza continued to glare at the rock-boy for a

moment before slumping her tentacles in defeat. "I suppose you are correct."

An Ossmendian official with a red sash clanked across the arena to where M'Frozza and N'Gatu stood. "Come this way, Captain M'Frozza. You will have an excellent view of the Ossmendian victory from the section where the two Earth boys are sitting."

25

Tyler looked up at the scoreboard. There were now two red X's on the board—the upper-left square won by El Gatito and the lower-right corner, which Weez, Felix, and Tomoko had won in a lunar approximation of three-on-three soccer. Six other squares were still filled with blue Ossmendian O's. Only the center square remained open, which would make three in a row for either team.

"Your team still has a chance," said M'Frozza from her spot next to Tyler in the stands. N'Gatu stood on her other side in the aisle, fiddling happily with a variable shower nozzle he'd brought from the plumbing convention.

"It's not my team anymore," Tyler told the Mrendarian captain. "It's Tomoko's team now."

"You cannot give up your team that easily, Tyler Sato!"

Tyler shrugged.

M'Frozza popped her nostril-holes a few times before speaking again. "I did not know about this challenge before it happened. Father-Parent kept it a secret from me."

"I believe you," said Tyler.

"We Mrendarians have a reputation for being tricky. We find ways to bend the rules without breaking them. I thought I was good, but Father-Parent has outdone me."

"Do the Ossmendians have a reputation?" Tyler asked.

"Yes," said M'Frozza. "Ossmendians are known for being unnecessarily cruel. I'm afraid this game is no exception."

On the field, Stonifer announced his next move. "Ossmendia challenges for the triple-win, preempting initiative."

"OSSMENDIA CHALLENGES FOR THE GAME. INITIATIVE IS PREEMPTED TO OSSMENDIA," boomed the grinding voice of the announcer.

"What does that mean?" asked Tomoko.

The Ossmendian flashed his enormous teeth. "The triple-win is the rarest and most devastating victory in a Galaxy Games contest. For us, it will mean starting the tournament with a huge boost to our reputation. For you, the losers, it will mean an eternity of shame. No worlds will trade with you, and no off-worlders would ever visit your system again."

"Would previously abducted children be returned?" asked Weez.

"Please ignore my underling," Tomoko told the Ossmendian boy. "What are the rules for this triple-win challenge?"

"I choose the rank and you choose the challenge, with no amendment allowed," said Stonifer.

Tomoko gathered her players into a tight circle. "All right, which of us do you want to play against?"

"I choose a captain-level challenge," Stonifer stated.

"CAPTAINS RANK," said the announcer. "TYLER SATO VERSUS STONIFER REDVEIN."

"But I'm not captain anymore," Tyler shouted from the stands. "I gave it up!"

"Did you register your resignation with the Galaxy Gaming Commission?" asked M'Frozza.

"I didn't know I had to!"

"I told you the first time we met that the commissioners control every aspect of the game."

"Tyler Sato," said Stonifer, as he strode toward Tyler's section of the stands. "You are the greatest child athlete on your world, just as I am the greatest child athlete on mine. This contest can only be decided between us. You must know this." The stone alien kept walking up into the stands until he loomed over his human counterpart. One of the floating silver balls hovered around his head as he spoke. "Do I intimidate you, Tyler Sato of Earth?"

"Maybe a little," said Tyler.

"Good. Ossmendia's victory would be incomplete unless I took you on directly, so I can make no other choice. You pick the contest. Anything you want. And I will defeat you."

Tyler looked over at the other Earth players and thought he saw relief on Tomoko's face. He knew what she was thinking: If Earth had to lose and be shunned by the entire galaxy, at least it would be Tyler's fault and not hers.

"WHILE THE EARTH CAPTAIN PONDERS HIS CHALLENGE, LET'S PLAY DRONES AND HOOPS!"

Tyler groaned. "Not another gimmicky game!"

"WE'RE LOOKING FOR THE LUCKY GALAXY GAMES FAN SITTING IN ROW ALPHA-ALPHA, SEAT TWELVE!" A spotlight from the top of the dome swept across the crowd. "IT'S . . . IT'S . . . IT'S . . . *HIM?!*"

"What?" asked Daiki. "Why is that spotlight shining on me? Did I do something wrong?" A tall Ossmendian game official ushered Daiki down onto the field.

"THE EARTH CHILD WILL HAVE TEN THROBS TO PILOT A HOLOGRAPHIC DRONE THROUGH AN OBSTACLE COURSE OF SPINNING HOOPS. THIS GAME REQUIRES REFLEXES, TIMING, AND MANY HOURS OF TEDIOUS PRACTICE. OF COURSE THE EARTH CHILD

DOESN'T HAVE A CHANCE, BUT LET'S ALL PREPARE TO GIVE HIM A ROUND OF APPLAUSE FOR TRYING."

"Oh, thanks." Daiki accepted a handheld controller. "What is this for?"

"READY? BEGIN! LET'S TRY NOT TO LAUGH AT THE EARTH CHILD'S PATHETIC ATTEMPTS TO—WAIT, WHAT'S THIS? HE'S ALREADY PILOTED THE DRONE THROUGH THE FIRST TWO HOOPS!"

"Amazing!" M'Frozza exclaimed.

"Go, Daiki!" shouted Tyler, and his teammates joined in the cheering as well.

"THIS IS UNBELIEVABLE!" said the announcer. "THE EARTH CHILD IS MOVING HIS DRONE THROUGH THE HOOPS WITH FLAWLESS PRECISION. WHERE DID HE LEARN HOW TO DO THAT?"

"Level cleared," Daiki announced, as his drone completed the course. "All that time I spent playing *RoboMaze* at the Pack-Punch really paid off!"

"Hmm . . . hoops," Tyler mused as he watched Daiki return with his prize for winning the game: a year's supply of Doctor Bezzle's brand of luxury grinding stones. "The challenge can be anything? Anywhere?" Tyler cautiously asked the Ossmendian captain.

"Of course," said Stonifer. "The Galaxy Games are flexible enough to accommodate almost any challenge. Leaving the arena would be permissible only if I agree, but I will not refuse any reasonable request."

Tyler smiled. "In that case, we're going to need a ride back to Earth."

PLATTE BLUFF, NEVADA:

Tyler had to ring the doorbell three times before Eric Parker peeked out through the mail slot. "Tyler? Why aren't you in Greece?"

"Hi, Eric. I need a favor."

"Forget it! I'm not doing any favors for you, Space Boy." The mail slot squeaked shut.

"Wait, Eric, listen! I'm sorry for not inviting you to my pizza party."

"It's way late to apologize for that. Stars have been named, pizzas have been eaten, and I wasn't there. What could change any of that?"

Tyler shook his head and whispered to the man standing next to him on Eric's front porch. "See? I told you he'd still be mad at me."

"Let me try." The man stepped forward. "Eric? Eric Parker?"

"Who's there?" asked Eric.

"It's the President of the United States, Eric."

"Nuh-uh!" Eric shouted. Then in a quieter voice he asked, "Really?" Tyler heard the lock click, and the front door swung open. "It really is you!" Eric exclaimed.

"Eric," said the president, "we need your help. The future of our world may depend on it. And you can consider it a personal favor to me as well."

"Of course, Mr. President. What can I do for you?"

"We need to use your basketball hoop," said the president.

Eric blinked. "The future of the world depends on my basketball hoop?"

"Yeah," said Tyler. "We're playing against the Ossmendian Galaxy Games team, and the match is down to the final square. It's me against the captain of the other team, and somebody blew up our complex in Greece. I need to use your hoop because I shoot better here than anywhere else."

Instead of listening to Tyler, Eric looked past his front porch at the warped landscape beyond. The normally flat road that ran past Eric's house was now an incline of steps upward in both directions. The city of Platte Bluff was arranged all around them in terraced lots on the inside of an enormous bowl that included homes, businesses, the hospital, the school, public parks, and the nearby university campus. The bowl extended a half mile outward and upward, with the whole thing covered by an opaque blue dome large enough to hold several news helicopters, the Burger Barn Blimp, and a cloud of floating silver balls.

"What the—" Eric stepped forward in a daze and

stumbled down his front steps. He recovered his glasses and gaped up at an enormous tic-tac-toe board that covered the sky. A streaming video in the center square showed a slow-motion replay of his awkward fall.

Tyler helped Eric to his feet. "Are you all right?" A sound system broadcast Tyler's voice to all the city residents looking down from their surrounding lawns, trees, or rooftop perches. Eric nodded, and a cheer echoed back at him like halftime at the Super Bowl.

"I forgot to mention," said Tyler. "The Ossmendians have turned Platte Bluff into a temporary arena for our game. It's Eric's Driveway Stadium, just like we always imagined!"

Eric lowered his gaze to the field level of stadium bowl, directly surrounding his house, driveway, and yard. "I'm pretty sure I never imagined all those Easter Island statues on my front lawn."

"And we never imagined you, either!" one of statues shot back.

"Yeep!" Eric slumped onto the grass with his eyes glassed over in a waking daze.

Daiki stepped forward to help Tyler lift Eric back to his feet. "Cousin Tyler-kun, I think your friend's brain is broken."

"This is probably a lot for him to take in all at once," said Tyler as he and his cousin each grabbed one of Eric's arms and led him to the VIP lawn chairs at the edge of the driveway. "Just relax, Eric. Take deep breaths and you'll get over the shock in no time. Here, I saved you a seat between M'Frozza the Mrendarian and Stephen Falconer the multibillionaire."

"Call me Steve," said Mr. Falconer, offering his hand.

Eric looked around the lawn-chair gallery to see Brayden, John, Lucas, Amanda and the rest of Tyler's family, Technician N'Gatu and Pilot R'Turvo, a dozen world leaders, Earth's entire Galaxy Games team, a bunch of people Eric didn't recognize, and a woman who looked like rock star Amy Thrush. "This is doing nothing to reduce my level of shock!" Eric shouted.

In front of them on the blacktop, Stonifer tapped two of his metal omniroots together to make the *tick tick tick* sound of a clock. "Can we get on with my winning this contest now?"

Tyler picked up Eric's basketball and dribbled it toward the hoop. Stonifer clambered after him. The rock-boy's root tips cracked and broke the pavement as he walked, to Eric's visible dismay. "The rules are simple," said Tyler. "We take turns shooting from this painted line until we 'break the ice.' After that we rebound for shooting positions. The first shot in any turn is worth one point, then you shoot from the line for two points until you miss. Winner is the first to get twenty-one points. Okay?"

Stonifer nodded. "That is acceptable. And so we will play for a slot in the Galaxy Games Tournament, and quite possibly the only chance your species will get to ever move out into the civilized galaxy."

"And you're going to do all this on my driveway?" Eric shouted.

"Of course," Tyler called back to him. "I've never lost a game on this driveway."

"That's because you use time-travel sneakers!"

"Really?" asked M'Frozza. "You allow time-travel footwear?"

"It's a custom rule," Eric explained.

Tyler stepped to the line, aimed, and threw up a brick. It didn't even touch the rim. It hit the garage door under the hoop with a loud *thunk*. "That's how you do it," he told Stonifer, "except you want the ball to go through the hoop."

The Ossmendian thumped to the line, and Tyler threw the ball to him. Stonifer caught it between two of his root tips. His first shot swished through the net. "Did I just break the ice?" he asked.

"Yeah. That must have been beginner's luck." Tyler grabbed the ball and threw it back to him. "It's one to zero. Now you get to shoot again for two more points."

Stonifer threw another swish. Tyler couldn't believe it. Beginner's luck couldn't strike twice in a row, could it?

"That's three to zero?" Stonifer asked. Tyler nodded. The Ossmendian shot another two-pointer from the line, and another, and another. He was like a basket-shooting machine! "Nine to zero," he said. "And I get to keep shooting until I miss?"

At the front of the VIP gallery, Brayden cupped his hands to his mouth. "Great strategy, Tyler! Way to lull him into a false sense of confidence!"

Stonifer kept shooting from the line, and the ball kept going in. Eleven, thirteen, fifteen, and then seventeen points, all in his first turn. He hit one more and was only one basket from winning.

"Hold on," said Tyler. "When you go for the win, you need a special trick shot. A double turnaround jump shot from the end of the driveway."

"A . . . jump shot?"

Tyler grinned. "What's wrong, Stonifer? Can't get your three-ton body off the ground now that we're not in lunar gravity anymore?"

The alien boy tucked his omniroots under his stone body and— *Pop!* Stonifer shot into the air and did a flip before coming down. Every human in the crowd stared in awe.

"I should have warned you," M'Frozza called out. "Ossmendians have a lot of strength in their limbs, even in gravity as strong as Earth's."

"Yeah, he's not bad." Tyler tried not to sound too impressed even as every ounce of his confidence drained away.

Stonifer stepped to the end of the driveway. Tyler passed him the ball. "This one's for game."

"Okay, Tyler!" Brayden shouted. "Now's the time for phase two of your plan!"

"How do you know there's a phase two?" asked Section Chief Jelassi.

"Every plan has a phase two," Brayden replied. "Otherwise it wouldn't be much of a plan."

Eric rocked back and forth in his seat. "Miss it, miss it, miss it."

Stonifer spun around twice and jumped into the air. He let the ball fly . . . too far to the left. His turn was over, and Earth still had the slimmest chance to win. All Tyler Sato had to do was score twenty-one points to win the game.

26

Tyler dribbled across the pavement and narrated to himself, like he always did when playing his A-game in Eric's driveway. "Tyler Sato goes to the line with the fate of the world on his shoulders." It was something he might have said months ago when he and Eric played, except that now it was true.

"Was I supposed to talk like that when it was my turn?" Stonifer asked the VIP gallery.

"It's optional," Eric told him.

Tyler put his toes on the line and tried not to trip over the chunks of driveway that Stonifer had dislodged with his metal root tips. "Sato bounces the ball and tries to steady himself. Fifty thousand fans lean forward in their seats."

"Yay, fans!" shouted Lucas. "He's talking about us!"

"No, he isn't," said Eric. "If I know Tyler, he's blocking

the rest of us out. That's what Eric's Driveway Stadium was always all about. Everywhere else, Tyler's been acting all grown-up and serious, but here, Tyler can goof off and be silly for the fifty thousand invisible fans that only he can see and hear."

"Fifty thousand invisible fans that only Captain Tyler can see and hear," M'Frozza repeated to herself in her native Mrendarian language.

Every tentacle on N'Gatu's body suddenly snapped to attention. "Invisible fans? Are they Dwogleys? Can Captain Tyler actually see Dwogleys?"

"Hush, N'Gatu," M'Frozza scolded. "There are no such things as Dwogleys."

"But—"

"These invisible fans must be a localized Earth phenomenon."

"Oh." N'Gatu flapped his face-tentacles in thought. "Then it is good that Tyler Sato can tell us what they are doing."

"Tyler takes his shot, and it's good! All around the stadium, fireworks light up the sky!"

M'Frozza looked up at the dome scoreboard above them. "The fireworks are invisible too?"

"Why not?" asked Eric. "The game might end before we have a chance to light the visible kind."

Stonifer tossed Tyler the ball to take another shot.

"It's up and it's good!" Tyler exclaimed. "Sato is closing the gap and the fans are on their feet!"

The Ossmendians on Eric's lawn checked under the bushes and behind the fence for invisible fans.

Tyler recovered the ball and sank another shot. "The score is nineteen to five, and everyone is screaming for Sato to win."

"It is amazing," said M'Frozza. "Even with my language implant and perception field, it all just sounds like empty air."

"Sometimes I feel that way about Congress," said the president.

Tyler kicked at the line under his feet. "Sato is going for two more and . . ." The ball bounced off the rim twice but didn't go in. "Awww!"

Stonifer grabbed the rebound. "What now?" he asked.

"It's your turn again," Tyler told him. "First you shoot from where you got the rebound. If you make that, you can try the trick shot again for the game."

"All right." The Ossmendian tossed the ball in, and the score was twenty to five. Stonifer stepped out to the end of the driveway and lined up for a possible winning jump shot.

"A fan runs onto the court!" Tyler shouted while Stonifer was in the air.

"What? Where?" The Ossmendian twisted around and fell with a *thunk*, hard enough to shake the ground.

"Oh, man!" Eric exclaimed. "Mom's going to kill me when she sees this driveway. And I'll probably get blamed for messing up the rest of the city, too."

Stonifer's shot missed the basket. Tyler got the rebound and ran over to the Ossmendian. "Are you all right?"

"I am fine. Did I injure the fan?"

"No, that was a false alarm. It was just an invisible janitor. He wanted to clean some of the debris off the court."

"What a strange thing to do," the Ossmendian said.

Tyler went back to where he'd gotten the rebound. "Sato tosses in his shot and it's twenty to six. He'll go to the line to shoot for two."

"Take your time," shouted Tomoko from the front lawn. "Just relax. Don't even think about how the entire human race is counting on you."

"I can't even look." Daiki hid his face behind his hands.

Tyler made the next basket. Then he made three more after that. That was five in a row, counting the rebound shot, which really showed the power of Eric's driveway. He was so glad he'd insisted on coming here!

Then Tyler missed the next shot and Stonifer got the rebound. The rock-boy tossed the ball in but the score remained the same, since only a tricky jump shot from the end of the driveway could win the game.

"The score is twenty to fourteen," the Ossmendian said. "It is getting closer but Stonifer can end the game with his next shot. A lifetime of training, five blue stars in the Ossmendian Junior Games, exhibition contests on a dozen worlds . . . all of it has prepared him for this moment."

"Only five blue stars?" M'Frozza jeered. "Pathetic!"

"Stonifer wipes the loose sediment from his eyes and steadies his front feet for the jump. The paved arena grows quiet, except perhaps for the invisible fans of Tyler Sato. Only Captain Tyler knows for sure whether his fans are being respectfully quiet or not."

"Most of them are being quiet," said Tyler. "Except for the guy in Section 12 who keeps yelling for more peanuts."

"Stonifer closes his eyes and tries not to think about the fifty thousand invisible Earth fans, the thousands of genuine Earth fans, or the eight billion Ossmendians watching the game on quantum transmission."

"Eight billion what?" Tyler asked.

Stonifer glanced up at the sky.

Tyler looked up and saw a swarm of the same softball-sized metal balls that had been hovering over their game on the moon. "Those are Ossmendian cameras?" Tyler asked.

"One of them is Mrendarian," said M'Frozza. "It was

short notice, but I managed to find an expert camera operator."

N'Gatu, the Mrendarian technician, waved to Tyler. Two of his arm-tentacles held a controller that looked a lot like the one Daiki had used on the moon.

"Yes, sorry, I forgot about that," said Stonifer. "Stonifer closes his eyes and tries not to think about the fifty thousand invisible Earth fans, the thousands of real Earth fans, the eight billion Ossmendians, *or the twelve billion Mrendarians* watching the game on quantum transmission."

"Or the billions of humans watching on TV," said the president, nodding at the television helicopters way up in the sky.

Tyler's mouth went dry. All the games he'd ever played with Eric combined had as many imaginary spectators—and these people were all completely real!

"Stonifer jumps, turns, shoots . . ."

Tyler watched the ball fly toward the hoop. If it went in, he'd spend the rest of his life on Earth with the rest of the galaxy forever beyond his reach.

The ball bounced off the backboard into Tyler's hands. Earth still had a chance.

"Sato shoots and, um, yeah," Tyler was now so nervous about the cameras that he could barely think. Somehow, the rebound shot went in. "Twenty to fifteen. Sato will go back to the line."

Above the roar of Eric's Driveway Stadium and the buzz of camera drones, Tyler became aware of some individual voices in the VIP section.

"Come on, Tyler!" Eric shouted.

"You can do it, honey bear!" his mother added.

"Make us proud, Tyler!" called the president.

"Booo!" shouted Amy Thrush. "Go, alien rock dude!"

Who invited her? Tyler wondered. Then he saw Amanda give the pop star a high-five. *Yeah, that figures.* Tyler tried to ignore the cameras in the sky, but that was impossible. Twelve billion Mrendarians with three eyes apiece—that was thirty-six billion eyes! Plus five or six billion humans and eight billion Ossmendians . . . how many eyes was that?

His heart pounded in his ears. He took a shot and looked away before it reached the basket.

"It's good!" shouted Eric. "Twenty to seventeen! You're coming back!"

Tyler got the ball again and tried to calm his heartbeat. He took another shot.

"It's good! Twenty to nineteen! Unbelievable!"

"Hey, Captain Stone-Face!" M'Frozza called to Stonifer. "Did you actually doubt that Tyler Sato was the best child athlete on Earth? This may become one of the greatest come-from-behind victories in the history of galactic sports!"

"Yeah, as if I could ever hit that double turnaround jumper with so many people watching," Tyler mumbled to himself. To his dismay, the sound system picked up his mumble and broadcast it around the stadium and out across the galaxy.

"You can do it, Ty!" Eric shouted. "I've seen you make that shot a hundred times before!" It sounded like Eric was Tyler's friend again, so maybe everything Tyler had been through had been worth it after all.

Tyler spun around twice at the end of the driveway and threw the ball as hard as he could. The shot went so wide that Tyler knew from the moment the ball left his hands that it would miss the basket. And the backboard. And probably the garage it was mounted to. Tyler winced as the ball hit the Mrendarian camera-ball. He winced again as the ball bounced off Eric's house. Then it bounced off the wooden fence. Then it hit the backboard.

And then it went in.

"We won!" Eric shouted. "We actually won! Hooray for Earth!"

During the wild celebration that followed, Tyler pulled M'Frozza aside. "That Mrendarian camera—"

"Do not worry, Captain Tyler. The camera was unharmed by its impact with your masterful shot."

"But I wasn't aiming for the camera. Why was it exactly where it had to be to deflect my shot into the hoop?"

"As I said, I found an expert camera operator."

Tyler followed her gaze to Daiki, who was waving hello with the camera controller in his hand.

In the aftermath of the game, the entire city of Platte Bluff rumbled back to its original landscape as the Ossmendians retreated back into space. Tyler's celebrating teammates spread into the zone between the police barricades at the end of Eric's street and the military blockade at the start of Eric's driveway. Some players gave interviews about how thrilled they were to play on the same team as the great Tyler Sato. Other players called their families or recapped the game with friends back home. Weez took the opportunity to record a podcast for *UFO Believers Home Journal*.

In a tree fort across the street from Eric's house, Technician N'Gatu placed a quantum call to an interplanetary hotline. "My name is N'Gatu. I am a technician employed by the Mrendarian embassy," he whispered, peeking one of his three eyes through a knothole in the fort to ensure that nobody with a language implant got close enough to overhear. "Is this the Dwogley Tip Line?"

"This line is for official business only," snapped the voice on the other end of the quantum.

"Yes, yes, I can imagine so," said N'Gatu. "I have a tip about Tyler Sato, captain of the Earth team. During a game against the Ossmendians, Captain Tyler claimed to see and hear a vast number of invisible creatures even though no other player or spectator could detect them. I believe . . . that is . . . I think it's possible—"

"*What* do you believe?" snapped the voice.

N'Gatu swallowed hard. "I believe Tyler Sato is the being you have been looking for. He is the one who can speak with the Dwogleys."

After a long pause, the voice sounded much calmer

than before. "You have served us well, Technician N'Gatu."

"Thank you!" N'Gatu beamed with pride. "You have no idea how good it feels to finally have someone believe me. If you'd like, I can have Captain Tyler ask his Dwogley friends what they want, and nicely request that they—"

"No!" the voice insisted. "The accursed messenger of the Dwogleys shall not be allowed the time he needs to corrupt the Galaxy Games Tournament. Captain Tyler shall be dead by the opening of the first round."

"Wait, what?" N'Gatu demanded. "I didn't mean for you to kill him. Hello? Hello? Mr. Dwogley Tip Line Person sir? Is anyone still on the line?" N'Gatu tried to reestablish the connection, but the other node had vanished from the network. Trembling, he dropped the quantum receiver and covered his eyes with his arm-tentacles. "By the Great Spawning, what have I done?"

27

PLATTE BLUFF, NEVADA:

Three days after Tyler's victory, pounding music expertly spun by A Guy Called Guy rocked a hall on the campus of the Platte Bluff Institute of Science. Disco balls threw constellations of stars around the crowded room. Over the stage, an enormous banner ensured that everyone knew the reason for the celebration and exactly who the center of attention should be. The banner read "Happy Sweet Sixteen, Amanda!"

From under the banner, Amanda Sato looked out over her birthday proceedings. The turnout was decent, the deejay had everyone on their feet, and the entire Platte Bluff High School Cool Cliques Coalition had decided to attend: Madison DuMont and her DuMontourage; Keith Courtland and the rest of the Jock Straps; Meg Lopez and her Fashion Cops; Tad Silverman and the Silver Boys; Monique Richmond and the Shiny Dancers; and all five

Flatliners. Finally, after months of Tyler this and Tyler that, Tyler on the Wheaties box and Tyler on the cover of *Newsweek*, Amanda was having a day of her own—at least in theory. "If one more person asks me to introduce them to my little brother, I'm going to scream," she said through gritted teeth. Then she returned to smiling so everyone would see how much fun she was having.

Suddenly, the song changed to an extended mix of "Go, Tyler Sato, Go (And Don't Come Back!)" by Amy Thrush, and time seemed to stand still. On the other side of the room, Tad Silverman stepped out of the huddle of Silver Boys. *The* Tad Silverman—Honors Society senior, captain of the Platte Bluff High School football team, and Hollywood-quality hottie—was looking directly at Amanda. If the latest gossip were true—and Amanda had no reason to disbelieve Brandy, who'd gotten a text from Heather, who'd overheard a conversation between Tricia and Madison DuMont herself—Tad was back on the potential-boyfriend market, having just dumped his cheerleader girlfriend for being too materialistic.

Amanda ran manicured fingernails through her new $70 hairstyle and brushed past the diamond earrings she'd borrowed from her mother just for this party. "Good thing I'm not materialistic. Oh jeez, he's coming over here! Quick, Amanda, look cute!"

Tad smiled at Amanda as he stepped closer. The left

side of his mouth curved upward while the right side opened just enough to display the straightest teeth that orthodontic services could create, capped with the whitest ceramic veneers. Colored lights played across his dimpled chin and product-enhanced hair. His voice oozed confidence to match the swagger in his hips. "Hello, Amanda. Great party."

"Th-thanks!" she stammered, feeling her face flush.

The dazzling smile widened. "Could I ask you a question?"

Amanda's heart raced like a pack of wolves. Or like a deer being chased by a pack of wolves. No, it was more like an eight-legged mutant deer being chased by a pack of elephant-sized wolf-monsters. *Tad's going to ask me out,* she thought. *Or no, he'll probably skip the whole "going out" part and just ask me to marry him because we're so obviously meant to be together. I'll be Amanda Sato-Silverman . . . or Amanda Silverman-Sato? Hmm. Maybe we should flip a coin.*

Tad cleared his throat, waiting for an answer, but Amanda was still lost in her daydream.

Sure it'll be tough to be married so young, but Tad could drop out of school and wait tables to support me through medical school. Or even better, he could get work acting in a series of cologne commercials, and I'd get to see him shirtless every time I turned on the TV! We'd laugh and laugh and laugh until— "I'm sorry, what was your question?" she asked, realizing that Tad was tapping his foot and checking his watch.

"I said, is that your brother over there in the corner?" Tad nodded at Tyler. "I thought it was him because he was hanging out with that Mrendarian and all, but I also thought the great Ty Sato would be a whole lot taller."

"Tad Silverman-Sato, you and I are through!" Amanda shouted. Unfortunately, that was the exact moment when A Guy Called Guy turned off the sound system to make an announcement. Amanda's raised voice echoed off the back walls of the suddenly silent hall for everyone to hear. "And I don't care how many cologne commercials you would have made, or how cute our dimple-chinned children would have been, or— Why is everyone staring at me?"

"Whatever," said Tad with a flip of his perfect blond hair. "See you around, psycho." He rejoined his friends, and the entire Cool Cliques Coalition snorted and giggled their way toward the exit.

"Tad! Call me!" Amanda shouted after them.

"Okay, that was awkward," A Guy Called Guy said into his deejay microphone. "I'd like to interrupt this episode of teen angst to bring you a very special presentation. Everyone please gather around Amanda at the center of the hall."

"What is it? What's going on?" Amanda glanced sideways to make sure Tyler was still far off in the corner of the room with his alien and human friends. Satisfied that Little Brother Space Explorer wasn't going to upstage her, Amanda stepped into the spotlight in the middle of the crowd of high-schoolers.

Two members of the catering staff pushed a car-sized, car-shaped, tarp-covered object toward her.

"No way!" Amanda exclaimed. "No. Way. I wasn't expecting a car for my birthday. A car is worth at least a dozen Tad Silvermans. A dozen Tad Silvermen? Oh, whatever. This is so"— she yanked the tarp away to reveal a car-sized, car-shaped, frosting-covered cake— "unexpected." She blinked at the sight. "All right, who covered my brand new car in buttercream icing?"

Tyler and his friends wove their way toward her, grinning like little maniacs, but at least for now the party guests were still appropriately focused on Amanda. Still, she felt as if she'd overlooked something important. Amanda poked a finger into one of the cake's marzipan tires and felt nothing but cake. "I don't get it. There's no car under there. Are my keys inside?"

"No, but I am!" proclaimed a voice from the cake's interior. To Amanda's absolute horror, Boffo the Clown exploded out of the car-cake's trunk. "Dum-diddley-doo, it's a Boffo birthday for you! I'm the Clown Prince of Fun and you must be"—Boffo checked the name written on a card taped to the inside of his wrist—"Wee Widdle Mandy-Pants!"

Tyler leaped forward and snapped a picture of his big sister's dumbstruck face. "It was a lot of work, but the slap-happy grin makes it all worthwhile," he told her with a genuinely slap-happy grin on his face.

"Tyler Sato, I'm going to kill you!" Amanda shrieked.

Tyler dodged through the crowd of laughing partygoers, out a service exit, and into the night.

Tomoko Tomizawa, Daiki Shindo, Eric Parker, and M'Frozza the Mrendarian caught up to Tyler at the campus center, near the academic building where Tyler sometimes snuck into his father's undergraduate astronomy lectures. "Human birthday parties are so much more fun than Mrendarian skin-shedding ceremonies," M'Frozza proclaimed.

The star-filled desert sky stretched above them like a blanket. "Which one is Mrendaria?" asked Tomoko.

M'Frozza pointed with one of her arm-tentacles. "You can't see Mrendaria from here without instruments, but that blue one is Ossmendia." M'Frozza made a sad, tentacle-waving shake of her head. "They suffered such a shameful loss. Their empire won't recover for a long time.

Certainly Mrendaria will never trade with them again, but my people were greatly impressed by your victory, Tyler Sato. Your winning shot is being celebrated in song, and I have Father-Parent's word that there will be no further challenges to Earth's place in the Galaxy Games."

"That was a pretty sweet shot," Tyler admitted. In Japanese, he added, "Even if there was some technical interference involved."

Daiki blushed and turned away.

"I'd like to take credit for providing the driveway," Eric stated.

"Yes, of course," said M'Frozza. "We also have a song about Eric Parker of the miraculously paved vehicle storage area, but it's not quite as popular. And maybe after tonight I will write one about Eric Parker's mother-parent's brother-sibling and his amazing bakery of clown-bearing desserts! There is still much I have to learn about your planet's culture!"

That reminded Tyler of something he'd been wondering about. "M'Frozza? Why did you come to Earth, of all places? If you were looking for a Galaxy Games challenge, there must have been a hundred other worlds as good as ours, or even better."

M'Frozza looked away. "It is embarrassing."

"What?" asked Tyler.

"Back on Mrendaria, when I had the celebration party

330

for my third skin-shedding, my father-parent gave me this as a present." She held out an arm-tentacle with a gold disk on it. A ball of lights hovered above the disk like a glass globe filled with fireflies. All the lights were white except for one, which was bright red.

"Modern art?" asked Tomoko.

"No, this is a star map," M'Frozza told her. "That red light represents your sun. In the Grand Stellar Repository, it is called M'FROZZA. My father-parent named it after me as a present."

Eric and Tyler looked at each other for a long moment. Then they laughed so hard that M'Frozza and Tomoko must have thought they'd lost their minds.

TO BE CONTINUED . . .

AUTHOR'S NOTE: JAPAN

DAIKI SHINDO'S NEIGHBORHOOD:

Daiki's neighborhood in Japan is based on an area of Tokyo called Takadanobaba, where I lived for a while. My tiny apartment overlooked the concrete banks of Kandagawa, the Kanda River, which seemed depressingly tame until cherry blossoms gave the flowing water a fresh spring wardrobe.

Takadanobaba means "high field for the horses" and was named when the area lay outside the city walls of Edo, which is what old Tokyo used to be called in ancient times. Today, the horses are long gone, and the former fields are crammed with homes, apartment buildings, offices, and shops. Takadanobaba has busy streets and a large train station but also quieter areas with twisty narrow roads that are almost too small for cars.

When I wasn't exploring the city by foot, you might have found me in a video arcade. The Pack-Punch isn't a real place, but resembles the kind of establishment where I got quite good at a game very much like *RoboMaze*. Video arcades are still everywhere in Tokyo, even though their popularity has waned in the United States. Among the souvenirs I brought back to America was a *Ranma ½* cartridge for the Super Famicom game console. I used this game as my inspiration for *Tekno-Fight Xtreme* because it includes a character who wields a two-handed battle spatula as a weapon. No frog-demons, though.

JAPANESE NAMES AND HONORIFICS:

There are four main ways in which personal names in Japanese culture are spoken and written differently than personal names in Western cultures:

Name Order

In Japan, a person's family name comes before their given name. Daiki and Riku, brothers in the Shindo family, would introduce themselves as Shindo Daiki and Shindo Riku. Their Uncle Hiroshi called himself Sato Hiroshi until he moved to the United States. Then he began using the Western version of his name, Hiroshi Sato, to make sure his American students would know to call him Professor Sato instead of Professor Hiroshi.

If Tyler Sato visits Japan or if he talks by phone or Skype to somebody in Japan, he might call himself Sato

Tyler to avoid confusion—or at least he would have before everyone got to know his namesake, TY SATO.

In this book, I've used Western name order everywhere but in dialogue, where I've gone with whatever order would be natural for the character who is speaking.

Honorifics

In Japanese society, it's customary to tag a person's name with an honorific title that shows the relationship between the person speaking and the person being addressed. As the relationship between two people develops and changes, they may also change the form of address they use. When Tomoko first meets Daiki, she calls him Shindo-san. As they become closer friends, she calls him Daiki-san at first, and then Daiki-kun.

This chart doesn't include all the ways in which Japanese honorifics may be used, but I hope it's useful in deciphering the ones that appear in this book.

HONORIFIC	MOST COMMON USE	EXAMPLE
-san	To address someone of roughly equal status.	Jun Takeda's classmate, Ataru Hashimoto, addresses him as Takeda-san because they are on the same social level but not very close as friends.

HONORIFIC	MOST COMMON USE	EXAMPLE
-sama	To address someone who is older or has a higher status.	Daiki Shindo, several years behind Jun Takeda in school, addresses him as Takeda-sama.
-sensei	To address a teacher, coach, or instructor.	Tomoko Tomizawa considers Jun Takeda to be her video-gaming instructor and addresses him as Takeda-sensei.
-sempai	To address a person with a slightly higher status in a school or other organization.	Riku Shindo, one or two years behind Jun Takeda in school, refers to him as Takeda-sempai and may address him more simply as Sempai.
-kun	To address a boy or male teenager.	Mr. Mori, the adult owner of the Pack-Punch Video Arcade, addresses Jun Takeda as Takeda-kun. Close friends or family members would call him Jun-kun.

HONORIFIC	MOST COMMON USE	EXAMPLE
-chan	1. To address a baby or toddler of either gender; 2. To address a girl or female teenager; or 3. To address a family member by a familiar, babyish name.	1. When Jun Takeda was a baby, his parents called him Jun-chan. 2. Tomoko's great-grandmother addresses Tomoko as Tomoko-chan. Daiki also addresses her as Tomoko-chan as their friendship develops. 3. Tomoko also calls her great-grand-mother Obaa-chan.

Formalism

Japanese forms of address tend to be more formal than American forms of address. Because of this, people in Japan are more likely to be called by their last names. At school in Tokyo, Daiki's classmates typically address him as Shindo-san, except for good friends like Katsuro. At school in Nevada, Tyler's classmates call him Tyler or Ty. They would never think to address a fellow student as Mr. Sato.

Kanji

Japanese names are usually written with Chinese-based characters called *kanji* that each have specific meanings. Many *kanji* characters are pronounced the same as other *kanji* characters with different meanings, and some *kanji* characters may be pronounced differently in different words or names—for example, the "hon" in Honda and the "moto" in Hashimoto are both the *kanji* symbol "本" meaning "origin, root, or book."

The most common way for Sato to be written in *kanji* is 佐藤. "佐" is pronounced "sa" and means "help." "藤" is pronounced "tō" and means "wisteria," a type of flowering vine adopted as a symbol by families with ties to the powerful Fujiwara clan that influenced Japanese politics for hundreds of years.

MANGA AND ANIME:

After a while in Japan, I had a massive collection of manga—which are Japanese comic books—stacked in every nook of my Takadanobaba apartment. I snagged more than a few books from the curbside recycling, much like Riku and Daiki do in chapter three.

Manga is extremely popular in Japan for readers of all ages. There's manga for boys, manga for girls, manga for younger readers, manga for teens, and manga for adults. There are even manga cookbooks!

Manga is usually published in thick black-and-white collections with chapters from several different ongoing stories all packed together. The most popular stories are then collected into paperback books called *tankōbon*, and the most popular *tankōbon* might get translated into other languages, including English. Japanese manga have become popular in the United States, so your local library or bookstores probably have a selection of translated manga and illustrated novels inspired by the style of Japanese manga.

Popular manga are often adapted into an animated form called anime. Anime and anime-inspired animation are enjoyed around the world. Some anime shows you may have seen in the United States include *Pokémon, Dragon Ball Z, Yu-Gi-Oh!* and *Naruto.* Some of the humor in *Galaxy Games* was inspired by manga or anime that I have liked.

The anime series that Daiki and Tomoko like to watch, *Hunter-Elf Zeita,* is not a real show, but it *was* created in Japan. One day in Tokyo after overdosing on manga and anime for a few months, I invented my own imaginary anime series about an elf, some dragons, and a whole lot of magical mischief. I sent some of my *Hunter-Elf Zeita* stories back to friends in the United States, and I'm thrilled that I can now reference this piece of my Japan-era writing in *Galaxy Games.*

GLOSSARY

arigato (*Japanese*): "Thank you" in a way that's more polite than saying *domo*, but less polite than saying *domo arigato*.

dozo (*Japanese*): The "please" in "please have a seat" or "please come this way."

Dwogleys (*Galactic legend*): Noncorporeal beings who are believed by some to live on every civilized planet in the galaxy while remaining undetectable by any known means. Legends say that Dwogleys can predict the future and are able to communicate through dreams, an ability they use to influence galactic history and bet on sporting events.

entanglement engine (*Galactic technology*): The method by which spacecraft and other objects pop from one star system to another. Each entanglement engine contains a large number of qutrit particles, which exist simultaneously in many different places at the same time. Any object with an entanglement engine can instantly trade places with any other object it shares a qutrit particle with.

Father-parent (*Mrendarian*): Literal translation of the term Mrendarians use to mean father. They also have several additional types of parents, listed by M'Frozza in chapter fifteen. Children are called daughter-child, son-child, other-child, etc.

freen (*Mrendarian*): A waxy substance that builds up in the Mrendarian gullet-sack. If freen is allowed to accumulate, it will eventually be expelled through the throat-hole. Most Mrendarians find it more pleasant to use a "freen juicer" to flush out the gullet every morning.

gambatte (*Japanese*): "Do your best!" or "Kick some butt!" More formally, you might say, *"Gambatte kudasai!"*

gato/gatito (*Spanish*): As Tyler notes, El Gatito Grande means "The Great Kitten" with *gatito* being a cuter and smaller form of *gato*. As with all things *luchador*, the use of this name is surrounded by mystery.

gleezers (*Mrendarian*): The highest set of slime-pores on a tentacle. To be up to one's *gleezers* in work is to be seriously busy.

gomen nasai (*Japanese*): An apology you might use when you inconvenience a family member or close friend.

To apologize more formally to most other people, you would say *sumimasen*.

gruud (*Mrendarian*): A snack food made from translucent worms. They're best when served live, but most *gruud* encountered off Planet Mrendaria is reconstituted from *gruud-paste*.

guten tag (*German*): "Good day!"

hai (*Japanese*): Yes

J-pop (*Japanese*): Pop music from Japan, upbeat and fun to dance to, often with lines of English mixed into the Japanese lyrics just to be cool.

jujitsu (*Japanese*): A Japanese martial art designed to allow an unarmed or lightly armed person to take on a more powerful opponent. Judo is one kind of *jujitsu* but there are many others that have developed over the past few centuries.

Kaeruyasha (*Japanese*): *Kaeru* means "frog" and *yasha* are nature spirits from Japanese mythology. The *yasha* are usually depicted as good and gentle but my Kaeruyasha has a bit of an attitude, so I'm calling him a frog-demon.

kawaii (*Japanese*): *Kawaii* rhymes with Hawaii and means "cute."

konnichiwa (*Japanese*): A polite "good afternoon" greeting.

language implant (*Galactic technology*): An organic computer linked directly to the brain of a Galaxy Games player, allowing two-way translation to and from any other language in the Galaxy. This advanced technology is strictly controlled by the Galaxy Games commissioners and reserved only for players and former players. Everyone else must use clunkier systems that might establish common language zones on a spaceship or two-way language filters on a communications channel.

luchador (*Spanish*): A masked Mexican wrestler who fights in the *lucha libre* style.

makenai (*Japanese*): For most people this means "I cannot lose" or "I will not give up," but in Jun Takeda's case in chapter 3 it seems to mean "I am in complete denial that I've already lost."

manga (*Japanese*): Japanese comics, usually printed first in black-and-white anthologies and later collected into paperback books.

moshi-moshi (*Japanese*): A Japanese greeting used almost exclusively when answering a phone.

nani? (*Japanese*): Can be used as the "what" in "What is the capital of North Dakota?" In chapter 3, Daiki is using it more like the "what" in "Whaaaaaat did you just say?!"

ne? (*Japanese*): This word, added to the end of a statement, turns that statement into a question—but not just any question. This is the type of question where you're expecting someone to agree with whatever you just said. Use it like *"verdad?"* in Spanish, "right?" in English, or "eh?" in Canadian.

Nekomecha (*Japanese*): *Neko* means "cat" and *mecha* means "mechanical" so the Nekomecha character in *Tekno-Fight Xtreme* is a "mechanical cat." The *mecha* that appear in manga and anime are often battle robots, which also might transform into vehicles or join together to form giant battle robots.

Obaa-chan (*Japanese*): *Obaa* means "grandmother," but the *chan* honorific makes it cuter and more like "Granny" or "Gran-Gran." Tomoko uses this term to refer to her great-grandmother.

ohayogozaimasu (*Japanese*): The polite way to say "good morning." A more casual way to say good morning is *ohayo*.

Onee-san (*Japanese*): Big sister, the female version of *Onii-san*.

Onii-san (*Japanese*): Big brother. More accurately, "nii" means "big brother," "-san" is an honorific term we've seen before, and "o-" is *another* honorific added at the beginning of some words. Younger siblings are usually just addressed by name.

Otooto (*Japanese*): Little brother.

perception field (*Galactic technology*): A sensory enhancement given to Galaxy Games players, allowing them to see, hear, or smell languages they might not otherwise be able to perceive. Even a perception field does not allow a person to see or hear Dwogleys, assuming that Dwogleys even really exist.

Smazzroot! (*Mrendarian*): An exclamation meaning "rotten fruit!" referring to a famous Mrendarian story about a young podling whose deliciously rotten fruit rolled into a ditch and out of reach.

squooshums (*Mrendarian*): Literally "a person who is entirely engulfed in another person's tentacles." Used as a term of endearment.

sumimasen (*Japanese*): A respectful apology to strangers or nonfamily, somewhat more formal than *gomen nasai*.

tatami (*Japanese*): A rice straw mat used as flooring in a traditional Japanese home. Rooms are often measured by how many tatami mats can fit inside them.

Torro! (*Spanish*): *El torro* is a bull, and yelling *"Torro!"* is one way a bullfighter might taunt an animal into attacking. It's like when the rest of us say, "Here, kitty, kitty!" as we thrust a hand in front of the claws and teeth of a housecat, except that the bull is bigger and angrier. In my opinion, the *torero* who gets into a ring with the bull has already proven his or her bravery beyond any doubt—actually fighting the bull is entirely unnecessary.

Yatta! (*Japanese*): "I did it!"

yen (*Japanese*): The basic Japanese unit of currency. Over the past few years, one yen has been worth a bit more than an American penny, so a Big Mac at a Tokyo McDonald's might cost around 320 yen. There are one yen coins and other coins up to five hundred yen. The smallest paper money starts at one thousand yen.

ABOUT THE AUTHOR

GREG R. FISHBONE serves as Assistant Regional Coordinator for the three New England chapters of the Society of Children's Book Writers and Illustrators. In addition to the GALAXY GAMES series, he is also the author of the novel *The Penguins of Doom*.

Fishbone developed a healthy obsession with science fiction at an early age. Between (and often during) classes, Fishbone doodled spaceships and plotted out his own early efforts at writing.

Fishbone attended law school in three countries, including Japan, where the term for "foreign attorney working in Japan" could also mean "outhouse." This made for many awkward conversations including the line, "I am studying hard and hope to become an outhouse someday."

Fishbone lives in the Boston area, practicing law by day and writing by night. He still sometimes thinks about moving to Tokyo to become an outhouse. You can find out more about him at gfishbone.com.

For more information about the Galaxy Games series, use your smartphone to scan this code! Or go to galaxygames.com.